Here Comes
COWBOY
CLAUS

T0191177

Published by Kensington Publishing Corp.

Here Comes
COWBOY CLAUS

DIANA PALMER
KATE PEARCE
DELORES FOSSEN

ZEBRA BOOKS
Kensington Publishing Corp.
www.kensingtonbooks.com

ZEBRA BOOKS are published by

Kensington Publishing Corp.
900 Third Avenue
New York, NY 10022

CONTENTS

COLORADO
CHRISTMAS CAROL

DIANA PALMER

CHAPTER 1

One of the assistants in the kitchen turned her head and the bells in her earrings jingled. Estelle Grancy chuckled. It was the holiday season and she loved Christmas.

The hotel where she worked, and lived, in Benton, Colorado, was a homey place. It was beautifully decorated, with holly and ivy running up the elegant staircase bannisters and Christmas trees in every meeting room. The biggest Christmas tree was in the lobby, a dreamy combination of red bows and golden balls, with white lights climbing up the tree and presents under it.

The staff got along well. And Estelle was a wonderful cook. She had a cushy job with plenty of free time, thanks to the retired cook who loved to fill in when Estelle wanted a day off.

But Essa, as she was called, wanted something more from life than spending it in a kitchen, regardless of how much she loved her job.

She was twenty-three and alone in the world. Both parents had succumbed to a killer virus three years previously and the grieving twenty-year old was left to take charge of their estate and do what was necessary to probate it. She was mostly over the shock, but the grief still hurt.

She pushed back a loose strand of pale golden hair from the tight bun atop her head, and her green eyes twinkled as she glanced toward the laptop computer on a lone table near the kitchen door. She'd left her file open, after saving it. She was writing a novel; a mystery novel. Her one great ambition was to be a novelist, and she loved to read mysteries, so she hoped she might be able to write one that would sell.

Her late father had been a deputy sheriff, and he was a wealth of information about solving crimes. She'd listened to him by the hour, enjoying the methodical way he went about turning up lawbreakers. He hadn't had much experience with murders, but he knew people who did, in big cities.

He'd wanted to sell a book, too. He'd worked hard at it, but none of his material was good enough. He had poor grammar skills, so Essa, even in her teens, was his copy editor. She polished his prose and made it literate. But his ideas were too run-of-the mill. They never sold.

Essa's, on the other hand, were unique and complicated. She'd had two notes from actual editors on proposals she'd sent in. The book she was working on now had interested the editor of a publishing house that specialized in mystery novels. So it was a chance, at least, to be published. They say if you start getting personal notes from editors, who were notoriously busy, it was a sign that you might be able to sell a book. Essa hoped so; she didn't really want to spend the rest of her life in front of a stove. She spent her breaks working on the book. It obsessed her these days.

She turned back to the dishes she was making for the evening meal, her head still in the clouds. She'd been floating since early that morning, when she'd opened the note from the editor.

She pulled her perfectly baked homemade rolls out of the oven and turned it off, admiring their lovely color. Just perfect.

". . . it was a dark and stormy night?" came a curious little voice from the doorway. "You have got to be kidding!"

Essa turned. A young girl of about ten was standing at the computer, frowning as she read. She was tall for a child, very skinny, with short, straight, thick, blond hair and big brown eyes that suddenly pinned Essa's. "You're joking, right?" she asked. "I mean, starting a story with '. . . a dark and stormy night . . .'?"

Essa's eyebrows arched. Talk about precocious kids! "It's sarcasm," she said, surprised by the comment.

"Oh! I get it!" The child laughed and her whole face lit up.

"Who are you?" Essa asked.

"I'm Mellie," came the reply. "Mellie Marston. My dad's name is Dominic, but everybody calls him Duke." She cocked her head and smiled. "Who are you?"

"I'm Estelle Grancy. But people call me Essa."

"I'm very precocious," Mellie announced. "And I'm also ob . . . obnox . . . something."

"Obnoxious?" Essa asked, amused.

"That's it! Obnoxious! I drive Daddy nuts. He says he needs to carry duct tape around so he can shut me up."

"Do tell." Essa laughed. "Precocious and also obnoxious. It sounds very interesting."

"Does it, really? Thank you!" Mellie said. "I'm going to try to be incorrigible next," she added proudly.

What an odd child, Essa was thinking, but how refreshingly different.

"Why are you in here?" Essa asked. "It's sort of off limits, you know."

"Sorry. I'm hiding from Daddy."

"Why?"

"Well, he has this iPad," she said, "and he was putting stuff in it for work. I sort of messed it up." She winced. "I just wanted to play mahjong, but I think I accidentally deleted the icon on the home page." She sighed. "So can I stay here until he stops using words I'm not supposed to hear?"

"Is he doing that?" Essa asked, fascinated.

"I'm afraid so. He has a very bad temper. And there's a boy at school who used those words, and they suspended him." She frowned. "But I don't think they can suspend Daddy. He's too important to the agency."

"Agency?"

"Daddy's a senior investigator for a detective agency," she explained. "He's here investigating somebody who might have killed somebody."

Essa's eyes widened. "Wow."

"That's what I said." Mellie chuckled. "Daddy has the neatest job! We go all over the place when he's on a case. It's school holidays at the private school I go to, so I get to go with him."

"Does your mom go too?" Essa asked pleasantly.

The little girl's face fell. "I don't have a mom. Not anymore. She got cancer."

"I'm so sorry!" Essa said, and meant it.

"I don't remember her very well," Mellie replied, moving closer. "She was real pretty. Daddy has a photo of her and me in our living room back home."

"And where's home?"

"It's in . . . Oh, dear."

A deep, irritated voice was calling, "Mellie Marston, where the hell are you?!"

Mellie winced. "Oh, dear, he's found me!"

She ran behind Essa. "You have to save me!" she whispered. "I'm too young to die!" she added in a theatrical tone.

"You should go on the stage," Essa murmured as angry footsteps came closer.

A tall, husky man came into view. He had thick, pale-gold hair like his daughter and the same dark eyes. He was very good-looking, but very somber. Make that homicidal.

"Are you harboring a fugitive?" he asked curtly.

Essa cleared her throat. He was intimidating. "Can you describe her?"

"Four feet tall, blond, brown-eyed, guilty expression . . ."

"Precocious?" Essa asked.

"Extremely."

Mellie peered around Essa's apron. "I'm really sorry," she said. "I just wanted to play mahjong."

"And destroy my career?"

"No, Daddy, honest," Mellie said plaintively.

"What have I told you a hundred times about the iPad?"

She sighed. "Don't touch it without permission." She gave him a mischievous smile. "But you always say we should be curious about everything and explore things we don't understand."

"Not my notes when I'm on a case," he replied curtly.

"She's just little," Essa interjected slowly.

He glared at her. "I'm talking to my daughter, not to you," he snapped.

She drew herself up to her full height, which was far short of his. "In my kitchen," she pointed out, "and you're both trespassing!"

"Aren't you a little young for a chef?" he asked.

Her eyes flashed. "You can ask the boss that," she replied.

"Come on, Mellie," he said, gesturing to his child. He glared again at Essa. "Before she curdles something."

Essa gave him a mock smile. "Careful you don't get something curdled thrown at you," she said sweetly.

He made a rough sound in his throat and turned as his daughter followed him.

Mellie looked back at her. "Help!" she mouthed.

Essa just winced and waved goodbye. *Poor kid*, she thought as she turned to the stove. *Imagine having a father like that!*

* * *

The next morning, Essa was making rolls for lunch when Mellie peered around the corner, past the other cook and two helpers dressed in holiday motif.

"Can I come in?" she asked.

Essa grinned. "Of course. Make yourself at home." She glanced at the child. "How did you escape?" she teased.

"Daddy was on a conference call about the case, so I slipped out." She chuckled gleefully.

"What sort of case?" Essa asked idly as she kneaded dough.

"A murder. Daddy said he found evidence that the killer came this way."

"What sort of murder?" Essa was interested.

"A really bad one," she replied. "Daddy won't tell me much, just that there was a woman they found who'd been hit with a bat many times. There were two other bodies. One was a little boy, and one was a man. Daddy said the boy was an old murder, but the man wasn't. And the woman was killed very recently. Daddy thinks the murders are all connected and there's a suspect. But he won't say who."

Essa whistled softly. "That's quick work."

"Daddy knows his business," Mellie said proudly. "His boss says it's a coincidence that all the victims are together, but Daddy says it could be a serial killer."

"A serial killer," Essa said under her breath. "That's scary."

"But Daddy's boss said it was a coincidence." She

laughed. "Daddy hung up and said that the killer already had a support system and didn't even know it!"

Essa chuckled, too. "Sounds like it. Why does he think the killer might be in Benton?"

"Because his father came from here. There's supposed to be an old ranch house somewhere that he inherited. It's not in town. Out in the country. Daddy is going out there with the sheriff to have a look later."

"So his boss isn't going to make him go home?"

"Daddy wouldn't leave. He said they could give the case to somebody else, that he'd just hire on as investigator for this sheriff's department and go right on working it."

Essa laughed out loud. "Your dad's stubborn."

"Oh, yes. He grounds me for two weekends sometimes if I'm bad."

Essa stopped kneading, up to her elbows in flour, and glanced at the child. "When you're bad?" she asked absently. "How old are you?"

"Ten."

"How bad can you be, at your age?" Essa exclaimed.

Mellie beamed. "Well, I don't think it's bad at all, telling a teacher that she shouldn't pick on kids because they're a little slow." She grimaced. "I got sent to the principal's office. But our principal's nice, and he didn't even suspend me. It made the teacher really mad. So now I have to toe the line, so she doesn't get me expelled." She pushed out her lower lip. "But I'm right, and she's not. Nobody should pick on people who are different."

"Mellie, you're a nice person," Essa said, and meant it.

The child's eyes lit up. "You really think so? Thank you. Most people just say I'm irritating," she added on a sigh.

"It's that you're intelligent," Essa explained as she went back to kneading. "It intimidates grown-ups."

"I don't intimidate you, and you're a grown-up," Mellie pointed out.

"No, I'm not," Essa assured her with a grin. "I'm only twelve. I never grew up. It's boring, being an adult, so I'm not going to be one. Not ever."

Mellie almost gurgled with glee. Her dad was so busy that he never noticed her, and she had no other family. Kids at school didn't try to befriend her because they were afraid of the teacher who persecuted her. So she was mostly unappreciated. How nice to find a friend in such an unlikely place!

"Could you teach me how to cook?" Mellie asked.

Essa grinned. "Not right now."

"I mean when you have time. It looks like fun."

"It is. It's about my only talent. Well, I have a way with words, if my English teachers weren't lying." Her eyes were dreamy. "Someday, somehow, I'm going to sell a book. It's the dream of my life."

"I'm spelling-challenged." Mellie sighed. "And math challenged. And I hate having to read stories about people I don't even like!"

"You'll graduate one day. Then you can read what you like. But spelling is very important. If you ever want to learn a foreign language, it's a lot harder if you don't have spelling skills."

Mellie's eyes widened. "Do you speak languages besides English?"

"Oh, yes. Chinese, Japanese, Spanish, German, and enough Italian to get me arrested in Rome."

"Wow!"

"I love languages." Essa sighed.

"So does my dad. He speaks Spanish and German."

"Well!"

"Not much, though," Mellie said. "He likes archaeology. He says most of the antique papers and books on archaeology are written in German. He learned it because he wanted to research. He got his degree in anthropology, though."

"And he's a detective?"

"He didn't want to teach. And spending his life in a big hole with a toothbrush didn't appeal to him, he said. But crime-fighting did! So here we are."

Essa just shook her head. *What a fascinating man*, she thought.

And sadly that thought went into eclipse when a deep, furious voice called, "Where the hell is my daughter!" Essa grimaced, glancing at a worried Mellie.

"Oh, dear," Mellie said in a small voice. "I forgot to mention that he said I couldn't leave the room."

"Bad time to forget that," Essa said under her breath as six foot one of solid muscle and wondrous man walked into the room in tan slacks and a green designer short-sleeved shirt. He ignored Essa's small staff, working in the back of the kitchen.

"I thought I'd find you here," he muttered at his daughter. He glared at Essa. "Hiding out with the future Nobel prize-winning authoress," he added in a savage drawl.

Essa just glared right back at him. "Said the man who can't speak without resorting to foul language as a substitute for good grammar," she countered. She even smiled.

The glare got worse. "Well, my English skills are probably still superior to your writing skills. Or have you sold something in the past few hours?" he added in a sarcastic tone.

Essa turned, her hands caked with flour, and replied, "When I win the Nobel Prize for literature, I'll remind you that you said that," she said with a sweetly snarky smile.

"That's the very day that I'll be elected president, too," he shot back.

They glared at each other while Mellic cleared her throat.

"Uh, Dad, didn't you have a phone call to make?" she asked.

He blinked and glanced at her, as if he'd forgotten she was there. "Phone call? Oh. Yes." He glared at Essa. "Let's go. And stay out of the kitchen. I don't want the staff's bad attitude rubbing off on you," he told his daughter.

"It's not rubbing off, it's rubbing out," Essa told him with furious eyes. "And you are so lucky that I don't have a hit man who owes me a favor as a friend!"

"Good luck affording one on what you probably make working here," he said insolently.

"Hit men come cheap if you look in the right places!"

"I wasn't talking about hit men. I meant friends." He smiled as he said it, and Essa could have thrown something at that smug expression. It was almost as if he knew she didn't have friends.

She just glared. "Do be careful when you drink coffee at meals," she said with poisonous sweetness.

"Poisoning guests will get you fired."

"Extenuating circumstances," she returned.

He ignored her. "Let's go, Melinda."

"Yes, Daddy." She glanced back at her fuming new friend and made an apologetic face. The kitchen staff was doing its best to smother laughter. Their cool as a cucumber boss was flaming up.

Essa almost ruined the boeuf Bourbonnais. She was burning with fury; she'd never been so angry in her life. She hated Mellie's dad. She absolutely hated him!

She finished her preparations for the next day with the help of the kitchen staff. They got everything ready for the next morning. She wished them a happy night, took off her apron, and moved warily out of the kitchen, searching to make sure she could avoid the big, blond barracuda who was ruining her life.

But all she saw was a slight, blond man in khaki slacks and a button-up shirt. He stared at her curiously.

She managed a smile and started to walk away.

"Excuse me," he said in a soft tone, "but I seem to be

lost." He smiled apologetically. "It's such a big hotel and I'm supposed to be in a meeting room . . ." He looked at a piece of paper in his hand. "The Martinique room . . . ?"

The manager had a wild sense of humor. He had three meeting rooms in the hotel for convention goers, and each one was named for one of his favorite islands. Talk about eccentric! The owner of the hotel was equally so, though, she recalled.

Essa laughed and her whole face lit up. "Our manager names rooms after islands," she explained. "They aren't numbered. That one is up that staircase"—she indicated it—"and immediately to the right. There's a palm tree on the door."

"Oh!" He laughed. "Thank you. You're very helpful." He lifted a shoulder. "I'm not used to women being polite," he said, and then flushed, as if he thought he'd offended her.

She laughed, too. "I know what you mean! Common courtesy seems to have gone right out the door in our society. I'm frequently shocked at the way people will talk to total strangers. And online . . . !" She rolled her eyes. "I can't believe the comment sections!"

"Me, too," he said, warming to his subject. "Perfectly nice people turn into keyboard monsters online!"

"Exactly!"

He smiled warmly. "I'm Dean Sutter."

"I'm Essa," she replied, and shook the hand he held out.

He had an odd handshake, not limp but not assertive, and his palms were sweaty. He was only a little taller

than she was, and of a slight built. But he seemed nice.
She noticed the pin he was wearing on his collar, which
had a karate symbol on it.

"Are you into martial arts? Sorry, if that sounds nosy,"
she said.

He touched the pin. "Yes," he said. "I do tae kwon
do. Do you study martial arts?"

"Not anymore. I don't have time," she said sadly. "I
did tai chi," she added.

He beamed. "My father made me take it up. He said it
would teach me not to be afraid of people." He laughed
apologetically. "I guess it sort of worked." The smile
faded. "That's where he met my stepmother," he added,
"at a dojo." And his face closed up.

His stepmother must be awful, she thought, *judging
from his expression*. But she didn't say it. "What sort of
workshop are you here for?" she wondered, because
there were three this coming weekend.

"The forensic one," he said excitedly. "It's being
taught by a forensic expert from the crime lab in Denver.
I can't wait! I love forensics."

She smiled. "I do, too," she said. "I never miss those
crime dramas."

"Some of them are pretty good, but there's no substitute for the real thing," he said with enthusiasm. "You
can learn so much from even a few hours in a class. And
this one has a reconstruction expert."

"You mean those people who use skulls and clay to
reconstruct a face for identification?" she asked. "That's
an amazing skill!"

"It really is." He hesitated. "Are you coming? To the workshop, I mean?"

She grimaced. "I really would like to, but I just don't have time," she said sadly. "I'm the head chef here. And it's the holidays, so I stay pretty busy."

"Oh, you cook! Wow! I wish I could!"

She smiled. "Anybody can cook, honest. It's just learning the steps. Forensics, that's hard! Do you work in law enforcement?" she added.

He smiled oddly. "Well, yes, in an affiliated way. It helps with my work."

"Lucky you."

"No, lucky you! I love food. I just can't make it!"

She laughed. "It was nice to meet you . . . ?" She couldn't remember his name.

"Dean," he supplied.

"Dean," she said.

"And you're Essa."

She nodded. "Yes. I'll see you around the hotel, I expect?"

"Yes, you will," he said, and smiled from ear to ear.

She smiled back and waved as she went down the corridor. She didn't realize that he watched her every step of the way.

The next morning, she was up to her ears in breakfast with her helper, Mabel, who could make the best sausage and scrambled eggs she'd ever eaten, and the two maids, Jessie and Jennie, who took orders and served.

There had been a sous chef until last week, when he

got into an argument with the manager and was fired. So now Essa was doing it all. She hoped a replacement would be forthcoming. There was also an ex pastry chef, so the hotel was leaning heavily on the local bakery for desserts. So many people these days had an attitude problem. The manager didn't. He was nice.

"How in the world do you make a biscuit?" Mabel grumbled as she worked. "Honestly, I'm fifty, and I've spent twenty whole years trying to make one that didn't bounce. And here you are, and you don't even measure anything, and you make the most wonderful biscuits on earth!"

Essa laughed. "The secret is to watch someone make them, someone who knows how. The second trick is heat. It takes a very hot oven to cook biscuits properly."

"Well!"

"I just love to . . ."

"Where the hell is my daughter?" a deep voice boomed.

"Oh, no, not again," Essa wailed softly while Mabel gaped at her.

The big, blond barracuda was back. He stormed into the kitchen. "Where is she?"

"I have not seen your daughter, and this is not a public space. Out!" she raged, pointing to the door behind him.

He didn't move.

"Out!" she repeated, "or I will have Jeff Ralston come right over and remove you forcibly! He's our sheriff," she added in a soft, deadly tone, "and he likes me."

"I'd need convincing, and I know who he is," the man huffed. "Where is she?"

"I told you, I don't know! I cook, I don't babysit!"

He glared at her. "If you're hiding her, I'll have your head on a stick."

"Good luck trying!"

He made another rough sound and left.

"Who was that?" Mabel asked, shocked.

"A man who has a sweet little girl, God help her. Imagine having a barracuda like that for a dad!" Essa grumbled.

"He sure is handsome."

"So are sharks!"

Mabel hid a smile. Essa went back to work, too busy to brood about Mellie's ill-mannered dad.

After the breakfast rush, Essa was leaving the kitchen when she spotted Mellie apparently being hotly lectured by her father. He pointed a finger at her and then walked out of the dining room.

Mellie sat there, depressed and near tears, picking at what was left of her bacon and eggs.

"Dear, dear," Essa said softly as she paused by the table. "At it again, is he?"

Mellie looked up and her face brightened. "Oh! Hi!"

"Hi."

Mellie made a face. "Daddy was looking for me and he couldn't find me, so he got real mad. I was outside talking to this nice guy who was looking at rocks. He said he was hoping to find a fossil or something."

"A fossil. Is he a paleontologist?" Essa wondered, interested.

"He says he's in law enforcement," came the reply. "He's here for a forensic workshop. You know, blood spatter and reconstruction and trace element collection stuff. I wish I could go but Daddy won't let me near it. He says I'm too young," she huffed.

Essa chuckled. "That's too bad. I'd love to go, too, but I have to work."

"The nice man looking for fossils says he knows a place out of town where there are Native American ruins," Mellie said excitedly.

"That I'd love to see." Essa sighed. "I did a couple of courses in archaeology during summer semester at our community college."

"He says he has a degree in ant . . . anthr . . ." She struggled for the word.

"Anthropology," Essa said helpfully. "Archaeology is a sub-specialization of it. He must be very smart," she added.

"He seems to be." Mellie made a face. "Daddy has a degree in anthro . . . whatever it is, too. But he isn't in- terested in going on digs. I am. I wish I could go look for artifacts. That man was nice. But Daddy always warns me about men."

"My dad always warned me about them, too," Essa replied. "He was a deputy sheriff, so I guess he knew a whole lot more than I did about life."

"A deputy sheriff," Mellie said, sighing. "Daddy

used to be an FBI agent, but he said Mommy didn't like him traveling all the time, and us having to move to new cities when he was transferred. She said it was like being in the army."

FBI. Nice background, Essa thought, but she didn't say it. Heaven forbid that it should get back to the blond barracuda that she found anything interesting about him.

"Oh, look, there he is," Mellie said, nodding toward a slight man coming in the door.

"Well, my goodness." Essa laughed. "And I was just talking to him last night!"

"Do you know him?" the child asked.

"Sort of."

He'd spotted both of them meanwhile and came right to the table, smiling easily. "And here are my new friends," he said in a soft, almost shy tone. "Essa, isn't it?" he asked the older of the two. He smiled down at the child. "And you're Mellie."

"And you're Dean Sutter," Essa replied, watching the surprise and delight on his face when she remembered his name.

"You make me feel valuable," Dean replied slowly. "I'm not used to people remembering me. I sort of fade into the background wherever I go."

"Me, too," Essa confessed. "I don't mix well."

"Same here," he said heavily.

"He knows where ancient artifacts are!" Mellie said excitedly.

Essa's eyes lit up. "So I heard!" She shook her head. "You must be one of those really brainy people if you know anthropology. I did two classes in archaeology and barely was able to pull a C. It's hard!"

"Not if you love it, and I do," he said. "My specialty is forensic anthropology. It's a relatively new field, or it was when I took it up. Now it's gaining popularity."

"Wow," Essa said, impressed.

Dean looked conflicted, but he smiled from ear to ear. "They were leveling ground for apartments over near Ralston when they found remains and called in anthropologists."

"It's freezing outside, and there's snow . . ." Essa began.

He laughed. "Yes, but construction never ends, apparently. Anyway, I noted the digging and stopped to ask questions. They found human remains. That's my specialty, so I helped with identification."

"That was nice of you," she said, smiling.

He flushed with pleasure. "Anyway, after the workshop tomorrow, if you might like to go with me, the ruins are probably Woodland period, nothing older than two thousand years . . ."

"I'd love to!" Essa said at once.

"Oh, I want to go, too," Mellie wailed. "But Daddy would never let me!"

The blond barracuda had come up behind them unexpectedly, so that when he spoke, the woman and the girl both jumped.

"Go where? And for what?" he asked abruptly.

CHAPTER 2

"This nice man knows where there are some ancient ruins outside town," Essa said when the other two remained silent. "I took two classes in archaeology."

"They're probably just Woodland ruins," Dean told him easily. "But they are interesting."

"You know about archaeology?" Duke asked abruptly.

"Yes. Dean Sutter," he held out a hand and the men shook. "I do forensic anthropology for a private foundation that deals with law enforcement."

Duke's eyebrows arched. "Heavy stuff."

"Yes, it is," Dean replied. "It's sort of a cop-out profession," he added self-consciously. "I don't like blood and guts. Mostly what I deal with are skeletons. I sleep better." He chuckled.

"I had a few courses in forensics myself," Duke replied. "So I gather you're here for the workshop?"

Dean nodded. "I'm particularly interested in the reconstruction artist's work. I saw a documentary that featured her. She's very good."

"Coincidentally, I know her," Duke said. "And yes, she is. Very good." He glanced at his daughter. "You really want to go dig up old artifacts?" he asked. "In the snow?" he added, because it was coming down.

Mellie's eyes lit up. "Oh, yes!"

"It's a recent construction site," Dean explained, "or they certainly wouldn't be out in this. And they have a very limited time for the dig. I understand that the construction site manager is raising Cain daily about the delay."

"I hear that."

Duke glanced at Essa, his eyes narrowing. It caused an odd sensation in her nervous system, and she lowered her gaze quickly. "I guess you want to go, too?" he probed.

"I would like to," she stammered, glancing at Dean and smiling. He smiled back, apparently fascinated.

"Okay, Mellie," Duke said. "If she goes," he indicated Essa with a shoulder lift, "you can go. But I want to know when you leave and when you'll be back. And make sure your damned cell phone is charged this time, so I won't have to send out search parties!"

"It was just the once, Daddy," Mellie defended herself.

"You got lost in Chicago," he muttered. "There are places in the city where you could vanish in a heartbeat and never be found. And your battery was dead!"

"A very nice policeman rescued me," the child protested. "And drove me all the way home."

"Lucky," he replied, "for you!"

She grimaced.

"So we don't want a repeat of that, right?" he persisted.

"Absolutely not," she agreed.

"And especially we don't want to have Destiny 2, and the Xbox both taken away for two weeks again?"

Mellie stood up and crossed her heart. "Oh, no, we don't!"

"Destiny 2?" Essa was all at sea.

"It's the best video game on the planet," Dean said before Mellie could reply. "I loved Destiny 1. I still play it, in fact, but Destiny 2 is out of this world."

"And Starfield is coming soon!" Mellie added.

Dean chuckled. "I know. I preordered it."

She grinned. "I'm hoping I might get it for Christmas," she hinted, glancing at her somber dad. "But I have to have the new Xbox model to play it," she added sadly, with another pointed look at her parent.

"We can talk about that later." Duke checked his watch. "I have phone calls to make. You through with breakfast?" he asked his daughter.

"Yes, sir." She stood up. "It was delicious," she told Essa.

"Thanks," she replied. "But Mabel cooks breakfast. She's talented!"

"I'll say!" Mellie added.

"We can go tomorrow after the last workshop, if you two are agreeable," Dean suggested. "About four o'clock?" he added. "And we'll be back here about six."

"That works," Duke said.

"Okay. I'll see you both then," Dean said, smiling.

When he was out of earshot, Duke glanced at Essa. "Do you have a cell phone?" he asked.

"Of course," she said curtly, and displayed it.

"Charged?" he purred.

She flushed. "I've been cooking . . ."

"Be sure you charge it before tomorrow afternoon," he interrupted.

She glared at him. "I do not need a keeper!" she raged.

"Fat chance," he muttered, glowering. "I'd rather keep rats."

She started to speak, but he'd already gone toward the door after motioning for his daughter to follow him.

Essa watched them go. If looks could have wounded, that big, blond man would have been looking for medical assistance!

The next day Essa had her phone charged and ready by four, and since it was a slow day and Mabel was willing to cover for her, she had two hours free.

"But I absolutely must be back by six," she told Dean as she slid into the passenger seat of his modest car, with an excited Mellie in back. "Mabel can't do meats like I can," she added with a chuckle.

"I promise I'll have you back here in two hours," Dean said, and smiled at her as he pulled out of the parking space and onto the highway.

"Okay. And thanks for taking us with you," she said excitedly. "I love anything to do with forensics!"

"It's been a hobby of mine for several years," Dean said. "I love detective work. I suppose it comes from watching too many Sherlock Holmes movies and TV shows."

"Me, too." Essa chuckled. "But I read true-crime books, also."

"So do I," he confessed.

He was a good driver. He didn't blow up if people pulled out in front of him abruptly, and two did, and he was calm and collected at the wheel.

"You drive really well," Essa commented. "Much better than I do."

"And you don't cuss like Daddy does when people do stupid things," Mellie gurgled.

He laughed softly. "I was taught by my stepmother." His face tightened. "She was a perfectionist in everything. Nothing could ever be out of place, even in a drawer."

"Did you have siblings?" Essa asked gently.

He took a long breath. "A brother. He had . . . they said he had health issues. He died when he was only three."

"I'm so sorry," she said.

He didn't reply. He seemed to be in the grip of some terrible memory. Essa felt sorry for him. He was a nice person, and it was terribly obvious that his stepmother had been a bad parent. She hoped that his dad had been kinder to him.

"What are we going looking for?" she asked, hoping to remove that expression from his face.

"Oh!" He laughed self-consciously. "Sorry. It's a bad idea to recall bad memories."

"I know what you mean," Essa said. "I lost both my parents at once, when I was twenty. It was such a good thing that I could cook! I never run out of job opportunities, even in a bad economy. There isn't a hotel or restaurant in the world that doesn't need cooks!"

He laughed. "Well, certainly not. Although I might not have realized that."

"It's small beans compared to being able to date ancient artifacts," she replied easily. "I'm so grateful that you're taking us with you! This is an adventure!"

He glanced at her to see if it was a sarcastic remark, because he'd grown used to them over the years. But it obviously wasn't. She was flushed with excitement, almost vibrating with it. So was his young passenger in the back seat. He felt . . . odd. New. Different. It was like something shifted inside him, all at once.

He smiled, too. Then he laughed. "I guess you're right. It is like an adventure."

"Exactly," Essa said. "I can't wait!"

He was amazed to discover that he couldn't, either. He took a long breath and felt reborn.

The site was on a hill, and there were several people working there already. Dean led his companions to the man who was obviously in charge. They shook hands.

"I hope you won't mind two observers," Dean added after greeting Professor Blake. "They're fascinated with forensics, and we do have at least one physical artifact here."

"We found two more this morning"—Blake chuckled—"and we'll be grateful for your expertise in identifying them. Your companions are more than welcome." He greeted them. "Dean will tell you what you're not allowed to do," he teased.

Essa grinned. "Thanks! This is so exciting!"

The professor sighed. "I wish my students were so enthusiastic," he said in a confidential tone. "One woman is upset because her manicure is being destroyed by the work, and another is furious because I asked her to stay off her cell phone while we're working. She reminded me that it's the holidays." He shook his head. "Another one is posting everything we find on her social media accounts, with emojis of reindeer, which has led to at least one indigenous group threatening litigation! Times have changed."

"Oh, yes, they have. But you can be confident that we won't post any confidential information," Essa assured him. She smiled. "I don't have any social media accounts of my own. I just live on YouTube, watching animal videos."

The professor chuckled. "So does my wife."

"I like the funny ones," Mellie said. "And especially the ones about Belgian Malinois. Did you know they can actually run across full swimming pools and even climb trees?!"

"Yes, I did," Professor Blake told her. "My wife and I have one. He's smarter than we are. But he doesn't climb trees," he added.

"I had a dog once," Dean murmured, but he quickly turned away, looking for the new dig site.

His companions excused themselves and followed him. Essa was getting vibrations about Dean. She'd been ultrasensitive all her life to other peoples' emotions and to sound and light. It caused issues from time to time. She sensed that there were horrible things in Dean's past.

"Here it is," he called to the others, and motioned. He got down into the pit and studied the skull and partial skeleton with keen eyes.

"Okay," he told the student who'd just mapped the site and was waiting for input on its skeletal remains. "Male—note the brow ridges—and likely Native American"—he had the skull in his hands and was noting the dentition—"due to the presence of shovel-shaped incisors."

He put the skull down and picked up first the right and then the left skeletal arm. "He was right-handed—note that the right side of the skeletal remains is larger than the left. Also, the way we deduce the gender of the remains is through examination of the pelvis. To put it simply, it's larger in a female, smaller in a male."

He took his time examining the other skeletal remains the students had uncovered, and everyone around him seemed fascinated. Essa certainly was.

"That's so cool," Essa exclaimed. "How do you learn all that?!"

He grinned from ear to ear. "From hard work and a lot of time spent with my nose stuck in a book."

"Or in a dig pit," the student taking notes said with a glance at the professor. "For hours on end!"

"It goes with the title of forensic archaeologist," Dean chided the student. "And yes, it's worth all the agony."

"Where did you study?" the student asked.

Dean glanced at his watch. "My goodness, did you say you had to be back by six?" he asked Essa. "I'm so sorry! We're going to be late! We'd better leave."

"Time goes by too fast," she wailed.

"We only just got here," Mellie added.

Dean chuckled. "It's been an hour," he told them. "But I'm glad it seemed like just a little time to you two."

"Come back when you can," the professor told him. "You're a great help!"

"Thanks. I won't be in town much longer, but I'm happy to help while I'm here. See you later."

Dean led the way past the other students, who stopped to ask him several questions about the new dig site and the skeletal remains inside.

They had barely thirty minutes to get back to the hotel, but Dean drove at a steady pace and without rushing.

"You're always so calm," Essa said admiringly. "I just go nuts when I'm late, or when I'm in a bad situation. You make everything seem so easy and simple."

He beamed. "Thanks. I really mean that," he added.

"Oh, I enjoyed today. Thank you so much!"

"Yes, thanks a million," Mellie enthused. "I loved every minute of it! I think I might want to study anthropology when I'm older!"

"I'm glad you both had fun. So did I," Dean said, and seemed really surprised by the thought.

Essa wondered if he'd had much fun in his life. He seemed tormented by his own brain. But she didn't mention it. People often responded badly when she blurted out very private things she'd discerned by her own sensitivity.

Dean left them in the lobby and went up to his room. Duke was waiting for Mellie.

"Ready for supper?" he asked the child.

"Oh, very! We had such a good time. Dean knows a lot about skeletons! He was teaching one of the students at the dig site!"

"About what?"

"Gender and race in skeletal remains," Essa piped up. "He seemed very knowledgeable."

"How did he discern those?"

"Gender by size of pelvis, race by dentition," she said.

Duke pursed his lips. "And what if the remains were a mixture of two cultures, or even three?"

She just stared at him.

"One of my friends is a forensic anthropologist," he explained. "He said that it complicates things if you have mixed-heritage people, and there are a lot of them these days."

"Well, I guess it would be pretty hard. But these are at least two thousand years old," she commented.

"Different set of circumstances," he conceded.

"It was still fun!" Mellie said.

Essa sighed. "And now it's back to the real world. I have to get to work! See you, Mellie."

"See you!"

Essa glanced at Duke and didn't say a word to him. He didn't speak, either.

Mellie just sighed. It would be nice if her two favorite people liked each other. What a shame that they seemed to be enemies from their first meeting.

After the supper rush, when the kitchen was clean, breakfast preparations were made, and she was through for the night, Essa trudged out of the kitchen, drooping.

To her surprise, Duke was waiting for her in the lobby. The giant Christmas tree in its red-and-gold trim was gathering admiring glances, along with the twin golden reindeer flanking it, both with red velvet bows around their necks.

"Can I speak to you for a few minutes?" he asked.

She looked at him with visible reluctance. "It's so late . . ." she moaned, because it had been a long day, and she was really tired.

"This won't take long."

She shrugged and followed him into the bar.

"I don't drink . . ." she began.

"Well, I do. Have a seat." He put her into a booth while he went to fetch a gin and tonic from the bar. He came back and slid into the seat. "Want coffee or something cold?" he asked as an afterthought.

"No thanks. I had a Coke in the kitchen."

He sat back in the booth, staring at her evenly. He took a sip of his drink before he spoke. "Give me your impression of Mr. Sutter," he said.

She stared at him, surprised. "Can I ask why you want to know?"

"No." He took another sip.

She really wanted to blow up at him. He was terse, unpleasant, mildly arrogant, and conceited. But, on the other hand, he was really gorgeous, and she wasn't used to being singled out by gorgeous men.

"He seems very self-contained," she said after a minute. "There's something simply horrific in his past, something that torments him constantly . . ."

"How do you know that?" he asked, shocked.

She blinked. "I don't know. It's a . . . well, a sort of sensitivity. I'm extremely vulnerable to sound and light— I have migraines. But it works with people, too. I sense them. Sort of."

"Go ahead." He nodded, encouraging her.

She wondered what he knew about Dean and why he was so interested in the man. Then she remembered Mellie. He was concerned as a parent, of course. He wanted to know about a man who had befriended his daughter as well as Essa. Of course he'd checked him out.

"Well, he's incredibly controlled. Never loses his temper, never gets angry when another person might. He said that his stepmother taught him those things, but he didn't sound as if he cared for her. I got the impression that she frightened him. He's methodical, highly intelligent . . ."

"And extremely dangerous," Duke interrupted coldly. She gasped faintly. "What?"

"Never mind what. But if he invites you anywhere

away from here, where you'd be completely alone with him, find an excuse to not go with him."

"Why?" she burst out, stunned.

He ground his teeth together. "I can't tell you. It's confidential information. Suffice it to say that I know what I'm talking about. Most people are far different from the public faces they assume."

He irritated her by fingering Dean as dangerous. It was absurd! The man was gentle and kind. Unlike this barracuda!

"So, is your private face sweet and kind, then?" she retorted, throwing down the gauntlet.

"My private life is none of your business," he said pleasantly. "Any more than yours is mine—what you have of one," he added with faint sarcasm.

She glared at him. It was an insult. He assumed that since she wasn't pretty or what he would call intelligent, she never got out of her room. It was true, but she wasn't admitting that to him!

"I can go out any time I like!" she returned hotly.

He just raised an eyebrow and smiled. Smugly.

She got up, feeling cold and devalued; like the young teen who'd been the target of half a dozen unkind people who enjoyed tormenting her. Her father had said she had to learn to deal with people—so she'd tossed one of her tormentors into the backstop on the baseball field and been expelled. Not for long, because her father did get involved then. But she felt just as miserable now, with this blond idiot making her feel like an insect.

The jolly surroundings of holly and tinsel and golden bells didn't put her in any sort of holiday mood. They were a reminder of the joy she'd lost. And here was Mr. Perfection reeling off all her disadvantages.

She glared at him. "I'm tired and worn out. If you need any other information, you can text me," she said angrily. "And if I wanted to find someone dangerous, I wouldn't be looking for him at a dig site!" she added icily.

She turned on her heel and started walking.

He started humming the theme song to the Pink Panther. She walked faster.

She threw things around in her room, absolutely out of her mind with fury. The Pink Panther theme indeed! She wasn't Inspector Clouseau, and just because she went to a dig, she wasn't trying to be a forensic detective.

She could hardly think for the anger. So to counter it, she pulled out her laptop and sat down to work on her novel.

It was about a serial killer. She'd read countless books on them and hoped she had learned enough background to make the antagonist believable. The hero wasn't the usual muscular sports-type hero. He was more like Raylan in the *Justified* TV series—lanky and smart and afraid of nothing. He'd started out to be dark-haired and light-eyed, but lately he looked more and more blond in her mind's eye.

No connection to that conceited man downstairs, she thought quickly, and felt even more sorry for Mellie, who had to live with him.

But no worries about that right now. She had a new

idea for a scene, and she was going to write it before she lost the thread.

So far she had six chapters of what was probably going to be a sixteen-chapter book. It was more fun than she'd realized to write a novel. Now her only problem was going to be who would buy it. Well, that was a problem for later. Right now, the only thing she needed to consider was working on it. Which she did.

The next morning, Mellie came into the kitchen where Essa was working, morose and upset.

Essa stopped what she was doing and went to the child. "What's wrong?" she asked softly. "You look like the end of the world!"

"Dean said I could go to the dig with him today if I wanted to, and Daddy said no way."

Essa sighed, recalling what Mellie's dad had told her in confidence about Dean. She didn't believe he was dangerous, but taking a child alone to a dig site sounded a little bit off. He might mean to ask Essa to go along as well, of course. But if he did ask, would she go now, after talking to Duke?

"We just went yesterday," Essa said gently. "And your dad may have someplace special that he's going to take you this afternoon, did you think of that?"

"No!" Mellie looked at her plaintively. "He doesn't take me places, Essa," she said softly. "That's why it was so much fun to go with Dean. Daddy doesn't . . . he just doesn't do that sort of thing. It's work, work, work, all the time," she added sadly.

"Yes, but he might realize that, after seeing how much fun you had yesterday," Essa told her.

Mellie brightened. "Really?"

She smiled. "Really. So you should stay here, just in case," she added.

"Okay. I will." Impulsively, she hugged Essa tight. "You're so nice. You're like my mother was," she added quietly. "She was nice, too. Well, sort of nice."

"Did you lose her a long time ago?" Essa wanted to know.

"I was five," Mellie said. "Daddy's been different since then," she added. "He never laughed a lot, but he was different. Now, he never even smiles."

Except when he's taunting me, Essa thought irritably, but she didn't dare say it.

"I have to get back to work, but I'll see you later," Essa promised, smiling.

"Okay. Thanks, Essa," Mellie said, smiling back.

"You're very welcome!"

She was just finishing a complicated sauce when Duke walked into the kitchen, flaming mad.

"What the hell did you tell my daughter?" he demanded, hands on his hips, face taut with anger.

"You can't be in here!" she said quickly, darting a glance at the rest of the kitchen help.

"I'll leave when you answer me!"

"Oh, gosh . . . !"

She rushed him out of the kitchen. Time was of the

essence. She could get fired, even though the manager liked her.

"What do you mean, what did I tell her?" she asked under her breath.

"You said I was planning to take her someplace this afternoon! I am not, the hell, taking her anywhere. I'm working!"

She gave him a speaking glance. "If you don't take her someplace, Dean will!" she said harshly. "He asked her to go with him to the dig, just the two of them. So I told her you might be planning to take her somewhere, so she wouldn't try to sneak off with him!"

He looked shocked. He blinked. "She didn't say that."

"She doesn't tell you a lot of things, does she?" she asked shortly. "She's a lovely, sweet child, and you're too busy to notice! One day you'll wake up and she'll be grown and getting married or working somewhere in a profession!"

He hesitated.

"I don't have time for this. I have to finish the lunch menu!" Essa said, and started to leave.

He pulled her back around gently by one arm. "All right, I'll take her somewhere," he muttered. "But you have to come, too."

Her eyes widened like saucers. "Why?"

He gave her a glowering look. "Because if you're still here, he'll probably substitute you for her," he said shortly.

"He hasn't talked to me today."

"That doesn't mean he won't," he said doggedly.

"You can't go anywhere with him alone. Not you or Mellie."

"But he's such a nice man! Why?"

"I can't tell you," he said shortly. "I wish I could. It would make matters a lot clearer."

She drew in a quick breath. "All right. Where are we going, then?" she asked curtly.

"Someplace . . ." He stopped dead. He didn't know. "It's a surprise!" he said. "It's a birthday surprise," he added.

Her eyebrows arched. "Whose birthday is it?"

"Somebody's," he said. He thought. "My great-uncle's."

"Oh. Does he live here?"

"He died two years ago."

"But we're celebrating his birthday . . . ?"

"Nobody knows he's dead but me. So we're going to see him and eat cake," he said stubbornly.

"In the cemetery?!"

"Get out of here," he muttered.

She tugged at her arm, which he was still holding.

"If you don't come, Mellie will refuse to go," he added.

She shrugged. "Okay. I'm game. I love celebrating dead peoples' birthdays. Should I bring a cake?"

"Only if you want to end up wearing it," he said as he released her.

She smiled sarcastically. "Or you could wear it."

His eyes narrowed.

"Okay. I'm gone. I'm already a memory . . . !" She headed back to the kitchen.

"In the lobby, at four!" he called after her.

She threw up a hand and kept moving. She wondered if she'd lost her mind. She also wondered what he knew about Dean . . .

CHAPTER 3

Mellie, all excited, was waiting for Essa in the lobby at exactly five minutes to four. But Duke wasn't there.

"Where's your dad?" Essa asked, looking around.

"On the phone in our room," Mellie said. "But he said he'd only be a minute. You look nice," she added in a faintly surprised tone.

"It's the way I usually dress," Essa protested, glancing down at her jeans and Save the Cobras T-shirt, with sneakers.

"Your hair," came the amused reply.

"Oh." Essa had left it long. It came to her waist in back, pale blond and thick and beautiful. She wasn't sure why she'd worn it down. She usually didn't.

"It looks pretty," the child told her, smiling from ear to ear.

"Thank you," she replied gently, brushing back a stray strand of Mellie's blond hair. "Yours always looks pretty."

"Thank you," was the quick reply.

"Hello there," Dean said, coming down the staircase. "Both of you down here?"

"Yes, Daddy's got a surprise for me! And I wanted Essa to come, too." She lowered her voice. "Daddy wasn't pleased," she confided.

Essa laughed. "Yes, well, we're not exactly sociable," she agreed.

Dean shook his head and chuckled. "I'm sorry you couldn't come today," he told Mellie. He cocked his head. "You're a nice child," he added in an odd tone. He glanced at Essa. "And you're a nice woman. Not just nice. You have . . . you're odd. I don't mean that in a demeaning way . . ."

"I am odd," Essa said softly and with a smile. She studied him. "And I think you are, too. In a nice way. You have a . . . a sad background. But it's nothing you can't overcome."

He looked downcast. "That might have been possible," he said, "if I'd met you two sooner. But there are things we have to do that we don't want to do."

"I understand," she said, still smiling kindly at him.

He sighed and smiled back. "You really are exceptional. Don't think too badly of me in the future," he said, surprisingly. "I didn't know the right people at the right time. It might have changed everything."

"I see."

"You don't," he corrected. "But you will." He smiled at Mellie. "I've enjoyed knowing you. I'm sad and happy that you couldn't come with me today. You're a sweet child. I hope you have a wonderful life."

"Thank you. I think you're nice, too," Mellie said warmly.

Dean looked torn. He glanced at Essa. "I think

maybe her dad has a sixth sense," he commented. He smiled. "Or maybe you do. What a lucky thing. Or maybe it's just fate. See you."

He left them with a wave.

"That was a strange conversation," Mellie told Essa, moving closer to her.

"It was," Essa said, spooked by it. The man was saying a lot without saying anything.

They were still discussing it in whispers when Mellie's dad came down the stairs. He was wearing his usual indifferent expression, except that it changed to a tight-lipped one when he spotted Essa.

She glared at him and didn't say a word. He glared back.

"Essa is my friend. You don't really mind that I asked her to come with us?" Mellie asked in a plaintive tone.

He took a deep breath. "Of course not." He glanced at Essa. "I thought you were going to another dig with your friend Dean?"

"He invited Mellie," she said, "and then he invited me. But Mellie said you had someplace special for her to go that was secret. And she wanted me to come."

He scowled as he pulled out his car keys. "Why were the two of you whispering?"

"It was something Dean said," Essa told him. "He said you must have some sort of sixth sense. We didn't understand what he meant."

"And he said he was happy and sad that we couldn't go with him," Mellie added.

Duke knew something, Essa could tell. But she didn't question aloud the sudden change of expression that he hid very quickly. Obviously he wasn't sharing any information with the enemy, she thought wickedly.

He looked down at her with a strange expression. "Your hair," he said. "It's very long."

"Too long for my profession," she said, tongue-in-cheek. "It caught on fire once, before I learned to put it up before I went into a kitchen."

He actually laughed, but he covered it up at once by coughing. "Well, you won't be near any fires today."

She and Mellie followed him out to his car. Mellie quickly claimed the back seat. An amused Duke insisted she move to the front seat. He climbed in and glanced at both of them to make sure their seat belts were on before he put on his.

"I always wear a seat belt," Essa remarked. "It saved the life of one of my friends. He was in the passenger seat in a wreck. It was the only thing that kept him from going through the windshield. His mother said he had bruises where the seat belt dug into him."

"Better bruises than dead," Duke replied as he drove out onto the highway.

"Where are we going, Daddy?" Mellie asked excitedly.

He glanced at his daughter and smiled secretively. "Wait and see."

"Oh, Daddy!" she wailed. And then she grinned.

* * *

They drove to a neighboring town, about halfway between Benton and Denver, to, of all things, an ice-skating rink.

"Oh, Daddy, you remembered!" Mellie exclaimed, and hugged him tight. "I thought you said you hated ice-skating now and would never do it these days!"

"I didn't say that." He noticed her glowering at him. "Well, I didn't mean it, when I said that," he corrected. He handed her a bill. "Go rent some skates."

"Aren't you going, too?" she asked Essa.

"I don't imagine the would-be novelist here could stand up on them," Duke said with a bland expression.

Essa just looked at him with an expression that could have stopped a charging bull. She went with Mellie to get skates.

"Can you really skate?" Mellie asked. "'Cause Daddy gets real snarky with people who don't do it well. He has his own skates, too."

"I get by," Essa replied, not adding that she'd won a regional championship while she was still in high school. She also had skates, but she'd had no idea they were going to an ice rink on this surprise trip for Mellie.

"Okay then."

"Are you good at this?" she asked Mellie.

"Not as good as Daddy thinks I should be." She sighed. "He and Mommy used to skate all the time."

They both sat down to put on their skates. Mellie noticed how meticulous Essa was about lacing up the skates; it was something a beginner might not even know how to do.

"At least these have toe stops," Essa muttered, "but

they've really been worn. I guess I'll escape blisters. Some, anyway." She laughed.

"You do know how to skate," Mellie said enthusiastically.

"I might. Just don't mention it to your dad, okay?"

"Okay!" Mellie agreed. It sounded like great fun, helping her new friend get one up on her dad. So few people ever did.

They went out onto the ice and were surprised to find Duke already there.

"I thought we might have to pick your friend up off the ice. Several times," he murmured, waving the red flag at the bull.

Essa smiled. "You're so kind . . . oops," she said, and pretended to slip. She recovered her balance. "These things aren't too stable, are they?" she asked. "Gosh, it's a lot different from roller skates."

"Yes, it is," Duke replied with a very superior smile.

"Well, no time like the present to get started, right?" She leaned forward just a little, her legs in position. "Somebody want to give me a little push . . . ?"

Duke gave her barrier a gentle push. She skated around the rink, very fast, and because there were only a couple of people skating, and at the other end of the rink, she jumped at top speed, and went into a triple salchow, followed by a toe loop, and finally ending in the unique layback that had helped earn her the medal in district competition.

She skated off the ice, out of breath. "Wow, thanks

for the push," she told a wide-eyed, silent, blond man. "It sure helped!"

"That was awesome!" Mellie exclaimed. "How did you learn to do that?"

"Years of practice. I won a district competition medal about four years ago."

"Why did you quit?" Duke asked.

"Both my parents died of a virus three years ago," she said quietly. "I didn't have the money to go into higher competitions. And I was too busy with . . . other matters." She choked back tears.

"Any siblings?" he asked.

She shook her head, fighting for control. "Just me."

"I'm sorry," he said, and it sounded genuine. "That would have been rough, both at once."

She took a long breath. "It's never easy, losing some-one you love. It's worse when there are two of them. But they went together." She smiled sadly. "You almost never saw them apart, except when they were at work."

"What did they do?" he asked.

"Dad was a deputy sheriff. Mom worked as a dispatcher for 911."

"Well." He actually sounded impressed.

"Dad always wanted to get a novel published. I helped him work on them, but he never did." She looked up at Duke. "If I ever make it, it will be like he made it, too. If that makes any sense."

"It does," he told her, and for once, he wasn't snarky.

"Aren't you going to skate anymore?" Mellie asked Essa.

"I was just catching my breath." She glanced at Duke.

"I forgot to ask—can you skate?" she asked, and with a really snarky smile.

"I do all right," he said easily. He pushed away from the barrier, sped around the rink as she had, jumped, and landed a triple salchow, a double toe loop, and a very nifty layback.

His cheeks red from exertion, his dark eyes glittering, he glanced at Essa's open-mouthed surprise. "I love skating."

"Daddy was asked to go to the Olympics, but Mommy got sick, and he couldn't go," Mellie said softly.

"I'm so sorry," Essa said with genuine feeling. "You really are an awesome skater."

"Thanks," he said, and glared at his daughter for saying something so personal to a virtual stranger.

"She's not like most people," Mellie said surprisingly. "She's . . . well . . ."

"Odd," Essa supplied. "I don't fit in with other people. I sort of sense things about people. It makes them uncomfortable."

He didn't comment. They all went back onto the ice and skated until they were out of breath and in danger of getting real blisters on their feet, something professional skaters had the equipment, and the know-how, to prevent.

"They have a cafeteria here. Want to get something to eat?" Duke asked when they'd turned in their skates.

"That would be great!" Mellie enthused.

"I'd love to eat something I didn't have to cook." Essa sighed. She glared at Duke. "But I pay my own way."

"Fair enough," he said.

"Daddy takes out girls who always want him to pay for everything, and they hate having me along," Mellie said on a sigh as she and Essa came out of the bathroom together.

"You go with him?" Essa asked, surprised.

"Oh, yes. He said he wasn't leaving me with any babysitters. Not after that first one."

"What happened?" Essa asked, angry to think that the poor child had been abused or something.

"Well, she had a headache, so she took some pills and went to sleep." Mellie's face dissolved into gleeful mischief. "First I went outside and walked in the mud, then I climbed all over Daddy's recliner. Then I went into the kitchen and threw tomatoes at the wall. After that, I unplugged Daddy's computer and all the other stuff, including the internet and the router. By the time Daddy got back and found the babysitter asleep, I'd done a lot of very bad things. So from then on, Daddy always took me with him on dates."

Essa burst out laughing. "Oh, I can see why he did that," she told the laughing child.

"So that's why Daddy can't get married again," Mellie said. "I'm obnoxious," she added with a big grin.

"Obnoxious, precocious, and very annoying from time to time," her father said curtly. He was carrying a tray. "I got you a hamburger with extra catsup and French fries, also with extra catsup, and a lemonade."

"My favorites! Thanks, Daddy!"

Duke looked at Essa. "You said you'd get your own," he reminded her.

"Yes, I did." She smiled at him and went to the counter, returning with yogurt and black coffee.

"You call that lunch?" Duke exclaimed.

"Well, I'm not really very hungry," she confessed. "I eat a huge breakfast, and it lasts me until supper."

"I eat a big breakfast, too," he confessed. "Of course, I have to cook it," he added, glancing at his daughter.

"You won't let me cook," she defended herself.

"It took a month to get the repairs done," he retorted.

"It only burned a couple of cabinets," she said defensively.

"Yes, and taught your father to never let you near a stove again!"

"Not nice," Essa chided. "She's a sweet child. You've done a magnificent job of bringing her up," she added, smiling at Mellie.

Duke, surprised, checked to make sure she wasn't being sarcastic. But she wasn't. She really liked the child. He was very surprised. None of his dates had liked her and made it evident.

"You don't really mind that I'm obnoxious?" Mellie asked with a big grin.

Essa chuckled. "No, because I'm obnoxious, too!"

They both gave Duke a smarmy smile.

He groaned and finished his meal.

* * *

On the way back, he turned off on a dirt road when they were near Benton.

"Where are we going now?" Mellie asked.

"It won't take long, will it?" Essa asked in a small voice. "I've really enjoyed today, but I have to be back in time to get the supper menu going."

"No problem. I just want to ask a couple of questions," he added.

It was a small ranch with well-kept paddocks and newly painted fences. The livestock looked well-fed, and the horses showed no signs of abuse. Essa, who was raised on a ranch, fell in love with it, especially the ranch house, which was flat and sprawling and seemed to blend into the forest that surrounded it. Sharp mountains, snow-capped, rose in the background.

"It's so lovely," Essa said in spite of herself.

"What, no comments about poor cows?" he asked.

She gave him a long-suffering look. "We don't eat cows, we eat steers. And if you noticed the menu where you're staying, we offer several beef dishes that I'm required to cook."

"What's a first-time mama cow?" he shot at her.

"A heifer."

His eyebrows rose. He didn't say anything but just got out of the car and went to shake hands with a man standing at the foot of the steps.

"I wish we lived here," Mellie said sadly, laying her arm over the back of the seat and pillowing her cheek on it as she spoke to Essa. "I hate living in Denver. Daddy hates it, too."

"I love Benton," Essa replied with a smile. "It's small, but we all know each other. And Benton during the holidays is extraordinary! We have a Christmas parade with floats and lots of horses."

"I like horses and cattle. And I'd love to have a dog and a cat." She made a face. "We live in an apartment. You can't have pets there."

"I live in the hotel," Essa replied. "I can't have a pet, either. I had to give up my dog and my cat after my parents . . ." She swallowed, hard. "Anyway, I don't have pets anymore."

"Do you know where they are?" Mellie asked, sad for her new friend.

"Yes. There's a no-kill shelter in town. I give them money every week for their keep. They aren't mistreated and they get plenty of attention from the people who work there."

"I guess that's better than having them go to a different kind of shelter."

"It truly is!"

Duke was shaking hands with the man again. He was smiling as he came back to the car.

"You look like the cat who ate the canary," Essa remarked.

"I just discovered something."

"What, Daddy?" Mellie asked, excited.

He glanced at her with a secretive smile. "This place rents horses."

"Oh, Daddy," Mellie exclaimed. "Could we go riding? Please?"

He chuckled. "Tomorrow, if you like. I don't work Sundays."

"Great! And can Essa come, too?"

"Oh, I have to work Sundays," she said at once, and

then flushed when Duke raised an eyebrow. It wasn't true. She had Sunday off.

"But you have to come, too. You shouldn't have to work all the time," Mellie argued.

"She might not know how to ride, honey," Duke said.

"I can ride," Essa blurted out.

The eyebrow was still raised. "Really?"

She glared at him. "Really."

"Then how about after lunch on Sunday?" He made it a challenge.

She ground her teeth together. She'd planned to worm her way out of it, but Duke's smile and Mellie's pleading eyes put an end to that.

"I guess I could," she said after a minute.

"We can even stop by a convenience store on the way back," Duke offered as he got behind the wheel.

"Why?" Essa asked innocently.

"To buy you some liniment. For after you go riding," he added with a big smile.

She counted to ten silently. It wasn't going to be the best weekend of her life. Although he was in for some surprises. He seemed to think he had the market cornered on sports. She was going to wipe that smug smile off his face.

She was just on her way up the staircase after cleaning the kitchen when Dean stopped on his way down.

"There you are," he said, smiling. "I was looking for you."

"Hi," she said, and smiled back. "I've been making up for lost time."

"I guess so. Did you have fun on Mellie's surprise trip?"

"We actually did," she said, with sparkling eyes. "Mr. Marston took us to an ice-skating rink. He thought I'd fall on my face."

"Did you?" he asked, and seemed really interested.

"Well, a double salchow and two double axels later he changed his mind."

He laughed wholeheartedly. "I'd love to have seen that."

"I just love changing peoples' opinions," she said with absolute glee. "It was great fun!"

"I'd have enjoyed taking Mellie to the dig." He sighed. "Not that you aren't fun to be with," he added quickly. "But she's so innocent, so bubbly, so excited about learning new things! I love seeing the world through the eyes of a child. It's like going back in time and being one myself. A different one."

There was a sudden darkness to his tone, a look on his face that was a little scary. And then he smiled, and Essa chided herself for reading things into his expression that weren't there.

"I don't guess she'd like to go Sunday?" he asked hesitantly. "I could postpone my next project."

She sighed and shook her head. "Her dad is now going to introduce me to horse riding 101 on Sunday afternoon," she said with a flash of angry eyes. "It's going to be a very interesting day. I guarantee, Mellie is going to love it!"

He laughed softly when he saw the mischief in his new friend's eyes. "Well!" He chuckled. "I wish I was going to be here to see it."

"Oh, are you leaving?" she asked, and felt and sounded sad.

He was surprised and pleased. People didn't usually miss him. He felt a deep sadness, an aching sorrow, for what might have been under different circumstances.

"You're such a nice person, Essa," he said after a minute. "I'd have loved having you for a friend when I was younger."

"What a nice thing to say!" she exclaimed, beaming. "Thank you. I . . . don't really fit in well with most people. I'm always the outsider, the person sitting in a corner at parties."

"That's me, too."

"It's a shame we didn't know each other years ago. We could have ganged up against the sarcastic people," she said with dancing eyes.

He chuckled. "Yes, we could have."

"If I give you my cell phone number, we could keep in touch."

He looked shocked. "I would have loved that. But it's unwise. On the other hand, your email might be possible. Could you write it down for me?"

"Sure!" She searched in her bag for the pad and pen she always kept for making notes on dishes when she changed the recipe. She wrote her email on a small sheet of paper and handed it to him. "How about yours?" she asked.

He studied her very carefully and saw nothing under-handed in the query. He laughed at his own suspicion. "I'll write to you first, how about that?"

She grinned. "That would be nice. I don't meet many people that I don't want to lose track of, if you get my meaning," she added ruefully.

"That's me, too," he confessed.

He checked his watch. "Well, I have things to do, and I have to pack. I'll leave first thing tomorrow. If I don't see you again, it's been really nice, knowing you."

"It's the same with me." She studied him long and hard, sensing the anguish in him, the sense of failure, of incompleteness. "I hope life is kinder to you on the road ahead," she said softly. "Much kinder."

He drew in a long breath. "That's not likely. But thank you for the sentiment. Always be aware of your surroundings," he added suddenly. "Safety is an illusion. You're never safe."

She laughed. "You sound like that old pioneer saying, 'If you do not see any enemies, then they are the thickest.'"

He smiled, but he didn't laugh. "They're right, you know. There are enemies all around, and they aren't always obvious. Never take safety for granted."

"I don't," she said.

He cocked his head and studied her. She wasn't really pretty, but inside, she was beautiful. "I'm sorry and glad to go," he said. "Take care of yourself."

"You do the same," she said gently.

He gave her one long, last look and went on down the stairs.

When she got to the top of the staircase, Duke was watching.

She drew even with him, curious.

"Is he leaving?" he asked.

She nodded. "On Sunday." She looked up at him. "He asked if Mellie might want to go out with him Sunday. I told him we were going riding with you."

He drew in a short breath. "If you see her when I'm not around, will you watch her for me, so that she doesn't sneak out?"

"I will," she said. She drew in a small breath. "There's something . . ." She frowned, trying to put it into words. "He has something dark and cold coiled up inside him, like an ice pack in a teddy bear." She looked up again, surprised at his expression. "I put that badly . . ."

"No, you didn't," he replied. "It's an apt observation."

"You know more about him than you're willing to tell."

"Yes," he replied quietly. "I know things I can't tell. But we must both make sure that Mellie doesn't go outside the hotel with him."

"He's not a mean person."

"There are compulsions that make intent useless, Essa," he said, using her name for the first time. "People do things they don't expect to do on the spur of the moment. Sometimes more than once."

The comment went over her head. She felt warm all over when he said her name, and her cheeks colored. With all her after-school activities, she'd had little time for boys, and she hadn't liked the boys she knew in school. She was a novice at romance, and it showed.

It showed very well to Duke, who'd never had a woman say no to him. This one, however, looked as if she would never say yes to anyone. It was a joke at first, then it was a curiosity. He didn't dare think of it as a challenge. He had a child to raise, and seducing her new friend wouldn't help their strained relationship.

"I'll watch out for her when she's with me," Essa said quickly. "Good night." She almost ran to get past him.

He watched her go, surprised that she was starting to have an effect on him. Of course, he didn't like it. Not one bit.

CHAPTER 4

Essa lay awake a long time, wondering what Duke knew about Dean. He was obviously not happy with the idea of Mellie going anywhere with him. There must be a reason.

He was a private detective. He'd been an FBI agent. They had ways of ferreting out information that nobody else could get. What had he found out that he couldn't share?

She scoffed at that idea. Dean was such a smart, kind person. He couldn't have a mean bone in his body. He'd obviously been put down most of his life, but it hadn't turned him bad. He was polite and patient even when he shouldn't have been. He was kind to everyone he met.

So why didn't Duke want not only Mellie but Essa, too, not to go anywhere with him? And why did he want Essa to help him make sure of it?

She worried the idea until she saw the time. She had to get up early to start the breakfast menu with her helpers. She turned off the light and went to sleep.

Only to have dark and scary dreams. There was a house where a small boy was beaten with a small shovel, beaten bloody, while a woman yelled at him over and over again. There was a little boy who was wrapped in a white sheet and put into a hole in the ground.

She rolled over restlessly as the nightmare continued. Now there was a young woman with a man. She stripped the clothes off the little boy and held him down in a tub of cold water with ice in it. She laughed while she did it.

She wore a blue bow in her dark hair, and she had on a pin of some sort, a colorful pin with a fist.

The boy was dressed now and shivering. The woman had on some sort of silky black pajamas. She was teasing the boy with her feet, with kicks and feints, and laughing wildly.

Then she was wearing a dress again. She looked funny, like a little girl dressing up, with a blue bow in her hair and a short skirt. But when Essa looked closer, it wasn't the woman in the skirt, it was the little boy. He had the blue bow in his own hair now. There was a man, slight and older than the woman, who cowered as the woman struck him. He was crying.

He turned and his face was a skeleton. And then, suddenly, the face was her own!

Essa awoke with a stark cry of alarm. She was sweating. What a horrible dream. She'd never had any like it. She sat up in bed, holding her head. If that was what she could expect tonight, she'd sit up and watch old movies, she thought.

* * *

The relief cook showed up on time, thank goodness, so she was free to go with Duke and Mellie to ride horses Sunday.

"Have you ever been on a horse?" Duke asked as they drove toward the ranch outside Benton.

"Once or twice," she lied.

"Good. Maybe you won't fall off going down the trail," he added in what she thought of as his mocking tone.

"Oh, I'll do my best," she promised from the comfort of the back seat. "Not to fall off, I mean," she added.

"I can ride really well," Mellie told her. "Daddy taught me. We used to live on a ranch."

Nobody said anything. It was obvious that it was a painful subject, because talking ceased for a few poignant seconds.

"Where did you go riding?" Mellie asked her friend.

"Around here," Essa said. "I grew up in Benton. Well, near Benton."

"It's pretty rural," Duke replied.

"Yes, and small towns are like big families," she said, smiling. "I've always loved living here."

"No inclination to go to Denver and find some great fancy restaurant with a name nobody can pronounce?"

"None at all. I don't want to live in a city. Not ever."

"Why?" he wondered aloud.

She sighed. "I watch television occasionally. Detective shows, CSI, stuff like that. It seems to me that the best of the cities these days is the worst of humanity."

Duke's pale eyebrows lifted.

"I'm just one opinion," she pointed out. "Everybody's entitled to one."

"Why aren't you married?" he shot back.

She drew in a breath. "I'm not the sort of woman who attracts men," she said with a shrug. "I don't move with the times. I don't watch much television, the subjects I'm interested in aren't exactly party talk, and there's a real limit to single men around here," she finished.

"The streets are full of men," he retorted.

"Sure. But most of them are married. The divorced ones run if you even look in their direction. The single ones mostly have two or three obliging friends, and the rest are gay." She smiled. "I adore gay men."

"They won't marry you."

She shrugged. "Big deal. They're good company, and I don't have to fight them off at my front door. Figuratively speaking. And should we be discussing this in front of you know who?" she added, jerking her head toward a fascinated Mellie.

"Are you kidding me?" Mellie burst out. "You should come to school with me. We got into a vivid discussion of sex right in my classroom until the teacher came back in and called the police! Daddy came and got me, and I got transferred to another school!"

Essa's mouth was open. "You have got to be kidding me!"

"I wish she was," Duke muttered. "Before that happened, one teacher corrected a student and wound up in the hospital fighting for her life."

"This is not how things happen in Benton," Essa said on a harsh breath.

"Not when I went to school, either." He laughed. "My teacher kissed her boyfriend outside the classroom and my dad called a conference with the teacher and the principal. She was disciplined. That's how school worked when I was in grammar school. These days, it's unreal what kids go through to get an education."

"He tried to put me in a private school, but I wouldn't go," Mellie said with a grin. "I need to be street smart to live in the modern world!"

"Not that street smart," he muttered, glaring at her.

"I don't blame you," Essa told him. She shook her head. "I still can hardly believe what's going on in the world today."

"My grandfather said that people born at the turn of the last century would run for their lives in any modern city. I guess he was right. It's not the world that generation grew up in."

"Times are just a lot harder," Essa ventured. "It's because we're so connected. I mean, look at the tables next time you're in our restaurant. Half the people there are staring transfixed into their cell phones. They come in with other people and never speak to them."

"I have to agree," Duke said. "The internet and social media have been both a blessing and a curse."

"Mostly curse," she replied.

"Now, now, could we really live without our video games?" Mellie interrupted. "Daddy?" she added with a pointed glare.

"It's just a couple of video games, and I have to relax

somehow." He glanced at her. "We both remember when I tried dating."

Mellie rolled her eyes. "We should forget that."

"Hell, yes, we should," he agreed at once.

Essa was all ears, her eyebrows almost meeting her hairline. Waiting.

Mellie glanced at her and laughed. "He brought home this lady who worked for the agency."

"Yes, and she took one look at my daughter, muttered something about excess baggage, and ran for her life," he said, his tone dripping sarcasm. "My baby! Excess baggage!"

Essa chuckled. "I think she's amazing excess baggage," she said, with a big grin at Mellie. "She's precocious, but she's smart, and she has manners. You've done a good job," she told Duke.

"The lady said she wasn't raising somebody else's brat." Mellie sighed.

"You're both well rid of her, then, aren't you?" Essa replied. "She showed her true colors before any real damage was done. I mean, imagine if your dad had just dated her at work and didn't bring her home until . . ." She swallowed hard at Duke's glare. "Sorry. Not my business. Shutting up now." She sat back in her seat.

They both burst out laughing.

"Yes, just imagine," Duke said, shaking his head. "To be fair, most people don't want anything to do with single parents." He glanced at his daughter with obvious pride. "And my baby will never be excess baggage to me."

"Thanks, Dad," Mellie said, smiling at him.

"Somebody who doesn't want a child in their lives isn't somebody I'd want to be around," Essa added. "Benton is full of families. They come in here on Sunday after church." Her eyes were dreamy. "The kids spill stuff and have fights, and get called down, and drop stuff—and our manager just laughs and calls one of the maids to help clean it up. He helps, too. This place is tailor-made for kids. Nobody fusses." She grinned. "Try that in some fancy restaurant in Denver."

"I don't have the insurance." Duke chuckled.

"And I don't have the inclination. I'll take Benton anytime."

"So would I." Mellie sighed. "Isn't it just beautiful here?" she asked, looking around at the lodgepole pines and aspens, at the long wide pastures and the sharp-peaked, snow-capped mountains in the distance. "It's heaven."

"I've always thought so," Essa agreed.

Duke pulled off onto a dirt road with shale stones. The car slid like mad until he got the handle on driving on it. "Damn," he muttered. "We could go skating!"

"Shale is awful, isn't it? I used to live on a road like this when I was a little girl. I learned a lot of new words when Daddy drove on it in the rain," Essa told them.

He grinned. "I don't doubt it. And we're here." He pulled into a long dirt driveway with, thank goodness, no shale, and stopped in front of a huge log cabin. Out back were lodgepole pines, outbuildings and fences.

Over the driveway, coming in, was "Circle Bar E Rally Ranch."

An elderly man came out to meet them, shaking

hands with Duke. "I'm glad you could make it. I don't do a lot of business here. Place is going to rack and ruin," he added on a sigh.

"It's hard to make ranching pay," Duke agreed.

"Come along. I'll take you back to the stable. Only have about six saddle horses now. With the fuel situation what it is, I've had to sell off a lot of livestock. It's like they're trying to kill agriculture these days."

"It's hard everywhere," Duke said. "All over the world."

"Too many groups trying to save the planet and killing people to do it," the old man muttered. "But, hey, don't pay any attention to me. I'm headed for the big sleep in the not-too-distant future. This will all be the problem of the next generation, and good luck to them. They'll need it."

Duke just nodded.

The horses were beautifully groomed, healthy, and tame. The saddles were hand-tooled leather with all the bells and whistles.

"Wow," Mellie exclaimed.

The old man grinned. "Pretty, aren't they? I had a leather smith working here for a few years. He made me some of the best regalia I've ever seen. Got two dress saddles in the barn that I use when we have parades in Benton."

"Parades?" Mellie was all eyes.

"Of course! We have a spring festival, when we have floats and show off our horses. Then there's the

Christmas parade, with more floats and more horses. You missed that one; it's just before Thanksgiving."

"That's the beauty of small towns," Duke said with a sigh. "Parades in big cities are a little more lively, and not in a way I like."

"I get that," the elderly man said. "Well, they're all yours for as long as you want to ride them today," he said, indicating the saddled mounts. "Might not be here much longer. I'm going to talk to a Realtor tomorrow. I'm too old to run this place, and I can't afford the help I need," he added. He shook his head. "Lived here all my life. Going to be rough, giving it up. See you later."

He left them to it.

"That's so sad," Essa said as she watched him walk away.

"We used to be a nation defined by agriculture. Now it's all going to corporate farms and ranches," Duke said. "That's not a step up, in my opinion."

"Mine, either, but they've got the money to buy people out. Family farms and ranches are going to be extinct in a few years. I hate to see it," she said.

He nodded.

Duke helped Mellie get on the smaller of the three horses and turned to Essa.

"Need a hand?" he offered.

She shrugged. "Thanks for the help," she said, taking the reins. "But I think I can manage."

She vaulted into the saddle, patting the horse gently on the neck. "We should have asked their names."

"Oh, do you think they have names?" Mellie wondered as her dad mounted his own horse.

"Of course they do." Essa laughed. "Anybody who pays this much attention to his horses surely names them. We'll have to ask when we get back."

"You know how to handle a horse," Duke mentioned as they went through two gates, indicated by signs, one threatening sudden death if the gates weren't closed after people went through them.

"I used to do rodeo," Essa said as they rode. "I grew up on a ranch. My parents had horses and a few cattle, lots of cats and dogs," she recalled, smiling sadly. "It was the most wonderful kind of life. Mom was a great cook. She taught me everything I know. They were good people, both of them. It was hard to lose them both at once." She said it matter-of-factly, not fishing for sympathy.

"That's rough."

"It was. But I have friends here in Benton and around the area, and I know just about everybody." She laughed. "Small towns are like big families. Everybody knows everything about you, but it's because they care. They're not nosey, they're . . . well . . . family."

He chuckled. "Exactly." He felt her eyes and turned his head. There was a long look that made her uncomfortable. She quickly shifted her gaze, feeling her heart go wild in her chest.

"I grew up on a ranch, too," Duke said, surprisingly.

"Down in Texas. I married a local girl who'd been away at university. We dated for two weeks, got married, and nine months later I was a father."

"Yeah, I was unex . . . unexpected," Mellie said, laughing.

"Boy, were you ever," Duke said, wincing.

"Daddy was over the moon, but Mom wasn't happy about it, not ever," Mellie said sadly. "She used to call me names and . . ."

"Not cool," Duke said, glancing at his daughter.

She grimaced. "Sorry."

"We don't air our dirty linen in front of guests."

"But she's not a guest!" Mellie protested, pointing at Essa. "She's like, well, like . . . family, sort of."

Essa melted inside at the compliment. But before she could open her mouth to speak, Duke did.

"She's company," he replied tersely.

"Oh." Mellie sighed and didn't speak anymore.

Essa was confused and felt shut out, all at once. Well, at least Mellie liked her, she thought. And then she wondered why it should bother her that Duke didn't.

They rode around the property until the heat and thirst got the better of them. They went back to the corral, left the horses with one of the cowboys, and stopped at the front porch to pay the bill.

"Your horses are in great shape," Duke said. "It's obvious that you love them."

The old man smiled. "Always have."

"Do they have names?" Mellie asked.

"Yes, all six," he said, smiling.

"What are they?" she asked. "Please?"

He chuckled. "You ever see *Snow White*, that old cartoon movie?"

"Yes," Mellie replied.

"There used to be seven of them, but I lost Dopey last year." He chuckled. "You can probably figure out the rest of their names from that."

"Wow," Essa said. "That's just way cool!"

He grinned. "I loved that movie. The cartoon girl looked like my Velza. She was beautiful, too." His smile was wistful. "Lost her four years ago. But I'll see her again before too long."

"Can I speak to you for a minute?" Duke asked the man.

"Sure. Come inside."

"No, out here's fine. Essa, can you walk Mellie around the yard?"

"Sure," she said, confused.

Mellie laughed. "I'm a horse. You need a bridle for me," she teased.

"No, I don't. I can catch you!" Essa said, making a feint at her.

"Want to bet?" Mellie took off at a dead run, with Essa right behind her.

By the time they got back, Duke and the man had finished their conversation apparently. They were both smiling.

Duke watched Essa, not running so fast now, still trying to catch the young girl, who ran like quicksilver.

"I yield!" Essa called out in a breathless whisper. "I just hope my life never depends on having to catch you!"

"You're old!" Mellie teased.

"Am not," Essa protested, leaning over to catch her breath, hands propped on her thighs. "Gosh, you can run!"

"She can," Duke agreed. "If it helps, I can't catch her, either," he added, and gave Essa an odd look that she didn't see.

He turned back toward the car. "Let's go, females."

"Females!" Essa huffed.

"Well, if I call you a girl, I'll insult you. If I call you a woman . . ."

"Let's just leave it right there so nobody gets offended," Essa said with a wicked grin. "And I won't call you a toxic male. Deal?"

He chuckled. "Deal. I'll be in touch," he called to the old man, who threw up a hand.

He pulled out onto the road. "Who wants lunch?"

Two hands shot up.

He checked his watch. "Make that supper." He glanced at Essa. "When do you have to be back?"

"I'm off all day and tonight," she said, grinning. "The manager thought I needed a day off. He's such a nice guy. His wife and two kids are every bit as nice as he is, too," she added without guile.

"Do you like everybody?" he asked her.

"Well of course I do," she said, faltering. "I mean, we have rude customers sometimes who want to yell at me for seasoning a steak or something, but most people are nice."

"Seasoning?" he asked.

"It's like this," she explained. "There are people who have all sorts of health issues, and they can't have seasoning, or salt, or anything cooked with or around peanuts. So I always have the wait staff ask first. This one waiter had an attitude problem and didn't ask. So the man had heart problems, and I'd salted his steak pretty nicely. He didn't actually yell, but he did protest rather unpleasantly. We cooked him another steak, minus salt, and the manager gave him his steak free."

"That was nice of him. What about the waiter?"

She wiggled her eyebrows. "Fired that same night. We all went into the kitchen, broke out the cake, and had a celebration. He was nasty to all of us, and one girl threatened to have him arrested for harassment. Nobody cried when he was gone."

"He didn't bother you?" He couldn't imagine how that slipped out.

"Me?" She sounded surprised. "He liked pretty girls," she said.

He glanced at her in the rearview mirror. He didn't speak. His eyes did.

"You are so, so pretty," Mellie said firmly. "And you're pretty inside, where it really counts!"

Essa had to bite down hard on tears. It was the kindest thing she'd been told since losing her parents. "Thanks," she managed in a husky tone.

Mellie just grinned at her.

* * *

They stopped at a small tea shop in the middle of nowhere between the ranch and Benton. Amazingly, for such a small, out-of-the-way place, it was crowded with people.

"The food must be wonderful here," Essa remarked. "Look at that parking lot . . . no! No! You can't get a parking spot right in front, nobody ever can . . . !"

Duke turned to her and grinned.

"Dad always gets one," Mellie replied. "Even in the pouring rain. He says it's magic."

Essa shook her head. "It must be!"

They got a table to themselves in back after a ten-minute wait.

"So sorry," the woman, obviously the owner, apologized breathlessly. "We're just inundated with customers today!"

Duke chuckled. "My companion says any place with a full parking lot must have terrific food," he said, nodding toward Essa. "She's a chef."

"Well!" the woman said, impressed. "Where do you work?"

Essa told her. "We're not big, but we do a big business on weekends," she added with a smile. "I wish we had someplace like this! It's amazing!"

"Thanks. My husband and I drove through here and had lunch one day, and the owner said it was a shame he'd have to close because his cook quit. We had both just retired, and we had our bonuses. So we bought it, hired a cook who wanted to live here, and the rest is history. We're always full! It's such a blessing! You try living on what you get for retirement," she added firmly.

They all laughed with her.

The menu was incredible. It was New York City-type dishes, very high class, with homemade bread and specialty homemade ice cream and pies and cakes.

"This is incredible," Essa remarked as she took the first bite of her steak. "Perfectly cooked, beautifully marbled, perfect seasoning!"

Duke laughed. "I can't comment on the cooking, but the food is lovely."

"Oh, yes!" Mellie enthused, chowing down on a hamburger and homemade fries.

"Peasant," Duke muttered at her. "I raised you to appreciate good food!"

"Hamburgers are wonderful food," she shot back, with catsup staining her cheek.

Essa laughed, taking her own napkin to dab at the child's cheek. "You look like you're wearing war paint," she teased.

Mellie grinned back at her and took another bite.

Duke, watching and listening to the conversation, felt his heart jump. His wife had never liked Mellie. She would never have done something like Essa just had. And it was so natural, not a contrived thing, not with any ulterior motives. Essa really liked the child, and it was obvious. Mellie returned that affection. It delighted him even as it unnerved him. He did not want to get mixed up with a woman. He'd had the cure. Or so he thought . . .

CHAPTER 5

All too soon, they were back at the hotel. Mellie wished Essa a good night, hugged her quickly, and went upstairs to the room she shared with her dad to watch a cartoon movie on pay-per-view.

"Nothing rated above PG, or you'll have trouble," Duke warned.

She just waved and kept walking.

"Oh, she's a mess," Essa said with a grin, watching the child go up the staircase. "You've done a great job with her."

He stuck his hands in his pockets and studied her quietly. "You love kids. But you don't want to get married and have some of your own?"

She gave him a droll look. "I'm everybody's big sister," she told him. "If somebody's girlfriend dumped him, here's my shoulder. If his wife is cheating on him, here's my shoulder. If he can't get a special girl to date him, here's my shoulder. That's me."

"You can't be the age you are and not have a single proposal of marriage."

"Well, I did have one," she said. She grinned. "But he was six years old, and his mother wouldn't let him buy me a ring."

He chuckled.

"Besides, I have these nightmares . . ."

His eyebrows arched.

"I mean really bad, howling nightmares," she added. "There was this one about a tiny little boy being beaten by a woman. She was wearing black pj's, like those martial arts people wear, and kicking him. He vanished. Then there was an older boy, but he was sturdier. She was hurting him. He ran away. He was older and he went back. He found something. He went mad. He had a weapon . . . his face was a skeleton. But when he turned around, it was . . . it was me." She looked up at him to surprise an expression on his face that she couldn't understand.

"When did you have this dream?" he asked.

"Last night. I almost came down and canceled today because I've had hardly any sleep. It was one of those three-dimensional nightmares that you wish you could forget."

He took her arm and led her to one of the couches and sat her down with him.

"There's a forensic workshop in Carnesville, about thirty miles south of here," he said. "Next Saturday. I have reason to believe that your friend who loves forensics will be there. Could you get off and go with Mellie and me?"

She frowned. "Dean?" she asked.

He nodded.

She was all at sea. "You don't think he's done something bad, do you?" she wondered. "He's such a nice man. Very gentle. I don't think he'd hurt a fly."

"Neither do I," he lied. "But I'm working a case, and I have to investigate anything out of the ordinary. He's not your typical forensic geek."

"Well, no. He knows too much," she agreed with a smile. "He's very intelligent,"

He nodded. "I don't think he's involved in anything, but he might be acquainted with someone who is," he said enigmatically. "I need to find out. But I don't want him to get suspicious. If you and Mellie come along, and you tell him that it was your idea to go to the workshop but your car wouldn't make it that far and Mellie wanted to go, too—and what a surprise, you didn't expect to see him there!" He gave her a long look. "Think you can pull it off?"

She made a face. "I had the lead in my school play in sixth grade."

"Great. Then can you ask your boss for one more free day? Tell him you're solving a case with the sheriff's department. It might help."

"I don't need to. He's just really nice. And one of the relief chefs needs the work," she added with a sigh. "His wife just left him and is suing for child support for their son. Honestly, doesn't anybody stay married anymore?"

"Some people don't and should. Some people do and shouldn't."

"Thanks. That gets you the Enigma Award for the year," she said sardonically.

He chuckled. "I'll find out exactly when the workshop starts. Thanks." He got up. "Mellie really likes you," he added, frowning, as if he couldn't understand why.

"Yes, strange, isn't it?" she asked. "I usually only attract drunk men."

His eyes widened.

"At parties, if I ever go to them," she explained. "I don't drink, so I'm usually sitting in a corner by myself. If there's a drunk man within fifty feet, he'll make a beeline for me. I did a dumb thing and danced with one once, and he passed out at my feet on a crowded dance floor. Was that fun!" she drawled, rolling her eyes. "So I stopped going to parties."

"That's sad."

She lifted an eyebrow. "You aren't exactly a party animal yourself," she pointed out.

He shrugged. "I don't have the time."

She smiled. "She's the best reason to not have time to party," she said.

He smiled back, without sarcasm. "I like to think so." He turned. "See you."

He was gone before she had a good reply.

During one free hour, Essa took Mellie outside the hotel for a walk on the grounds. Some of the trees were shedding pollen profusely, despite the cold. Mellie started sneezing her head off and coughing repeatedly.

"Back inside, right now," Essa said, herding her into the hotel lobby.

But the coughing didn't stop. Her face was turning red, and she seemed to have trouble breathing.

"Give me your phone," Essa said quickly.

Mellie dug it out. She was still fighting for breath.

Her dad's number was on speed dial. Essa punched it, but there was no answer. She called 911 instead, but the ambulance would take too long to get to the hotel, so she told them she was bringing Mellie right to the emergency room.

She told one of her staff on the way out what had happened and where she was going. She had the woman stay with Mellie in the lobby while she brought her car around. Then they got Mellie into the front seat and Essa burned rubber getting her to the ER.

She explained the situation to a clerk, who got Mellie right into a treatment room. Luckily, there were very few people who needed to be seen.

The young doctor examined Mellie, called in a nurse, and gave instructions.

"Your daughter will be fine," he told Essa, assuming she was responsible for the girl, "but she needs to see an allergist. This is an asthma attack, and I'm betting it's not the first one." He smiled. "People don't realize it, but pollen can be a problem year-round, not just in the warm months."

"But she was only coughing," Essa replied, not correcting his assumption about her relationship with her little friend.

"It sometimes presents that way, which is why

people don't see allergists. It's not uncommon. She'll be fine. We're giving her breathing treatments, and I'll prescribe an inhaler. You got her here in good time. Don't worry."

"Thanks," Essa choked. She was really upset. The child could have died.

"All in a day's work," he said.

"I'll be okay," Mellie said as she did the breathing treatments. "Really, Essa."

Essa hugged her. "I'm so sorry! I never should have taken you out when pollen was in the air . . . !"

"Yes, but we didn't know I had asthma, did we?" the child asked gently. "Really. I'm fine."

Essa swiped at her eyes. "Okay."

Mellie's phone rang. Essa plucked it out of her pocket and answered it.

"Where the hell is my daughter?" came a familiar voice.

"We're in the ER," she said. "She's okay," she added quickly. "She has asthma."

"She has . . . what?" he asked curtly.

"Asthma. She started coughing while we were walking under some trees, and it wouldn't stop. I was so scared . . . I rushed her to the ER. They're giving her breathing treatments . . . Here, she can manage a few words . . ."

She handed the phone to Mellie.

"I'm okay, Daddy," Mellie said in a rasping tone. "Essa took great care of me. Yes. Yes. I will. Okay. Bye."

She handed the phone back. "He's on his way here," Mellie managed.

"Okay." She smiled at the little girl, mentally hoping somebody, a doctor, a nurse, an orderly, somebody, would come to save her when he walked in the door. He was certainly going to blame her for the attack. And she blamed herself.

Duke walked right into the treatment room. Mellie, still doing the breathing treatment, gave him a smile and a thumbs-up from her perch on the examination table.

Essa, standing beside it with her arms crossed over her chest, looked devastated.

Duke hugged his daughter. Then, to her surprise, he pulled Essa into his arms and hugged her close.

"Thanks," he said huskily.

She felt funny. He smelled of spicy cologne and soap, and he was as solid as a wall. All muscle. He was much taller than she was, but they fit together perfectly. She never wanted him to let go. She sighed and smiled and nuzzled her face into his shoulder.

"Thank you," she whispered.

He lifted his head and looked down into her eyes with affection. "What for?"

"Not being mad at me," she replied solemnly. "I didn't know she had allergies," she said miserably. "She could have died, and it would have been my fault!"

"Or she could have had an attack when she was all alone, with nobody to help her. How about that?" he added gently.

She took a deep breath. "Thanks," she said. "That makes it a little better." She glanced at Mellie and smiled.

"She's a trouper," she added. "I went all to pieces, but she was just so calm!"

"I taught her never to panic but to assess the situation," he replied, smiling at his daughter. "She's sharp."

"She's also asthmatic," the doctor added, coming in behind them. "I gather that symptoms haven't presented before this?" he asked as they shook hands.

"Never," Duke said, letting go of Essa. "Of course, we've rarely been out of cities until now."

The doctor nodded. "I've called in a prescription for a rescue inhaler, a nebulizer, and meds to use if she has an attack this bad again. I'd recommend allergy shots as well. You'll need to get her to an allergist as soon as possible."

"Is there one in town?" he asked, surprisingly.

"Yes. He has a branch office here, and he comes two days a week." He gave Duke the doctor's name and the phone number of his office. "Your daughter has a very adult attitude toward emergencies," he added with a smile at Mellie. "Your wife, I daresay, may need sedation."

Duke just chuckled. "We'll take that under advisement," he replied, not correcting the doctor.

Mellie was finished with the breathing treatment. Duke helped her down from the exam table.

"Get that rescue inhaler asap," the doctor recommended. "The pollen count is pretty bad, even though it's practically winter."

"We'll do that. Thanks."

"My pleasure."

* * *

"Now. Tell me all about it," Duke said when they were in the car. He'd actually arranged with someone to pick up Essa's car and deliver it to the hotel and leave the keys at the desk. And this time, Mellie was in the back seat and Essa was in the passenger seat.

"I started coughing and couldn't stop," Mellie explained. "Essa tried to call you, but your phone didn't answer, so she drove me to the hospital."

"No ambulance?" he asked Essa.

"It was ten minutes away, according to dispatch, and I was pretty sure we didn't have ten minutes," she replied. "I got her there very quickly. I'm just so sorry . . . !"

"Nobody knew she had asthma," Duke interrupted. "And you very likely saved her life."

"Yes, you did," Mellie said. She beamed at the woman in the front seat. "You saved me."

"I just did what anybody else would have done," Essa said.

"You'd be amazed at how many people wouldn't have done it," Duke said somberly. "I've been in law enforcement most of my life. You can't even imagine the things I've seen. Compassion in our modern society is a dying thing."

"Not here," Essa replied, feeling warm inside as Mellie laid a hand on her shoulder.

"Thanks for what you did," Mellie told her.

Essa squeezed the little hand and smiled. "You're most welcome."

Half the hotel staff poured into the lobby when Duke came in with Essa and his daughter, all relieved that the child was all right.

Duke just shook his head as they all went back to work. "It's not like this where we live," he told Essa.

She grinned. "That's why I live here," she replied.

"I wish we did," Mellie said on a sigh.

Duke didn't answer her. He just smiled.

They drove to the site of the forensics workshop the next Saturday. Duke was distracted, nobody knew why. Mellie talked nonstop about what Dean had taught them at the archaeology site.

"I think I might like to do archaeology," Mellie said enthusiastically.

"Me, too." Essa sighed. "But I'm not smart enough."

"You are so," Mellie said firmly. "You can do anything you want to."

Essa smiled at her. "You're very good for my self-esteem."

"Only when she isn't brooding about the dog we don't have," Duke muttered as he drove.

"We could have just a little dog," Mellie warmed to her subject. "They wouldn't know he was in the apartment!"

"It's in the lease, honey," he told her. "No pets. I'm sorry."

"I can't have a dog, either." Essa sighed. "The hotel won't allow it."

"I saw an old lady with a little puffy dog going up the stairs," Mellie told her.

"Oh, that's Mrs. Greeley," Essa replied. She smiled. "She owns the hotel. She comes every other month to make sure the place is running well and everybody's happy with their jobs. And their salaries. She's one of a kind," she added softly.

"You like old people?" Mellie asked.

"Very much," Essa replied. "You can learn so much just by listening to them!"

"You do that?" Duke asked.

"I go to the nursing home on holidays and take cookies and pies and cakes," she said. "The manager donates them. There are so many who don't have family anymore. All they need is somebody to just listen to them."

Duke nodded. "One of our agents is retired from the CIA. Boy, can he tell some stories!"

"I'll bet." Essa chuckled. "We have a retired Texas Ranger, and she's got lots of those, too!"

"A Texas Ranger. Wow!" Mellie said.

"I wish we had time to visit," Duke said. "But I only have a few more days to wrap up my part of this case. Which my boss doesn't think I'm doing."

"Why doesn't he come here and do it if he doesn't trust his people?" Essa asked, outraged on Duke's behalf.

He noted that and felt warm inside. She was getting to him. The more he learned about her, the more she attracted him. And her actions with Mellie after the asthma attack were the biggest draw of all. She was one in a million. Stupid local men, he thought, letting a treasure like Essa get away.

He thought of his late wife and how different she was from Essa. The pregnancy had been an accident. She'd wanted to end it, but Duke dug in his heels. He wanted the baby more than anything. She could have it, and he'd have to raise it, she said hatefully. She wasn't being tied down to diapers and bottles and sleepless nights. Fine, Duke had said. He'd do all that.

And he had. Her death several years ago hadn't been the tragedy most people thought it was. She'd had nothing to do with her little girl. She was irritated by the noise the child made, reluctant even to change a diaper, and she hated the constant crying. The child cried when she was wet or hungry, but his wife never seemed to connect those things.

He held down a full-time job and was a full-time dad, while his wife went out with her girlfriends day and night and left her child in his care. He never understood why she was so angry. When she got cancer she refused treatment. She had nothing to do with Mellie even then. Duke buried her with her parents. Mellie was only five years old.

Then he thought of Essa, rushing his daughter to the hospital, staying with her, bawling because she was afraid of what might happen to Mellie—that was incredible to him.

He rarely dated, because once women discovered that he had a child, they wanted nothing to do with him. The fact that he was a widower didn't even give him points, because any woman he married would be raising another woman's child.

His own wife didn't want her own child. But here was Essa, who adored Mellie, and it showed. It was also mutual.

"One thing, and we won't discuss this outside the car," Duke said when they got to the site of the workshop and parked. "Nobody leaves the premises with Dean. Is that clear? Under no circumstances whatsoever," he added, emphasizing every single word. "And we didn't know he'd be here, also. Got that?"

They both nodded. Essa wanted to ask questions, but Duke's expression deterred her.

Mellie and Essa exchanged puzzled looks, but they didn't argue.

Mellie was left with a prearranged babysitter at the site, to her utter disgust, but Duke was firm. He also cautioned the woman, who was middle-aged and formidable, that Mellie was not to leave the premises without his express, personal consent. In person. She smiled and promised.

Duke escorted Essa to the workshop, handing her a program as he picked up one for himself.

"They have some heavy hitters here," he murmured as they scanned the handout while participants came into the room around them. "One of these is a former FBI forensics supervisor."

"Do you know him?" she asked.

He looked down at her, smiling. "No. I was just a case agent when he was there."

She smiled back. He was so incredibly handsome. It made her heart sing just to look at him.

They stared at each other until a loud cough interrupted them.

They turned.

"Dean?!" Essa said, giving a good impression of absolute surprise. "What are you doing here?!"

He chuckled. "I can't get enough of these workshops. Why are you here?"

"I didn't get to go to the one at my hotel. Duke saw this one and offered to drive me." She made a face. "My car won't make it past garages. I'd be on the side of the road hoping for rescue if I'd tried to drive here."

"Well it's good to see you," he replied. "Did you bring Mellie?"

"She's with a babysitter, complaining that we shut her out of essential learning for her future." Duke chuckled. "She wants to be a forensic anthropologist. She said you impressed her that much," he added with an easy smile.

Dean flushed. "She really said that? About me? Gosh." He looked odd. "Tell her thank you. That's, well . . . that's one of the nicest compliments I've ever had."

There was a speaker at the podium, calling for quiet.

"Better get to my seat," Dean said. "Want to get coffee at the break? They have a nice café attached to the hotel across the street."

"Good idea," Duke said. "We'll wait for you at the intermission."

"Good deal," Dean said, smiling at them both.

They all sat down, and the program started.

* * *

The workshop went on until lunch. The first hour was a presentation by a blood spatter expert who explained the patterns and how they helped forensics examiners pinpoint the particulars of an assault in murders. The second hour was a talk by the man from the FBI forensic lab and included information about how even a grain of pollen or a fleck of paint could help solve a crime.

Then it was time for lunch.

"My head is swimming," Essa said, shaking it as they left the auditorium. "I've never in my life been more fascinated with anything."

"It really is fascinating," Dean said. "I've studied it for years and it never gets old." He had a faraway look. "It's just . . . well, sometimes I seem to lose myself in it."

"That's not a bad thing when it's your career," Essa teased.

He chuckled self-consciously. "I suppose so."

Mellie spotted them and jumped up leaving the babysitter behind, who quickly disappeared. "It's you!" she exclaimed when she saw Dean. She ran to him. "I didn't know you'd be here! I'm so happy to see you!"

He looked very strange, as if he were choking on something. He swallowed hard. "Mellie," he replied, and smiled. "It's good to see you, too. How are you?"

"I'm great! Are you learning a lot here for your job?" She grimaced. "Sorry. I guess you don't really need to learn a lot more. You're awfully smart!" She looked up at him and grinned.

He was breathless. He'd been undervalued by most people in his life, abused by some, ignored by others. But here were these two females, a child and a woman, and they both looked up to him. In fact, they liked him, and it showed. He didn't know how to respond to praise. He'd rarely ever had any.

"You're embarrassing the man, Mellie," Duke chided, but gently.

"No!" Dean exclaimed, catching his breath. "Oh, no, it's not that. You see, I don't . . . well, most people don't like me . . ."

"Why not?" Mellie asked belligerently. "They must not be nice people, then."

"Absolutely," Essa agreed. "You're just different. Smarter than most people, and that makes them jealous, so they ignore you or put you down."

Duke's eyebrows arched. "You're more perceptive than most people."

"Indeed you are," Dean added. He smiled at her. "I wish I'd known you—someone like you," he corrected gently, "when I was young."

She cocked her head, puzzled, but smiling. He looked young. Perhaps he felt older than he looked. "Thank you. But, why?"

He drew in a breath. "That's a question with a very long answer."

"And I'm starved. Lunch?" Duke asked his companions.

"Oh, Daddy, you're always starved," Mellie teased.

"Said the girl who ate a whole sub sandwich that she was supposed to half with me," he muttered.

She grinned and hugged him. "You're just the best daddy! And 1 was really hungry," she added with a chuckle.

Dean, watching, grimaced. It was acutely painful to him to see what a normal family was like. It pointed out poignantly what he'd missed, what he'd lost. His eyes went from Essa to Mellie, and he hated what was inside him, what would be dangerous to them. No matter what, he had to keep himself together. He didn't dare let loose the demons inside. He had to fight them . . . !

"Are you okay?" Mellie asked him, worried by the expression on his face.

The child's concern hurt him. He managed a smile for her. "I'm fine. I'm really fine," he emphasized. "I'm just starving," he teased.

She grinned at him.

He grinned back, touched.

They ate sandwiches and then ice cream at a table in the hotel where the workshop was being held.

"This stuff is really interesting," Essa said between bites. "I've read about things like blood spatter and facial reconstruction for years, but it's different when you get to see it in person."

"It really is," Duke said. "I used to do it for a living. Sometimes I miss that part of my life. Now all I do is track down fleeing fugitives and hunt deadbeat husbands," he added with faint distaste.

Dean seemed to relax a little as he said that. He

laughed softly. "I suppose that would get boring. What do you do?"

"I'm with a detective agency," he said, sighing. "I thought it would be as exciting as working for the bureau." He looked up and grimaced. "It isn't."

"His boss is mean to him, too," Mellie said belligerently.

"Mellie," her dad cautioned.

"But he is," she argued. "You shouldn't let him yell at you, Daddy. You should yell back."

"Yelling rarely solves problems," Dean commented absently. "In fact, it often precipitates them."

"Absolutely," Duke agreed. "And neither does beating a child," he added coldly, his eyes on his coffee.

Dean seemed to draw into himself, as if he could feel welts across his body. In fact, he could. It brought back horrible memories of his insane stepmother, who was the soul of kindness around his own father but cruel when nobody was looking.

"Children can be reasoned with," Dean agreed after a minute. "Hitting children only provokes resentment and injustice. And those often translate into crimes." He glanced at Duke with a wan smile. "I imagine you've run across a number of victims of child abuse who became murderers."

"All too many," Duke said, and his voice softened as he looked at Dean. "The world can be a cruel place to a child."

"Not this one," Mellie sang out, laughing. "Daddy never hits me." She glowered at him. "But he takes away my video games."

"Just punishment," Duke said with a grin. "Effective, too!"

Everyone laughed.

Dean finished his coffee. "If you aren't happy in your job, you really should find one that does make you happy," he told Duke. "Life is . . . very short."

Duke's eyes narrowed. "Short, indeed. And good advice, also."

Dean flushed with pleasure. These people made him feel of worth. He liked them. It made what he'd done harder. It made living with it almost impossible. He'd done something insane in response to two insane acts. He hadn't meant to. It had been impossible to draw back, to stop himself. It had been an act of passion.

He'd thought about Essa and Mellie since he'd left the hotel. He'd missed both of them. He could hardly believe it when they walked into this hotel. He'd been looking for a way to get back to them. And here they were.

But now he was in a quandary. He didn't know what to do. Wasn't it dangerous for them to be near him? If he'd done something totally insane once, couldn't he do it twice? Could he stop himself?

He didn't want to hurt either of them. He hated himself. He didn't understand the stranger who'd taken over his body. How was he going to go on living? He looked at the child and shivered inside.

CHAPTER 6

Dean sat with the others when they went back in for the last few segments of the workshop. All around him were reminders that Christmas was coming. Stockings hung on garlands of fir and holly interspersed. A Christmas tree, highly decorated, in the corner of the room. Happy things. Reminders of wonderful holidays.

But not for him. His holidays had been filled with fear and apprehension. His poor father, after she'd fooled him into believing she was the perfect woman, became terrified of her. She tortured him.

He'd thought that surely one day his father would stand up to her, divorce her, leave her. He'd begged him to, especially when he went to college. He came home on holidays, and those were agonizing. She laughed as she tormented the older man, called him names, belittled him. She did the same to her stepson, dared him to do anything about it. All through college she'd made him feel worthless, despite his high scores on tests and his successes. She couldn't even grasp the basics of what he did, so she belittled that, too. But most of the attacks were personal. He was ugly, she said, he'd never find a woman who wanted him. He'd be alone forever. He was too stupid, too lacking, too disgusting. Over and over and over again, almost his whole life, he'd had to listen to such things.

Outside the house there was an unmarked grave. He knew. She hadn't realized that he knew who and why it was there. But when he found the second one, just a few months ago, he'd poured out all his fury and hurt and vengeance on her. She'd laughed. He was just like his father, she'd taunted. He wouldn't do anything except cower in the corner and complain. She was still laughing when he saw the baseball bat that his father had kept, a souvenir of his childhood. He was barely aware of picking it up . . .

The lecturer had raised his voice. Dean caught his breath. He'd been lost in the horror of the past. He was almost sweating with the fear. He felt the most intense sense of guilt.

He couldn't escape the guilt. It was running down his sweating face like tears. Tears. He couldn't bear to remember. So many tears. He wanted to tell someone. He wanted it more than anything. But it would require a kind of courage he didn't have. She had seen to that. She, with her screams and taunts and dares and humiliation over so many bleak years.

He thought of her, saw her face, and was sickened by what she'd done to him. Things so horrible that he could never share them with a single soul. His poor father had suffered as well, every single day until . . .

But he couldn't think about that. Not yet. Essa and Mellie made him feel differently. They gave him hope.

They made him feel that he wasn't worthless. If he could just have them close for a little while longer, just a few days. Then, he decided, he'd do what he had to do. Surely he could work up the nerve by then.

They gathered in the lobby to say goodbye.

"I thought I might detour by the hotel in Benton on my way back to Denver," Dean said to the others. "Maybe we could go to the dig one more time," he added with a smile at the females.

"Oh, yes!" Mellie exclaimed.

"That would be very nice!" Essa seconded.

Duke just smiled, as if in agreement.

"Then it's a date," Dean said, pleased. "So, I'll see you in a day or two perhaps?"

"In a day or two," Essa agreed.

Mellie nodded.

They both smiled.

Dean said his goodbyes and went up to his room to make everything ready for the trip. He hoped he could outrun his guilt for just a little while longer. He phoned his lawyer and made some changes to his will. Just in case.

"You two did great!" Duke told them on the way back to the hotel.

"Yes, but now what?" Essa asked. "You've already told us not to go anywhere with him."

Mellie nodded.

"I'll think of something," he promised.

"Oh, Daddy, you always say that." Mellie laughed.

He wrinkled his nose and smiled at her. "It gives me time to think up excuses." He chuckled.

Essa listened to the byplay. She was still in the dark about what Duke wanted them to do and why. He knew things that he wasn't sharing. She wondered what they were.

Duke dropped them off at the hotel and went on to Sheriff Jeff Ralston's office in town.

"Any news?" Jeff asked with a smile.

"Lots. He's coming back here. He wants to take Essa and my daughter out to the dig site again," Duke told him.

Jeff grimaced. "Bad idea. Very bad."

"Yes, I know. But I don't have any evidence that would hold up—just a sec," he excused himself as his phone rang.

He answered it and went to the other end of the room. He listened to the arrogant, prideful voice on the other end of the line.

"You've spent enough time lazing around that hick town and producing nothing of note," his boss said. "So you either come back now or you're fired."

Duke was barely able to hold his temper. "I've been following leads. The man is dangerous. He's already killed three people . . ."

"You have no proof of that," came the icy reply. "You have a theory."

"The same killing method on three corpses and you think it's a coincidence," Duke said through his teeth.

"You're chasing shadows. You're supposed to be getting evidence in a burglary, not tracking down phantom killers!"

"The man is a serial killer," Duke said shortly. "I know what I'm talking about. I worked forensics for the FBI."

"Obviously their recruiter was desperate when they hired you," came the reply. "As I've just told you . . ."

"Fine. Take your job and shove it," he said. "I'll send you my new address. You can forward my severance pay."

"You can't quit! This case . . . !"

"Is now your problem." Duke hung up. The phone rang again. He ignored it and went back to Jeff, his face taut, his dark eyes blazing.

Jeff studied him. "Lost your job, I'll wager."

"I quit," he replied. "The damned idiot wouldn't listen. He wants me to investigate a burglary! There's a serial killer on the loose, I'm this close to nailing him, and my boss wants me to throw away the investigation for a burglary!"

"Your boss is an idiot. Come work for me. My investigator got married and moved to Denver. I need an investigator, and you need a job. The pay's probably about the same, except that I'm a dandy boss. You can have holidays free and even an occasional free meal when we go to meetings at our local gun club—I'll nominate you for membership." He grinned.

Duke laughed. "Well!"

"How about it?" Jeff asked.

"I'm hired," Duke said.

"You'll need a place to live," Jeff continued.

"Got it covered," Duke replied. He became somber. "Now, let me tell you what I know about this man, and why I want to deal with him right now . . ."

They spoke for several minutes, during which Jeff winced as he realized just how much danger Essa was in. He knew her, having lived in Benton all his life. She was a sweet woman.

"One slip," he began uneasily.

"There won't be one," Duke said firmly.

Fate laughed.

The next morning, Dean was in the lobby very early when Essa came down with Mellie. It was Essa's second day off in a week, and she'd already apologized to her boss for having to ask for it. But he, a forensics buff himself, was eager to be a part of the investigation, even on the fringes.

Essa started. She hadn't expected Dean this early. Nothing was ready. Duke had gone by the sheriff's office to make sure he had all his support people in place.

"I only have a few minutes," Dean apologized with an easy smile as he looked from Essa to Mellie. He checked his watch. "I have to be in Denver in two and a half hours, so this will be a very quick trip."

Essa calmed a little. That didn't sound like a man with nefarious plans, although she'd never been able to get Duke to tell her exactly why he was investigating

Dean. He'd mentioned a burglary case once. That might be it, but why was Mellie involved at all?

"So, can you come with me?" He chuckled. "I've already phoned the head of the team to clear it with him. He said they'd made some very interesting finds yesterday."

Essa relaxed. This wasn't going to be anything worrisome. She and Mellie could drive out to the dig site and call Duke from there. He could meet them at the excavation.

She glanced at Mellie, who looked a little more concerned than she did.

"Dad said not to leave the hotel," Mellie said uneasily. "He had someplace he was going to take us first. He said you probably wouldn't be ready to go until later this morning . . ."

"It's barely eight thirty," Dean said easily, concealing his dismay. "I'll have you back here by no later than nine fifteen. How's that?" he added, smiling at them.

"Well, that should be okay," Mellie said. "But if he starts yelling, I'm hiding behind you!" she added to Dean with a chuckle.

"Fair enough," he said. "Shall we go?"

They ran into one of the two day receptionists on the way out. "Essa, you still off, you lucky devil?" he teased.

She grinned. "Yes, I am! Dean's taking us to look at old dead things," she said with mock drama. "Eat your heart out!"

He made a face at her. "I love forensics, you know that. Couldn't I go instead of her?" he asked Dean, pointing at Essa. "I know how to use a trowel and a toothbrush!" he added hopefully.

Dean forced a laugh. "Sorry. The head archaeologist only gave permission for Essa and Mellie. Maybe another time," he added.

"Thanks anyway. Have fun!" he called as they went out the door.

Dean already had the car in the front parking lot. He settled Essa in the front seat and Mellie in the back.

"I should call Daddy," Mellie said, pulling out her cell phone.

"Not just yet," Dean said, smiling. "I have a surprise first."

"A surprise?" Mellie asked, diverted, putting away the phone. "For me?"

"Yes, for you. Something special." He pulled out of the parking lot. "Essa, seat belt, please," he said gently.

"As if I need it," she teased. "You're one of the best drivers I know."

He flushed a little. "You make me feel so good about myself," he said, almost to himself.

"You're a nice person," she replied, puzzled. "Surely I'm not the only one who tells you that."

"You're very nice," Mellie seconded. "And we'll fight anybody who says you aren't!" She grinned.

He was breathing uneasily. His hands on the steering wheel were white from the pressure. Essa and Mellie were such unique people. Kind. Generous. Empathetic. He wanted to keep them with him forever, to forget the past, to have a future that included them. Never had anyone made him feel so good about himself, made him want to make amends. But then, there was only one way he could make amends. And he couldn't take these kind people with him. He didn't know where he might end up. It might be a very bad place, and then what? He'd have sacrificed his kind friends on a whim. A sad whim. He couldn't just go out and collect kind people and make them stay with him. What had he been thinking?

He drove on to the dig site while Essa and Mellie talked back and forth about the previous day's forensic workshop, with Mellie asking a dozen questions.

"That's right, isn't it, Dean?" Essa asked suddenly.

"Wh . . . what?" he stammered, trapped in his thoughts.

"The speaker said that one grain of pollen found on a suspect's clothing had matched with a flower in the lapel of the victim, and that it had been prime evidence in the conviction."

"Pollen." He was blank, caught in the fever of what was coming. "Yes. Pollen. That's right."

"Are you okay?" Essa asked softly. "Dean, you look terrible. If you don't feel like taking us out here . . ."

He wiped at his forehead, where beads of sweat had formed. "I didn't have breakfast," he said dimly. "And I didn't sleep well. I'm all right. Really. Really I am."

Essa drew in a breath. "Well, we wouldn't have complained if you hadn't felt like doing it, you know," she said with a gentle smile.

Knives. Knives in his heart.

"Of course we wouldn't!" Mellie agreed.

They were so kind. Possibly the kindest females he'd ever known. Definitely not like his stepmother! He hated himself for what he'd thought. They were so innocent. They had no idea what he planned for them.

But Mellie's father suspected him. He was a detective. Did he suspect him of what he'd actually done, or was it just some sort of apprehension that had no name, a detective's hunch that there was something not right about Dean?

"There it is," Essa said, noting the dig site just off the main highway on a dirt road, but visible from the highway. She frowned. "I don't see anybody . . ."

Dean ground his teeth together. He sped up to the dig site and stopped the car. "Get out of the car, both of you."

They stared at him, shocked.

"Please," he ground out, eyes shut tight. "Please!"

"Dean, what's wrong?" Essa asked. "Can we help?"

"No. Nothing can help me now." He took a shuddering breath. "Please. Get out. You have your phones. You can call . . . for help." He looked at Essa with wild, unseeing eyes. "Please! Hurry!"

She didn't understand, but she felt a darkness in him suddenly—a vicious, cold darkness that was beyond anything she'd experienced.

"Get out, Mellie," she told the child as she unfastened her seat belt and opened the door.

"What is it" she asked Dean when they were standing beside the car.

"You'll know. You will. Forgive . . . me," he choked,

his eyes going from one of them to the other. "I was once . . . a kind person. It was the shock. I didn't think she'd do it. Of course, it wasn't the first time. He didn't stop her then. Maybe it was . . . fated. But when I saw what she'd done, I . . . I just went crazy. I loved my father! Please don't . . . hate me."

"Of course we don't hate you . . ."

"Close the door," he said through gritted teeth.

No sooner had Essa done that than he turned the car with furious speed and jetted out onto the highway, spinning dirt and gravel everywhere.

Duke had just contacted the sheriff of another county in Colorado, and now he had enough evidence for reasonable suspicion to make an arrest. It had taken some quick work by Sheriff Jeff Ralston, but he had a warrant, signed by a local judge.

Now all he had to do was get his girls and ensure their safety before he arrested Dean. He walked into the hotel and stood very still.

They weren't in the lobby where he'd sent them before he left the hotel. His heart stopped. His blood ran cold. Surely Dean hadn't come early . . . ?!

"Hi, there," the desk clerk called gaily. "If you're looking for your little girl, she and Essa went out to that dig site with Dean Mr. . . . Marston?!" he exclaimed, because Duke's face was white. Sheet white.

He was punching in numbers like a wild man with hands that were unsteady. Please, God, he prayed silently as he waited for his daughter's phone to ring. Please, God . . . !

It rang once. Twice. Three times. He groaned out loud, holding up a hand to ward off the desk clerk, who was asking questions. Four times!

Mellie, he thought with horror. Please, *God, spare Mellie. Spare Essa*. He couldn't bear to lose them; either of them!

Five times . . . !

"Hello? Daddy?" Mellie asked.

He almost staggered with relief. "Baby, where are you?" he asked at once.

"We're at the dig site, but there's nobody here," the child said. "And Dean . . . what? Oh, sure, here."

"Duke," Essa said, "Dean left us out here at the dig site. There's nobody here. He was acting very oddly, and he drove away like a madman! What's going on?"

"I'll be there in ten minutes."

"It's a twenty-minute drive . . . Hello? Hello?"

Mellie looked up at her. "Daddy drives like a maniac sometimes," she explained. "But he's a really good driver. He used to race cars," she added with a grin. The smile fell. "Did he say what was wrong with Dean?"

"No." She handed Mellie back her phone. It was cold out here, and lonely. "I wish I knew what was going on," she added.

Mellie pressed close to her. "Me, too. I hope Dean is all right. I like him a lot."

"So do I," Essa said. She hugged the child close.

* * *

It was more like twenty minutes before Duke showed up, and he was followed by an ambulance and a sheriff's car with sirens going and lights blazing.

Duke stopped by Essa and Mellie, but the other vehicles kept going.

Duke didn't hesitate. He scooped up the most important females in the world and hugged them close.

While Mellie pressed close, his head bent, and he kissed the breath out of a shocked Essa. She melted.

"I can't remember the last time I was this frightened," Duke said, kissing Essa's eyes shut.

Mellie pulled back and looked up at him. He was very pale. "I don't understand, Daddy. Dean brought us out here to see something the archaeologist found, but there was nobody here. He told us to get out of the car and then he took off."

"Like a bat out of hell," Essa added, meeting Duke's eyes and still disconcerted by that very passionate and unexpected kiss. "He said a lot of things I didn't understand, about what his stepmother had done and he saw his father and went crazy and did something. He was very upset about it. He asked us not to hate him . . ."

Duke just looked at her. He looked down at his daughter. "I thought I told you two to stay in the lobby," he said in a choked tone.

"We're sorry," Essa replied. "But Dean came very early and said the crew had found something exciting. He promised we'd only be gone for about a half hour." She shrugged and smiled. "So we went with him. After all, he wasn't really dangerous, was he? I mean, you were investigating a burglary for your detective agency. Most burglars wouldn't hurt a fly."

"Let's get in the car," he said gently.

When they were situated, he started to speak, but a sheriff's car pulled off the highway onto the dirt road and stopped beside them at the dig site. Jeff Ralston, somber and quiet, got out of his car and came to Duke's window, which was powered down.

"You were right," Jeff said. "I'm going to write a letter to your former boss and tell him what a damned fool he is!"

"Former boss?" Mellie asked, her eyes lighting up.

"Right about what?" Essa asked.

Jeff produced a crumpled, stained note and a pin in a plastic envelope. "I'll transfer this into a paper bag when my deputy gets back, but you can handle it this way without damaging the evidence."

Duke took the bag and read the note. He ground his teeth together. "Dear God," he whispered, and his eyes closed.

Essa and Mellie were very quiet, both consumed with unanswered questions.

Duke turned to Essa and handed her the bag. It contained a karate pin like the one Dean wore on his collar, and a note written hastily on the back of an envelope.

She read the scribbled note locked inside the bag.

"I didn't mean to do it," the note read. "She killed my little brother when I was in grammar school. My father said they'd take me away if I told, that it was an accident, my stepmother hit him accidentally. So I said nothing. She treated my father so badly. I hated to see it. He loved her. He wouldn't leave her. But I came home for Thanksgiving, and I found him. His body was still warm. She laughed. She said she was finally free of him, she could go out and get a real man to marry. I just lost it. There was a bat close by. I picked it up and . . . I can't live with what I've done! Essa and Mellie, they're both so kind. I never had kindness. Not from anybody. My computer is in my room. It will explain everything. I spoke to my attorney last night and signed a document online. You'll see why. Hug the girls for me. Tell them . . . I'm so sorry. So very sorry. I loved them both. I can't live with what I've done. This is what's best for everybody. Take good care of them."

It was signed Dean.

Essa was frowning, oblivious to Mellie in the back seat asking to read the note.

She looked at Duke for an explanation.

He took a deep breath and glanced at Jeff Ralston for help. He was too choked up to speak, the first time he was so affected by a perpetrator.

Jeff looked at Essa. "Dean Sutter's car went over the side of the mountain at a high rate of speed. He wasn't wearing a seat belt, so he was thrown from the car before the gas tank exploded." He swallowed. "They're taking him to the morgue at the hospital pending autopsy."

Essa felt the blood drain from her face. "He's . . . dead?"

Jeff nodded.

Tears ran down her cheeks. They ran down Mellie's, too. Essa reached over the console and gripped Mellie's little hand tight in wordless sympathy.

"Why?" Essa choked on the word.

"I'll tell you when we get back to the hotel," Duke said.

It was a long story. They pieced it together from what was written on Dean's computer, and there was a lot of information there.

His father had remarried when he was ten years old. His stepmother had been a martial arts expert. She worked at a convenience store part time. She hated her two stepsons. She hadn't wanted children, and she would have insisted that Dean's father give them back to his mother. But his mother had died.

There had been another child, a little boy, Dean's brother. She'd killed him and threatened to tell the police that his father did it if he didn't help her conceal the crime.

Dean's extremely wealthy father was cowardly. He agreed and helped her bury the child. The story went out that he'd wandered off into the woods when his stepmother and father weren't looking. There was suspicion of foul play, but nothing could be proven.

Dean's father, a mousy little man, did whatever his wife told him to. When he wasn't home, she tortured Dean in ways that he only insinuated on his computer. She made fun of him when he wanted to play sports in grammar school, ridiculed him day and night. His father was afraid of her because she did crazy things. The murder of his youngest son cowed him even more. He didn't want to go to prison. She'd threatened to make sure he did if he ever talked. So Dean had no respite from her.

Despite all she did, Dean put up with her until he came home the day after he graduated from college. His father hadn't been at the ceremony, but he'd promised he would be. When he got home, he found his father in a shallow grave next to the place she'd put Dean's little brother the day she killed him. Dean loved his father.

They went back in the house, and she bragged about what she'd done, said she'd have a new life now, one with a real man. While she was talking, Dean's eyes fell on the baseball bat he'd had from playing in Little League, before the evil woman snared his father. He walked toward it like a sleepwalker, picked it up and . . .

He didn't bury his stepmother. He left her for the forensics people to go over, to hunt him. But nobody had contacted him, not since the day they'd found her, when the investigating officer asked where he'd been at the time of the crime. Why, in his dormitory, getting ready to come home.

Nobody could disprove it, and the family was wealthy. Very wealthy. So questions that might have been asked of a less-fortunate son weren't asked of him.

He was, of course, the least likely suspect. Dean had graduated with a degree in anthropology and had made straight A's. His paternal grandfather had died his freshman year and left him rich. Filthy rich. His father's death had only added to his fortune. He was rich beyond the dreams of avarice. But he was warped by his childhood. Hopelessly warped.

Other women had been mean—women with smart mouths and spoiled attitudes, but Essa had been gentle and sweet. Like Mellie. The two of them had overwhelmed him with their kind natures.

Mellie had pleaded to come along when he invited Essa to the dig site. The child's obvious, spontaneous affection for him, like Essa's, had knocked him back. Their kindness only heightened the guilt he felt at what he'd done in an instant's passion.

So the only solution had been to take himself out of the picture. He could no longer live with the guilt, no matter how fitting a punishment it was for his cold-hearted stepmother. He'd sent the car over the cliff to make sure he could never harm another person.

By the time Duke got through explaining in his hotel room, Essa and Mellie were both in tears.

Sitting on the sofa between them, he hugged them both.

"It's for the best," he told them softly. "I know that you both felt affection for him. But he couldn't have had a normal life in any event, considering what his life had been like. Losing his little brother and then his father to a madwoman's insanity destroyed something inside him. When he killed her, it only added to his desperation. He couldn't bear it."

They were pressed close against his broad chest.

"I felt so sorry for him," Essa said. "He was such a sad person."

"But he was nice to us," Mellie told her father.

"Nicer than you know, yet," Duke replied.

Essa lifted her head. "What do you mean?"

"Dean left a document on his computer. It was signed and notarized, authorizing his estate to be split between the two of you," he explained.

"Why?" Essa exclaimed.

"He probably felt that you showed him the only real affection he'd ever had," Duke said simply. "The document, I'm told, will hold up in court. They can't find a single relative, no matter how distant."

"That's so kind," Essa said. "So at least we can afford to give him a proper funeral, right?"

He smiled at her. "Among other things. His estate is worth ten million dollars."

Essa just stared at him.

Mellie burst into tears. "I just wish he hadn't died," she said. "We could have visited him in jail and sent him mail and stuff."

"It wouldn't have worked out that way," Duke replied. "I'll explain it to you one day. Meanwhile, I have two other announcements."

They pulled back and looked at him from reddened eyes.

"First, I just took a job with our local sheriff's department as their investigator."

"Oh, wow, we don't have to leave Benton?!" Mellie exclaimed. "We can stay here with Essa?!"

He chuckled. "I also bought the ranch where we went riding." He shrugged. "I planned on dedicating my life to paying it off . . ."

"I'll pay it off," Mellie said with a grin. "And we can share it, Daddy!"

"I don't need millions of dollars," Essa began warily.

"Yes, you do," Duke said. "You can marry me and live with us, and we'll fund an outreach program for mental health here," he added. "That was what Dean asked that a portion of the estate be used for—before your mutual bequests were added."

"What a sweet man," Essa said. "I know, he was a killer. But there were extenuating circumstances. And if he hadn't had the upbringing he did . . ."

"We'll never know." He was studying Essa. "I believe I just made you a proposal of marriage . . . ?"

Essa flushed.

Mellie grinned. "You have to marry him!" she told her friend. "Then you can come live on the ranch with us, and we can go riding all the time!"

Essa burst out laughing. "Now, listen here . . ."

Duke got up and pulled Essa into his arms. "Mellie, go play that handheld game of yours in the bedroom. With the door closed," he added. "Now."

Mellie laughed gleefully and went running to obey her dad.

Essa was kissed until her mouth was sore, and then kissed some more. It was the most delicious few minutes of her whole life.

"I love kids," he whispered into her parted lips.

"Me, too," she managed weakly. "And Mellie shouldn't really be an only child."

"So we can get married and raise kids and hell in Benton, Colorado."

"Most definitely."

"Is that a 'yes'?" he teased.

She pressed closer with her arms around his neck. "I might need just a little more persuading," she whispered. He chuckled.

"No problem at all," he whispered back.

A small Christmas church wedding, with Mellie as flower girl, poinsettias all around them for decoration, and a passionate wedding night and morning and afternoon and night and morning later, Mellie knocked on the door of their new ranch house. Beside her, one of the receptionists for the sheriff's department, whose family she'd been staying with during the brief honeymoon, grinned, as it seemed to take a long time for someone to answer the door.

Essa opened it, wearing sweats, with her long hair around her shoulders. "Mellie!" she exclaimed, and hugged the young girl, and then hugged her some more. "Oh, I'm so glad to see you!"

"And I'm so glad to have you as my mom!" Mellie exclaimed, hugging her back, hard.

Duke came to the door yawning, also wearing sweats. "I hate jogging," he said to nobody in particular. Mellie ran to him, and he hugged her.

"Jogging?" the receptionist asked.

"Jogging." He sighed. "Our new morning routine. I suggested coffee and toast, but the exercise guru here"— he jerked his thumb at his new wife—"said not until we did a mile. So we did a mile."

"It's great exercise, and we don't want you to go to fat, now do we, sweetheart?" she asked with a purr in her voice.

He just shrugged.

"Thanks for bringing her home," Duke told the visitor with a grin.

"My pleasure. And when Jack and I go to Yellowstone on our vacation, you get to return the favor," she teased. "Except that we've got four kids. You'll be calling us every day to see when we're coming home," she added with glee.

"Don't count on it." Duke chuckled. "I love kids."

"Me, too," Essa said. "You'll have to bring help to get them back." She chuckled.

"Am I going to get brothers and sisters?" Mellie exclaimed, all smiles.

"We'll do our best," Essa said solemnly. She grinned at Duke.

He laughed, too.

"We also think that our chef should retire and work on her profession," he told Mellie.

"Her profession?" the receptionist asked.

"She writes novels," Mellie said enthusiastically. "And she's great! I'll never forget that first amazing line of her novel!" She stood up straight and struck a pose. "It was a dark and stormy night . . . !"

Essa threw a wadded-up paper towel at her.

And two years later to the day she'd met Duke and Mellie, during the Christmas holidays, Essa sold her first novel. She showed the acceptance letter from her editor to Duke while she held their firstborn son next to the Christmas tree. "Told you I could do it," she teased.

He pulled her close. They watched Mellie chase their new German shepherd puppy around the front yard of the ranch with delight. "I think you can do anything you want to," he said softly, and bent to kiss first her, and then the baby.

"I think you can, too," she replied. "Merry Christmas," she murmured.

And the look she gave him was so full of love that he grinned from ear to ear.

Essa gave a thought to the troubled man who'd paved the way for so many changes in their lives. The mental health outreach program worked hand in glove with local, state, and federal agencies to get help to children with mental issues. It was off to a running start and had plenty of support.

Dean, she decided, as she thought about it, would be pleased with the project he'd outlined and financed with his estate. The children who benefitted were also eligible for scholarships if they decided to go into courses of study that dealt with behavior modification. Mellie had already decided on a career in anthropology when she grew up, inspired by Dean's example. All of this was due to the influence of a tortured boy who had been given no help when he needed it the most. Now, many children would be saved, because of him.

It was a good Christmas legacy, Essa thought as her eyes went from her husband to her new daughter, to the baby. They were all gathered near the Christmas tree with so many colorful presents under it while they looked out at the first flakes of snow.

THE MOST
WONDERFUL RANCHER
OF THE YEAR

KATE PEARCE

Thanks to Jerri Drennen for beta reading this novella and to Sophie for making sure I got Pen "right."

CHAPTER 1

Nilsen Ranch, near Quincy, California.
Christmas.

Pen Jones took a deep breath and paused to appreciate the silence. In front of her a swath of dark-green pine forest swept majestically up the foothills and onward to the snow-covered peaks beyond. Behind her was the Nilsen Ranch, where she'd come to meet her boss. She spent most of her time in her family home in Quincy or working various minimum-wage jobs in town and often forgot how amazing the world around her could be.

Not that it was quiet. She smiled as the sounds of the forest became more distinct: the rustle of pine needles and the critters flitting in and out of the tall tree canopy. She'd already seen a posse of squirrels gathering last-minute supplies, two woodpeckers, and some kind of raptor circling lazily in the leaden gray sky. The predator wouldn't have much luck today, as the first snow had fallen, covering everything in a patchy white blanket.

Pen didn't mind the snow, which was good, because

once it got going, it tended not to stop for months. The mountain peaks often retained their icy, white caps way into the summer.

"Pen!"

She turned to see a figure waving and hollering at her from the fence above the pasture where she stood. "What are you *doing*?"

It was a question Pen heard a lot in her life. . . . She started back toward the barn, retracing the tracks she'd already made on her way across the field. Her breath frosted in the air as she tried to increase her pace.

Her cousin Bernie, who was not only her boss but the person getting married to Luke, the owner of the ranch, waited for her to reach the fence. She was easy to recognize because of her red hair and beaming smile.

"Are you okay?"

"I was just admiring the scenery."

Bernie repressed a sigh—something else Pen was used to. For some reason, Pen's wayward attention span made people worry about her. She didn't mean to annoy anyone, but she never understood the urgency people had for the simplest of tasks.

"I thought I'd arrived too early because I couldn't see any other trucks," Pen explained as they walked up toward the charming, wood-framed ranch house. "Then the sun peeked through the clouds, and I had to check out the view."

"Perfectly understandable." Bernie patted her shoulder. "Anton's going to be late, and Rob's already here."

They entered the ranch house where the smell of

coffee and fried bacon fragranced the air. Pen's stomach growled.

"Have you eaten?" Bernie asked as they both took off their substantial winter coats and boots.

"I had some cold pizza at six this morning." Pen paused. "Or was that yesterday?"

"Come and eat, and then we can start making plans." Bernie ushered her toward the kitchen. "We've got to wait for Anton anyway."

Luke and his mom, who co-owned the ranch, were chatting away at the table while Rob, who rarely cracked a smile, and never in Pen's direction, sat quietly sipping coffee.

"Morning, Pen! Take my chair." Luke Nilsen, Bernie's fiancé, stood and offered his seat. "I need to get out to the barn and help Noah. With Max lording it up in England, we're a bit shorthanded."

Rob raised his hand. "I can help."

"Not until we've finished our planning session." Bernie wagged her finger at Luke. "Don't forget you work for me, Rob."

Rob sat up straight, his brown gaze serious. "I'd never forget that, boss."

Luke looked amused. "Don't worry—I'm way too scared to pinch your café staff, Ber."

"Good. Now, off you go while I sort out our wedding catering. You do want to get married, don't you?"

"Absolutely." Luke blew her a kiss and turned to the door. "Don't be a stranger, Rob!"

Bernie pretended to huff and turned to Pen. "Help

yourself to coffee. There's plenty of food being kept warm on the stove, so grab a plate and dig in."

Pen took a pancake, some syrup, and a deep, rich purple-colored berry compote.

"There's bacon and eggs in the other pan," Rob said as she sat opposite him.

She looked up into his brown eyes. He had such an *interesting* face; she could stare at him for hours. Unfortunately, he absolutely hated it when she tried.

"Thank you for mentioning them, but this is fine." She surveyed her plate. It was rare for him to initiate any kind of conversation, as he tended to keep to himself.

"You forgot your coffee." To her surprise, Rob went to fetch her some. "White with two sugars, right?"

"How do you know that?"

His eyebrows rose. "We work in the same coffee shop."

"But I don't know how you like your coffee," Pen pointed out.

"Black," Rob said. "Just as it is."

Pen nodded. "I would've expected that." She returned her attention to her food. "This is very nice."

"Glad you're enjoying it," Bernie said from beside her. "Luke's still cooking for three calorie-consuming cowboys, when he's the only one left."

"Noah's gone, too?" Pen asked.

"No, he's just moved into his new house with Jen and Sky," Bernie reminded her. "He's doing his own cooking now."

Pen was just finishing her pancake when Anton walked

in, complaining loudly about the state of the roads, the snow, and the unacceptable position of the ranch in the middle of nowhere. He'd grown up in a city, loved noise and crowds, and found life in the middle of a gigantic national forest somewhat trying.

Bernie let him grumble as she settled him at the table, dished him up a plateful of food, and brought him coffee. Pen continued to surreptitiously study Rob, who was pretending not to notice. He'd rolled the sleeves of his shirt up to his elbows, revealing some of his tattoos, which were mainly done in black. When Pen had asked him about the art, he'd clammed up and not spoken directly to her for days.

She was used to people avoiding her annoying questions and didn't take it personally. But she'd learned her lesson and tried to suppress her immense curiosity around him. From what she could make out, the tattoo on his left arm was a dragon of some kind. She wondered how far up his arm it went.

"Pen?"

She jumped as Bernie spoke to her.

"Sorry." She smiled at her cousin. "What's up?"

Bernie had her boss face on and was holding her tablet, which meant she was about to get all business. Pen still wasn't sure why she'd been included in the offsite café-staff meeting, as she was just a barista. Anton did most of the baking. Rob ran the online delivery business, and Bernie did everything else.

Bernie smiled. "Thanks for coming out here. I wanted you all to see my wedding venue so that we can work out the logistics of feeding and entertaining everyone."

"Uh, I think we've all been here before, boss," Anton said. "We did Noah and Jen's wedding last summer."

"I know, but summer and winter are very different here," Bernie said.

Anton glanced outside and shuddered. "I guess."

"Everything will have to be inside so space will be tight." Bernie looked around the kitchen. "The good thing is that the guest list is small because we're planning on holding a second party in town so everyone local can attend regardless of the weather."

Pen nodded. "That's very smart of you, Bernie. If it does get bad no one would get out here at all."

She loved the winters when the town got cut off and the tourists stopped passing through. She also knew that several members of her family relied on those tourist dollars to make a living including her parents' bookshop, her cousin Lucy's B&B, and Bernie's café in town.

"As I can't supervise the catering on my wedding day, I'm going to rely on you guys to make sure everything gets done properly," Bernie said. "Anton's going to manage the food prep, most of which we'll have to do offsite. Rob's in charge of the logistics of getting everything up here, and Pen . . ."

Pen looked up.

"You're going to be the public-facing member of our team."

"What exactly does that mean?" Pen asked.

"You're my troubleshooter." Bernie smiled. "You're going to make sure everything is running smoothly, deal with the guests, and support the rest of the staff when necessary."

"You want *me* to do that?"

"Yes." Bernie looked at her. "Why wouldn't I? You're perfectly capable."

"Most people wouldn't agree with you."

"Then here's an opportunity to prove them wrong," Bernie said without so much as a blink. "I have faith in you, Pen."

Pen looked at Anton and Rob, but neither of them looked surprised at Bernie's decision to give her an important job at the wedding. She'd expected them to object or outright laugh, because even though she was twenty-eight, most people didn't think she could do anything except be a blond airhead.

"You might want to take notes while I'm talking to Anton and Rob about their parts in this event," Bernie suggested. "Obviously I'll send you all the info, but you might have suggestions or insights of your own to add."

Pen picked up her phone and stared attentively at Bernie who was flipping through the pages on her tablet. If her favorite cousin trusted her to make sure her wedding went off without a hitch, Pen would do everything in her power to make that happen.

As the youngest of three kids and a member of a large and boisterous extended family of cousins and aunts, she was used to being considered the weird one. Seeing as most of the guests would be her family, she was looking forward to proving that maybe she had her uses after all.

Rob glanced surreptitiously at Pen, who sat diagonally opposite him at the kitchen table. She was hard not to look at with her blond hair, bright smile, and sparkling positive attitude. Inwardly, Rob grimaced at his own thoughts. Little Miss Sunshine was just too much for him to deal with, so he tended to keep away from her. Unfortunately for him, Pen had never known a stranger and had tried on numerous occasions to draw him out.

He'd resisted so far, but it was difficult. He didn't understand why she kept trying. They had nothing in common, and if she really did get to know him, she'd probably run away screaming when she found out what he'd done and where he'd been. He wasn't a good man, but he was trying to become one, and he didn't need any distractions from achieving that goal.

He took another look. She was pretty, though, and right now she was glowing with pride because Bernie had asked her to act as the wedding coordinator. He had a sense that the offer had come as a surprise, but he wasn't sure why. From what he'd observed at the café, she was good at her job, and great with the customers, which was exactly what Bernie needed.

"Rob, the logistics of ordering the food, and whether getting it prepped at the café or waiting until the day itself, will be on you," Bernie said. "I'm absolutely sure you'll ace this."

"I'd better," Rob said, shifting in his chair. "I don't want to be the one to ruin the boss's wedding."

"Oh, don't worry." Pen grinned at him. "That will definitely be me."

"It will be neither of you," Bernie said. "Because I have faith that this day will go off without a hitch."

"No pressure, then." Anton sat back. "I guess I'd better finish that wedding cake."

After the meeting, Anton gave Rob a ride back to town while Bernie went with Pen.

When they turned out onto the county road, Anton glanced at Rob. "Are you okay about working directly with Pen?"

Anton had recommended Rob for the job with Bernie, and Rob would never forget it. Getting a job after being in prison was always difficult, and Anton had come through for him big time. Rob loved his work. To his surprise, he also loved living within the great national park, the fresh air, and the feeling that he could run for miles and never see another human being. It reminded him of home. He never wanted to feel trapped again.

"Rob?"

He realized Anton was still waiting for an answer. He shrugged. "Not a problem for me."

"She's family. I guess Bernie thinks she'll be great at handling all the awkward relatives."

"Pen's good with people."

Anton nodded. "Yeah, she is. In her own particular way."

He lapsed into silence until they pulled up behind the café on Main Street. "I'll show you the menu Bernie and I have planned for the wedding buffet, okay?"

"Sounds good." Rob got out of the SUV. "The sooner I know what we need, the better, because I have a feeling, we're going to need supplies as soon as possible."

He glanced over at the snow-covered hills. "Last year this place got completely cut off again, as did the ranch."

Anton waggled his eyebrows at him. "Maybe you shouldn't have decided to move out of town, then."

"I think you needed your space back." Rob keyed in the code to the new extension at the back of the café that housed the state-of-the-art industrial kitchen. "And you snored."

Anton chuckled. "Yeah, and you hate my cat."

"Correction. Your cat hates me. I love cats. My mom had several. . . ." He stopped speaking. Talking about his family made him feel bad, and he needed to be positive and focused right now.

Rob took off his coat and boots, washed up, and made sure he was ready to enter the kitchen in a hygienic state. Since Bernie had expanded the business, they needed to do things to code, and as one of the team leaders, he had to set an example. He still couldn't believe he had a team working under him. At first it had been just him and Bernie, but the online café had taken off, and now he was managing real people with a substantial budget, and there was talk of a statewide expansion. . . .

Sometimes he woke up at night terrified he'd been found out and dragged back to prison, but so far so good. Bernie trusted him and his team seemed to listen to him. Back before he'd succumbed to the lows of painkiller addiction he'd worked in a Michelin-starred restaurant and ran a team of twenty. He'd been fired because he couldn't handle the pressure. After that, he'd slid slowly down the ranks from employed to unemployed, and then onto the streets, where things had gotten ugly.

"Hey, Rob!"

He looked over toward the large pantry where Matty was waving at him.

"Can you take a look at our chocolate chip supply? I think we're getting low."

"Can't have that." Rob walked over to Matty. "The customers would riot."

CHAPTER 2

Pen set her notebook on the kitchen table and found her pencil. Bernie had given her a list of guests and the basic layout of the ranch and asked her to work out how to fit everyone in for both the ceremony and the sit-down reception afterward. Thirty guests didn't sound like a lot until you tried to squeeze them into spaces meant for a family of four.

She walked through the kitchen and onward into the family room, where a basket of toys sat beside a large TV and a couch. Everyone who lived at the ranch was out, and it was blessedly quiet, which gave her time to think things through. The family room was the biggest indoor space available, and unless Pen could come up with an alternative that didn't involve remodeling the house, it would have to double as both the place for the actual wedding and the meal afterward.

Pen turned a slow circle and nibbled the end of her pencil. Clearing the room of furniture wouldn't be a problem, and introducing rows of folding chairs was very doable. But because it was the only usable large space on the ranch, they wouldn't be able to set up the tables for the dinner until the last minute, which left the problem of what to do with the guests while the transformation happened.

She went back into the hallway and contemplated the closed doors that ran down both sides. There were four bedrooms, but none of them were big enough to house the guests, so where was she going to put them?

Pen got out her phone and sent a text to Bernie, who was working at the café.

Does anyone have a tape measure up here?

Bernie replied quickly.

How would I know? I don't live there yet. ☺ Check in with Luke or Sally. Or try the second drawer on the right in the kitchen. That's where they keep all their junk.

Pen headed back to the kitchen and had just opened the drawer when the screen door banged, and someone came into the mudroom.

"Hey, Luke!" Pen called out. "I swear I'm not a burglar. I'm just going through your stuff." She started looking through the miscellaneous things stuffed into the drawer.

Behind her someone cleared their throat. "I'm not Luke."

Pen jumped and spun around, a ladle in her hand.

"Rob?"

He gestured at the ladle. "Do you want to put that down?"

"You startled me."

"Yeah, sorry about that. I wasn't expecting anyone to be home."

"Neither was I." Pen set the ladle on the countertop. "Are you here about the wedding?"

A crease appeared between his brows. "No, why would I be?"

"Because you're here."

Rob just stared at her.

Pen regarded him carefully. "And you look different."

"That's probably because I'm not in my work clothes."

He wore a tight black T-shirt, jeans, and socks, and his hair looked like it had been flattened under a hat.

"In fact, you look like a cowboy," Pen said.

His faint smile made her stare at his mouth.

"I guess that makes sense, since I live on a ranch."

"You live here?" Pen blinked at him.

"Yeah."

"Since when?"

"Since Luke offered to rent me one of the converted bunkhouses."

"I thought you lived with Anton in town."

"I did for a while, but he needed his space back." Rob looked out the window. "I like it here, and Luke gives me a break on the rent if I help out on the ranch."

"You do the cooking?"

"Nope."

"Then what do you do?"

"Cowboy stuff." He gestured at the ladle. "Can I help you find something? I know my way around this kitchen pretty well now. Sally insists I eat most of my meals with the family."

"I was looking for a tape measure," Pen said, aware that he'd obviously had enough of her incessant questions and certainly wasn't going to tell her how he knew how to cowboy up. "I'm trying to work out where to put the guests after the ceremony in the family room while we set up the tables for the wedding reception."

He glanced down the hallway. "Yeah, that's a tough one."

"I was thinking that if we took out the table in the kitchen there would at least be room to serve drinks." Pen frowned. "But then they'd be in the way of the food prep, and the kitchen staff won't like that."

"What about the mudroom?" Rob suggested.

"Too small, but it might work as a flow-through from the kitchen. Maybe if we put a narrow barrier between the dining areas and the actual kitchen and then remove the table, there would be enough space." Pen walked toward it. "Although I wonder whether we could rig up some kind of awning outside the house and send everyone out there."

Rob had followed her. "Not if it's snowing."

She sighed. "This isn't as easy as I'd thought it would be. Bernie's going to regret asking me to do anything."

"You'll figure it out," Rob said, and then paused. "I just came in to get something to eat before I go back to town. Can I get you anything?"

Pen checked the time. "I should be going soon myself. I've got a shift at the bookstore today while Mom's out."

"Just coffee, then?"

"That would be great."

She watched him deal with the coffee machine in his usual precise manner. He handed her a mug.

"Here you go."

"Thanks." She sipped her coffee as he looked in the fridge and got out some eggs. "Are you making an omelet?"

He got out a frying pan. "Yeah."

"Nice."

He turned to face her. "Are you sure you don't want one?"

"No, I'm good," she reassured him.

He frowned. "Did you have breakfast?"

Pen stared at him. "No."

"You should."

He started cracking eggs with one hand into a bowl, added various seasonings, and took a bag of cheese from the fridge.

"Why should I have breakfast?" Pen asked.

"It's good for you."

Rob put some butter in the heated pan and swirled it around, releasing a snap of salt and fat that made Pen lick her lips. She knew she should leave, but watching Rob cook was something else. His movements were so efficient and precise.

He added the egg mixture and swirled it expertly in the pan, flipped it, and sprinkled on cheese and fresh herbs. He set the omelet on a plate and looked over at Pen.

"Eat this."

"But it's yours."

"I made enough for two. Go ahead." He turned back to the stove. "I can't have you going hungry."

"I . . ." Pen moved closer to the table. The omelet looked perfect and smelled divine. "Are you sure?"

He nodded, all his attention on the pan. Pen sat down and carefully cut into the omelet. She ate the first bite and almost moaned.

"How do you get something so simple to taste so good?" she asked.

He offered her a quick smile. "Practice."

He joined her at the table and started eating his own omelet. Silence fell as they both dug in.

"Where did you learn to cook?" Pen asked.

He didn't look up. "Here and there."

He wasn't one of the world's great conversationalists, which made Pen want to fill the quiet with inane chatter. She determinedly didn't do that and continued to eat.

Eventually she finished her omelet. "That was delicious."

"You're welcome." Rob was still focused on his plate.

Pen rinsed her dishes, placed them in the dishwasher, and took the pan over to the sink.

"Don't worry about that," Rob said. "I'll take care of it."

She left the pan and turned to look at Rob. She was a totally easygoing person, but something was bugging her. His brown eyes reluctantly met hers, and he went still.

"What's up?"

Pen took a deep breath. "Do I annoy you?"

"No more than anyone else in the world. Why?"

"Because why go to all the bother of making me lunch and then ignore me?"

A crease appeared between his brows. "You looked hungry. I fed you."

"And that's it?"

"What more do you want?" He appeared generally confused.

"Most people make conversation while they eat. I'm told it's supposed to be a social occasion," Pen said. "I know you're shy, but—"

"I'm not shy," he insisted.

"Okay, that means you just don't like talking to me."

"Why would you want to talk to me?" Rob asked. "We have nothing in common."

Pen bit her lip. "I'd better get back. Thanks again."

She went into the mudroom, grabbed her coat and put on her boots. She was halfway to her truck when she heard Rob coming after her.

"Pen . . ."

"What?"

"I'm sorry. That didn't come out right."

She shrugged. "It's okay. I know I'm weird. It's the ADD. A lot of people don't like to talk to me."

"That's not it!" He looked appalled. "You're . . . great. It's me. I'm the problem." He shoved a hand through his thick, dark hair. "I'm not used to sharing stuff, and what the hell could I talk to you about that wouldn't make you regret asking? My bad behavior, my addiction to painkillers, or my prison record?"

"You were in prison?"

"Yeah." He finally looked her straight in the eye. "Are you still sure you want to talk to me?"

"If you can deal with me having the attention span of a gnat and for asking the world's most intrusive questions then, yes. I'm pretty sure I can."

"You can't help having ADD. I caused everything bad that happened to me."

"It's not a competition, Rob." Pen opened the door of her truck. "I'm sure both of us could do with a friend. Let me know if you change your mind."

CHAPTER 3

"Why did I decide to get married at Christmas?" Bernie wailed as they drove back up to the Nilsen Ranch. It was Sunday and Pen's day off. "It must be one of my most stupid ideas ever."

"It's not stupid." Pen was fairly certain her normally calm cousin was suffering from bridal nerves. "It's all going to be fine. Everyone has accepted their invitations, and there are no big storms forecast. It will all go according to plan."

At least she hoped it would because she'd been responsible for a lot of the planning. The wedding was a week away, and there were still a few details to get right, which was why she'd asked Bernie to come to the ranch with her. Rob would probably be there, and Pen knew he'd be horrified if they had to have another awkward conversation. He hadn't responded to her offer of friendship, which hurt more than she'd expected.

People thought she was oblivious to what went on around her, but it wasn't true. She'd learned through painful experience to be super aware of how people reacted to her. She'd had to acquire social skills that came naturally to other kids, and it had been hard. Even now she sometimes felt like an alien in a world where she never quite fit in.

She got out of Bernie's truck and turned to look down the slope toward the old barn, where she could hear whistling. Completely forgetting Bernie, she walked toward the sound, her attention on the man in the center of the field with the young horse.

Luke and Noah were standing at the fence in typical cowboy pose, one booted foot on the bottom rail of the gate, their arms folded on the top rail, providing a place to rest their chin while they watched whatever was going on in the field. Luke glanced at Pen and grinned.

"I didn't know Rob was a horse whisperer, did you?"

Pen shook her head and focused her attention on the man and the horse. From what she could tell there was some kind of conversation going on between Rob and the unbroken colt. As they watched, he slowly picked up a saddle blanket from the ground and showed it to the nervous horse, allowing it plenty of time to sniff the scary new thing.

"He's already got the halter on, which neither Noah nor I could do," Luke murmured. "If he can get the horse to tolerate the blanket on his back, we might be onto a winner."

Rob gently ran his hand down the horse's back in a repetitive motion that made Pen wish she were the one standing next to him. All the time his hand was moving he was talking to the horse and edging the blanket closer, touching the fabric against his neck and lower, letting him get a good sniff of it. With the economy of motion Pen was used to seeing from him when he cooked, Rob finally placed the saddle blanket on the horse's back, continuing the soothing motion of his hand over the woven fabric.

The horse flicked his ears a couple of times and looked around to check what was on his back but didn't seem to mind the intruder at all.

"That's . . . awesome." Noah had a big, deep voice that usually came out super loud and sometimes made Pen want to cover her ears. Even his whispering sounded like normal talking, but Pen appreciated him trying to keep it down. "We might be able to save this horse after all."

Luke called out to Rob. "That's probably enough for today."

"Yeah, I was just about to wrap it up," Rob said. He attached a rope to the halter and led the horse toward the gate. "I suggest you get out of the way. He's still skittish around people."

Luke, Noah, and Pen moved into the shadow of the barn as Rob led the horse out, their heads close together, the horse's ears constantly flicking in Rob's direction.

"Man, that's something to see," Luke said.

Behind Pen someone cleared their throat. She turned to see Bernie looking at her.

"Where did you go? I walked into the house talking away, and then I looked around, and you were nowhere in sight."

"Sorry, Bernie. I got distracted," Pen apologized.

Luke hugged Bernie and dropped a kiss on top of her

head. "You again? You might as well move in you're here so often."

"Not until you put in those extra closets you promised me," Bernie said as she kissed him back. "I'm here because Pen wanted to run something by me, but then she disappeared."

"We were watching Rob work his magic with a horse," Luke said.

"Ah." Bernie looked at Pen. "Now it makes sense."

"He's a horse whisperer." Luke grinned at them both. "I've never seen anything like it."

Bernie glanced over at the snow-covered paddock. "Why are you breaking horses in winter?"

"Ask Rob." Luke turned toward Rob, who was approaching their little group. "Want to tell them the story?"

Rob shrugged, his gaze drifting past Pen to fasten on Luke. "You tell it better, boss."

"Can we go back to the house first?" Bernie asked. "It's freezing."

Rob looked like that was the last thing he wanted to do, but he nodded, and walked beside Pen, his attention obviously elsewhere.

Pen risked a question. "Are you worried about leaving the horse?"

"Yeah. He needs all the reassurance he can get right now."

"You were very patient with him."

"After everything he's been through, he deserves to be treated well." There was a hard note in Rob's voice.

"I'm amazed he even let me try to get things back on track. People suck."

"I agree," Pen said as he held the door open for her to enter the ranch house. "But you were wonderful."

He shrugged. "Just some tricks I picked up from my old man, who can get any horse following him around in minutes."

"Your dad's a rancher?"

Rob went still, a pained expression on his face, like he'd accidentally revealed the codes to the nuclear arsenal. He gazed at Pen and slowly nodded. "Yeah."

"Which is why you know how to work on a ranch and have a talent with horses." Pen kept her tone casual. She had no idea why speaking of his father was so difficult for Rob, but from her intense study of normal people's faces she knew when she should stop asking questions.

She took off her coat and Rob hung it up for her while she removed her boots. Luke and Bernie had gone into the kitchen ahead of them. Sally had obviously been busy getting the Christmas decorations up, as the house was filled with holly, paper chains, and lights. The scent of pine sap from a recently cut Christmas tree permeated the air.

Rob followed her into the kitchen, his reluctance to be there obvious even to Pen. Luke handed them all mugs of coffee and leaned back against the counter, his attention on Rob.

"Tell Pen and Bernie what happened with the horse."

Rob looked down at his coffee. "Not much to tell, really. Someone put up a flyer in the coffee shop asking for help with a dangerous and unmanageable horse, so I went to take a look."

Luke waited a beat and then couldn't resist adding to Rob's story. "So Rob called me and asked if I could meet him at this horse barn on the Reno side of town. Apparently some millionaire bought an unbroken colt at one of the mustangs roundups in Colorado and, despite having no experience whatsoever, decided he could break the horse."

"Typical," Bernie muttered. She ran the town humane society and was well used to having pets dumped on her by clueless people. "I wish some places did better checks on their buyers rather than let some idiot buy a completely wild horse and screw up."

"This particular guy ended up in the ER with a concussion and a broken ankle," Luke added. "He intended to have the horse put down. The owners of the barn figured they'd try and find someone to take the horse before the guy got out of the hospital. They put notices up all over the place and on the internet, appealing for help."

"Good for them," Pen said.

"Which is how Rob found out about the horse, took me to meet him, and asked if we could bring him here and make things right." Luke looked over at Rob. "Once I'd squared it with the original owner, we were good to go."

"Did you buy the horse?" Pen asked.

"We didn't have to. The guy was just glad to get rid of the problem."

"How did you know Rob would be able to fix it?"

"Because he told me he could." Luke smiled at her. "And, as it's the longest conversation I've had with Rob in the six months he's lived here, I figured it was important to him."

Rob cleared his throat. "I was willing to buy the colt, but I had to okay it with Luke because it's his ranch."

"I'm glad you did," Luke said. "Because I got the privilege of watching a miracle unfold."

"Hardly that," Rob said.

"Dude, a week ago we barely managed to load that colt on the trailer without getting injured. He's a handful, and now you've literally got him eating out of your hand."

Pen smiled at Rob, who for once held her gaze. "I think it's wonderful."

"Yeah?"

"Do you have a name for him yet?"

"Not yet. I like to work out their personality before I name them."

"What a great idea. I wish humans did that, because some people have names that really don't suit them, don't they?" Pen asked. "I mean, what if we waited until we were old enough to make our own decisions? I bet we'd all choose something different."

"I guess." Rob blinked at her.

"I used to work with a person called Joy and she wasn't joyful at all, and some people just don't look like a 'Matt' or a 'Dave,' do they?" She studied everyone's bemused faces and reminded herself not to go off on a tangent. "It's a paint horse, right?"

"Yeah." Rob looked relieved that she'd gotten back

on track. "He's going to be a stunner when he's fully grown."

"Do you intend to keep him?"

"It depends how he does with the training," Rob said. "Not every horse wants to be ridden."

Pen nodded. "Some of them are free spirits and should remain so."

"Except this one can't go back," Luke said. "He's been away from his herd for too long."

"Poor horse." Pen sipped her coffee. "It's a good job he's found Rob then, isn't it?"

An hour later, after she'd worked through the minor issues with Bernie and come to some conclusions, Pen walked back down to the barn and went to find the paint horse, who had been put into the corner stall. The upper part of the door was open. Pen could see him happily eating hay, his tail swishing gently. He paid no attention to her at all.

"Don't go in there, okay?"

"I'm not that stupid." Pen didn't need to turn to know that Rob was behind her.

"It's always better to ask than to assume," he said as he joined her at the half-open stall door. "He looks pretty calm right now, but it's very superficial."

"He sounds just like I used to be," Pen said. "When I was a kid, I used to have these epic meltdowns, and my parents would have no clue why. I'd literally scream the place down, hit, bite, you name it, I'd do it."

Rob didn't immediately reply, and Pen kept talking.

"Sometimes it was that the label on my clothing was itching me, or there was a loud noise, or too many people, or . . ." She smiled. "No wonder my parents stopped wanting to take me anywhere. I always ruined it for everyone else." She glanced up at Rob. "I don't do that anymore, I promise."

"I guess you just found it hard to express yourself." Rob nodded at the horse. "Just like this guy."

"At least I wasn't torn away from my family and left with someone who didn't understand me. My parents were awesome. They took me out of elementary school and my mom taught me herself until I was ready to deal with the kids in school."

"You got bullied?"

"No, I just couldn't cope with the noise, and all the change, and . . ." She sighed. "Everything really. You can't learn if you spend most of your day trying to crawl under your desk and curl up in a ball."

She nudged his elbow with her own. "But I don't want you feeling sorry for me or anything. I had parents who cared enough to find workable solutions for my issues and eventually a school district that made things better for me."

Rob looked at her. "You make it sound way easier than it probably was."

"It wasn't easy."

There was a short silence while they both avoided each other's gaze and studied the horse.

"I had a great childhood." Pen held her breath as Rob started talking. "Two brothers, two sisters, and parents who brought us up to be hardworking, god-fearing people. My dad is third-generation Californian. His great-grandfather came from Mexico to work on a cattle ranch when he was fifteen and never left. Eventually his son bought his own ranch."

"That's amazing," she said softly.

"Yeah."

She glanced up at his face, and he wasn't smiling. "They sound like good people."

"They are."

"Just like you."

"I'm not good." He straightened up. "I think I hear Bernie calling. Are you supposed to be getting a ride back to town with her?"

Even Pen knew a dismissal when she heard one, but something made her keep going.

"Are they still in California?"

"I guess so." His shrug wasn't convincing.

"Will you see them at Christmas?"

"How could I? I'm working here." He walked toward the entrance of the barn. "Bernie's coming this way. She's definitely looking for you."

Pen followed him out, torn between her secret pleasure that he'd confided in her and confusion at his obvious desire to forget everything he'd just said.

"I bet they'd love to hear from you."

He stopped so suddenly she almost walked into him.

"Pen . . . just because you think the world is full of sparkles, love, and endless cupcakes doesn't mean it's like that for the rest of us."

She met his gaze. "But I don't think that."

"You just try and see the best in everything and everyone."

It was her turn to frown. "What's wrong with that?"

He blew out a breath. "It's not realistic."

"It's better than the alternative. Expecting everything to go wrong isn't healthy for you."

"That's . . ." Rob stared at her and slowly shook his head. "I don't have time for this. I've got work to do."

"And I'm not stopping you." Pen walked past him. "Have a great day off, Rob. I'll see you at the café on Monday."

Rob watched Pen walk up the slope and looked around for something solid to kick, seeing as he couldn't kick himself. What the hell was wrong with him? Sharing family stuff with a woman who thought life was a bed of roses and that everything would probably work out okay if you just had positive thoughts. Why had he even opened his mouth? It wasn't as if she'd forced him to talk to her.

Of course, his family was still at the ranch they'd owned for two generations. Where else would they be? The fact he wasn't with them was probably celebrated every year. He remembered the horror on his parents' faces when he'd been convicted and sent to jail. He'd refused to see them because at that point in his life he was so busy blaming everyone else for his own failures that he thought they were the ones who'd let him down.

They'd tried to write to him, and he'd returned their

letters unopened. After a while they'd stopped, and he'd convinced himself he'd done the right thing and set them free from worrying about him. When he got out, he'd moved to a different part of the state and started again as a dishwasher—the only job he'd been able to get. Eventually he'd met Anton, and life had improved.

Rob realized he was staring into space and tried to get a hold of himself. He was in a good place, he'd paid for his crimes, and he was on the road to recovery.

He grimaced. Now he sounded like Pen, who despite what he'd thought, hadn't always had an easy time of it. She'd tried to laugh it off, but he knew in his bones it must have been tough.

He reminded himself that assuming stuff about people made him the ass, not Pen, and that somehow he didn't mind her knowing about his family. He was certain she wouldn't pass the information on—not that there was anyone who cared enough to want to know about him. But even sharing that much had made him as nervous as the unbroken colt. But she'd listened and offered her opinion, and he hadn't minded one bit, which was a first.

He'd offered to help Luke and Noah with the winter prep up at the snowmobile barn, so he headed that way. The snow had settled in patches, but it wasn't deep enough to bother him, and he enjoyed the snap of the cold air. It reminded him of the years he'd spent working on his parents' ranch—until the day he'd confessed he wanted to be a chef and all hell had broken loose.

But now? Rob took a moment to stop and admire the

distant snow-capped mountains and the impenetrable green depths of the forest. He could see the beauty of both jobs. He chuckled to himself. Maybe Pen had come up with a whole new career for him—the cooking cowboy. He'd be on TV before he knew it.

CHAPTER 4

"Pen! Where have you been?"

Pen shut the door of the bookstore and looked over at her mother, Diana, who sat behind the cash register. She walked through the tightly packed aisles and bent to give her mom a kiss.

"I was at the Nilsens' with Bernie. I thought I told you."

"You didn't say you were going to be gone all morning." Her mom stood up. She was blond like Pen and just as petite. "And what on earth can Bernie want *you* for? You're only a barista."

For some reason her mom's words stung more than usual.

"I'm helping with her wedding."

"Doing what exactly?"

"Making sure all the pieces work together to deliver Bernie and Luke the best day of their lives."

"That sounds a little . . . complicated for you, darling."

Pen raised her chin. "It's fine. I'm enjoying it."

Her mom pressed her lips together as if there was a

lot more she wanted to say but was trying to be kind. "Can you take over this afternoon while I get some lunch and see Jake?"

"Jake's here?"

"He's back for Christmas." Diana smiled. "He's doing so well now."

"Of course he is," Pen said, ignoring the lingering worry in her mom's eyes. "I can't wait to see him."

"He texted me to say he's almost here. I told him to come to the store." Diana moved some of the book catalogues around. "Any more thoughts on going back to college and finishing your degree next year?"

"Not really." Pen had fielded the question a million times. "I don't think that environment suited me very well."

"But you've got to do something with your life, darling. You can't exist on low-paying part-time jobs and expect to have your own home one day."

"I know." Pen tried to smile. "Maybe I'm just waiting for inspiration."

Her mom sighed. "That's a lovely idea, but you know you must put in the real work, don't you? Your dad and I built everything we have from scratch."

"You did," Pen agreed. "And you did it while bringing up a family."

Diana reached out and took Pen's hand. "And that's what I want for you. A family of your own. I know you have your issues, Pen, but you are a lovely person."

"Thank you."

"And you shouldn't give up on trying to find a partner."

Pen didn't think it was a good time to tell her mom that the only man who interested her was an ex-con who barely knew she existed and who would probably run away screaming if he knew how she felt. She looked down at the floor, aware that everything she felt showed on her face and that her mom knew her well enough to pounce on any sign of weakness.

Luckily the shop bell jangled and there he was, her tall, handsome older brother, Jake. He grinned and opened his arms.

"Hey, shrimp!"

She rushed over to give him a hug. He smelled like coffee and faintly of cigarettes.

"Hey, you." She smiled up at him. "How's it going?"

"Good." He reached out and drew their mom into the hug. "Happy holidays, Mom. Kev sends his love."

"It's a shame he couldn't join us," Diana said.

"He has to look after the cat." Jake winked. "And his parents are close by, so he won't be on his own over Christmas."

"Next year, then." Diana patted Jake's arm. "Are you ready to go? We're having lunch at Bernie's."

"I hear she's doing great things in the cake world." Jake checked his cell. "Are you coming, Pen?"

"Nope, I've got to mind the shop."

"Can't you close for lunch, Mom, so Pen can come?" Jake asked.

"We can't afford to lose any customers, Jake. If the

store is closed when people think it should be open, they tend not to come back. And it's good for Pen to be responsible for something for a change." Diana blew Pen a kiss. "You don't mind, do you, darling?"

"It's fine."

Jake waited until their mom was almost out of the door before turning to Pen. "Well, I tried."

"It's all good. Have a nice time and bring me back a doughnut."

"Will do." He paused. "It's really good to see you, shrimp."

"You, too."

Her smile died as he closed the door behind him. He looked well, he seemed happy, and he was in a committed relationship, but they all worried about him because that's what families do. Her mom was still concerned about Pen finding her place in a world that wasn't built for people like her, and she had legitimate concerns about Jake, who always managed to look as if everything was fine even when it wasn't.

For once Pen didn't have to work in the evening. She was looking forward to a proper family dinner at home with Jake, her parents, and probably some of their immediate family, who all lived locally. Her cousins were starting to get married and find partners, and the family was growing larger by the year, which she loved.

Pen sighed and walked back to the desk. She imagined Rob sitting next to her at the family dinner, holding her hand, and looking at her adoringly. He'd confided in her today—something she sensed didn't happen often, so why shouldn't he come to care for her? Why couldn't she have the happy ever after that everyone else in her family expected?

Several hours later, she looked up as someone came into the shop. She blinked twice.

"Rob?"

He considered her for a second, and then nodded. "Your parents own this store."

"That's right." She grinned. "Did you think I was stalking you?"

He came closer. "It did cross my mind."

"What can I help you with?" Pen asked.

"Holiday cards," Rob said. "I haven't had anyone to give them to for years, but I guess that's changed."

Pen got up to show him the holiday merchandise at the back of the store. "When you're done, come and find me."

"Thanks."

Pen returned her attention to the fantasy novel she'd borrowed off the shelves and was so engrossed that Rob had to gently clear his throat to get her attention.

He pointed at the book. "I like that series."

"It's brilliant, isn't it?" Pen carefully closed the book. "I'm about two books behind so I always try and catch up when I work here."

She rang up his purchases on the old-fashioned cash register, and he paid with cash.

"I wish I could afford to buy some gifts, but I don't have the funds," Rob said as he put his wallet away.

"I know the feeling." Pen sighed. "I really should get myself organized and find a proper job."

"You seem pretty good at the event coordination thing," Rob commented. "Can you train to do that?"

She stared at him. "I don't know, but it's a good idea."

The shop bell rang, and her mom came in. For once, her attention wasn't all on Pen as she came forward with a charming smile. "Hi, are you Rob? Bernie said she thought you were in town doing some shopping, so I'm glad I caught you here."

"Yeah."

"I'm Pen's mom and Bernie's aunt," Diana said. "Bernie asked me to give you a message. She said she has to stay late tonight, so can she take you back to the ranch around nine?"

"Sure." Rob nodded. "I can hang out with Anton."

"Anton's not here today," Pen reminded him. "He's in Reno."

Rob grimaced. "That's right."

"Why don't you come and have dinner at our house?" Pen said the words before she realized what was going to come out of her mouth. "That will work, won't it, Mom? Bernie can pick him up when she's ready."

Her mom looked at her. "That's a great idea. It'll give us a chance to get to know you better, Rob. Bernie says such great things about you."

"If you're sure that's okay, Mrs. Jones. . . ."

"Please call me Diana." She patted his shoulder. "Pen, why don't you take Rob back to the house and start the prep while I close up? Jake's already there, but I think he's taking a nap before dinner."

"Typical," Pen said as she found her backpack and kissed her mom. "We'll see you at home."

Rob couldn't quite believe he was walking beside Pen as she chatted merrily away, or that he'd been invited to dinner at her parents' home. It all happened so quickly he hadn't managed to think of a convincing excuse and had found himself agreeing despite every part of his brain yelling *no*.

He didn't do families, and he certainly didn't need to spend more time with a woman who had the uncanny ability to draw him to her like a moth to a flame. The fact that good people like Anton, Bernie, and Pen existed gave him hope when he'd thought there was none. Deep in his heart, he wanted to believe he was redeemable, and they made him think it was possible. But that didn't mean he'd ever feel like he fit in or should even be given the chance.

He realized Pen had asked him a question, and he looked down at her.

"Say again?"

She stopped walking, her hands twisting together, her expression suddenly uncertain. "Are you mad at me? I didn't give you a chance to say no without sounding rude, and I know you'd never do that to my mom."

"Why did you ask me?"

Pen met his gaze. "This sounds stupid. But I never had the kind of friends who wanted to meet my family. I was always that kid—the one who got left out unless the parents insisted on inviting the whole class . . . the one never picked for a team. When I was a teenager, my social life became zero." She sighed. "I guess I just wanted to have my friend over."

"Are we friends?" Rob had to ask.

A flash of hurt crossed her face and was quickly concealed by a smile. "Okay, maybe I'm overstating it. How about coworkers?"

He nodded, his attention on the blueness of her eyes and the curves of her lips. He was starting to learn her body language, the way she defended herself with a joke and a smile, the expectation of being rejected already in place. She reminded him of the colt, and she needed the same careful handling. She deserved so much more than having to beg him to spend a pleasant evening with her family.

He took one of her restless hands in his, shocking them both.

"It's all good. Anton's been nagging me to be more outgoing, so this is a great place to start."

"Really?"

"Yeah." He squeezed her fingers, and they resumed walking, holding hands. "How far out of town is your house?"

"It's just up the street." She pointed at one of the large Queen Anne houses. "My parents bought it for a song thirty years ago and lovingly restored it."

"It's . . . nice." Rob stared at the enormous house. It had a railed porch all the way around the ground floor, steps up to the massive double front door, and fairy lights everywhere. "Someone loves the holidays."

"That would be me," Pen confessed.

"No." Rob deadpanned. "I don't believe that for a second."

She looked up at him and chuckled, which made something inside him want to reach out and give her a hug.

"You're teasing me."

"Yeah."

She tugged on his hand. "We'll go around the side to the kitchen. No one really uses the front door."

"Same at my parents' house," Rob said. "My mom would've had a fit if we'd gotten mud on her fancy carpet, and living on a ranch there was a lot of dirt."

When he was a kid, he'd loved Christmas and was the first to nag his parents to set up the tree and get on with the decorating. He wondered who did it now and whether they still hung the ornaments he'd proudly made at school, with his name front and center.

"You can put your jacket here," Pen said. She wore a sparkly blue knitted sweater over jeans and had her hair tied back in a ponytail.

Rob found a spare peg, took off his boots, and followed her into the kitchen. The cupboards were cream-painted pine, and there was a large island, perfect for food prep, in the center.

"Mom restored all the original cupboard doors by hand and repainted them. When she could afford it, she got someone to come in and take down the wall into the original pantry and scullery to enlarge the kitchen and design new features to match the old ones." Pen went to check the note on the refrigerator door.

"It's a great space." Rob automatically washed his hands and looked around for something to do. He had no idea how a guest was supposed to behave, but decided he'd rather participate than sit around trying to make small talk. "What's on the menu?"

Pen brought the note over. "Looks like some kind of massive chicken-and-veg stir-fry, which I guess is why Mom wanted someone to do the prep."

"We can handle that." Rob scanned the list. "Where are your knives?"

"In the block on the island." She pointed them out. "I'll get the vegetables out of the refrigerator and wash them."

Rob found a stack of chopping boards in a drawer below the knives. "How many are we feeding?"

Pen paused and started counting on her fingers. "You, me, Mom, Dad, Jake, and my sister Demelza. I think."

"Demelza?"

"My mom had a thing about the Poldark novels."

Rob nodded like that made sense. He'd never been a great book reader. He stared at the red pepper on his chopping board. What the hell was he going to do if Pen's parents started asking him questions about books? They owned a bookstore and probably expected everyone to be as well-read as they were. Not for the first time he wondered whether he should do the prep and then invent an excuse to head out. It was only a four mile walk up to the Nilsen Ranch. . . .

"It's okay." Pen put some onions and garlic at his side. "They try not to bring their work home with them."

"How did you know what I was thinking?" Rob chopped the pepper fast and set it to one side.

"I guess I've learned to study people's faces in case I miss something that would be obvious to everyone else. For example, I regularly remind myself that not everyone wants to listen to me go on about my interests."

Rob studied her. "I've never heard you talk about yourself. You're always the one asking the questions."

She shrugged. "I realized early on that it was a good way of not making everything about me."

Rob sliced the onion and crushed the garlic, releasing the rich aromas. "You have the right to your opinions."

"Oh, I have plenty of those." She grinned at him. "Shall I get the chicken or should we wait until we're closer to eating?"

For the first time he noticed how she always deflected the conversation away from herself. "If we do it now, we can stick it in some marinade so it will taste better," Rob said. "Just something basic like honey, soy sauce, fresh ginger, and sesame oil."

"You're a genius," Pen said.

"I wish."

He got out a new board and waited while Pen, with many exclamations of disgust, washed and patted the chicken breasts dry.

"Thanks. I need a large bowl or sealed bag." Rob

diced the chicken, added the marinade, and set it back in the refrigerator. "All your mom needs to do now is get the wok out and cook."

"I didn't know we had a new chef in town."

Rob turned to see a tall, dark-haired man coming into the kitchen.

"Hey, Dad." Pen finished washing her hands and went to give her father a kiss. "I invited Rob to dinner and somehow made him do all the prep work."

"That's very kind of you, Rob." Pen's father smiled at him. "I'm Stefan."

"Pleased to meet you, and thanks for inviting me into your home," Rob said as he continued cleaning up.

Pen touched his arm. "Why don't you go and get acquainted with Dad while I finish up in here? Mom's going to be back in ten minutes."

He tried to convey to her that it was the very last thing he wanted to do, but somehow, he was hustled out of the kitchen and into the family room, where Stefan offered him a beer, which he declined.

"So, Pen says you work for Bernie?" Stefan settled into what was obviously his favorite chair while Rob took the one opposite.

"Yeah, I manage the online side of the business, which means I don't get a lot of time to actually cook anymore."

"Do you miss that?"

"It's where I got my start, so yeah. I never thought I'd be managing twenty people, but Bernie's a great, supportive boss."

Stefan beamed, and Rob remembered that Bernie was his niece.

"We always hoped Pen would become someone like Bernie, but, alas, it was not to be."

"Pen's great," Rob said. "The customers love her."

"She is a very kind and thoughtful girl." Stefan nodded. "And I suppose there's still time for her to settle on what she wants to do with her life." He looked up as the back door banged. "Ah, I think Diana's back. If you'll excuse me, I'll go and make sure Jake is up."

Pen looked across the table at Rob, who seemed to be holding his own with her loud and boisterous family. The stir-fry had been delicious, and now they were onto pie, ice cream, and coffee, and no one seemed willing to leave yet.

Jake refilled his coffee and turned to Pen. "So what's this I hear about you managing Bernie's wedding?"

"She's hardly managing it, Jake," Diana said with a little laugh. "She's simply helping her cousin out."

Pen looked at Jake. "Actually, it's a lot more than that, Mom."

"Like a wedding coordinator," Jake said. "Good for you."

"I'm enjoying it."

"It was so kind of Bernie to give you something to do, darling," Diana said. "I didn't even have to ask!"

Everyone around the table laughed except Rob, who was looking at Pen.

"Pen's doing an amazing job," Rob spoke up. "She's

dealing with the logistics of setting the wedding up, managing the guests, the food, and the entertainment, and she hasn't had any hiccups so far."

Pen opened her mouth to do her usual jokey, self-deprecating denial, but something in Rob's eyes made her pause.

"It's very kind of you to say that, Rob, but I'm sure Pen would be the first to tell you not to exaggerate." Stefan chuckled. "My daughter doesn't have a managerial bone in her body."

Pen set her coffee mug down on the table, her face heating with embarrassment. Rob would think her family believed she was hopeless.

She stood up. "Excuse me. I left my phone in the kitchen."

"Pen?"

She ignored the concern in her mom's voice and escaped into the kitchen where she picked up her cell and kept walking until she reached the outside porch. She took several quick breaths and fought the desire to cry. Behind her the screen door creaked and someone came up behind her.

"It's freezing." Rob dropped her jacket around her shoulders. "Can't have you getting sick right before the wedding."

Pen took her time putting her jacket on and kept her head down as she zipped it up. "For the record, I don't come home every day and pretend I'm as successful as Bernie."

He considered her, his breath frosting in the air. "I never thought you did."

She put her hands in her pockets. "I'm well aware that I'll never run a business like her."

"You're definitely not Bernie," Rob agreed. "But there's nothing wrong with that."

"Bernie doesn't need her mom to beg for jobs for her." Pen sighed. "That's how I got my job at the café. Mom asked my aunt Linda if Bernie could help her loser cousin out."

"Bernie picked you to coordinate her wedding because she knew you could do the job."

Pen looked up at Rob, who was frowning. "You don't know that. Maybe Mom's right and Bernie just felt sorry for me, like everyone else."

"Bullshit." Rob stepped forward and put his finger under her chin, raising her gaze to his. "Don't put yourself down. You are *way* better than they give you credit for. I know because I work with you every day, and they don't."

She couldn't look away, mesmerized by the gold flecks at the edge of his brown eyes. She wanted to lean in, rest her forehead against his chest, and breathe in some of his quietness and certainty.

"Pen . . ." He lowered his head and kissed her firmly on the mouth. "Don't listen to them."

Pen brought her fingers to her lips. "Did you just kiss me?"

"Yeah." He nodded. "Someone had to."

Behind them, a horn beeped, and Pen recognized Bernie's truck.

"I guess my ride is here." Rob patted her shoulder. "See you in the morning."

CHAPTER 5

Two days before the wedding, Pen had basically given up working at the café to concentrate on solving the million little details that would make the event go off without a hitch. Neither Bernie nor Luke had time to hang out at the ranch and accept deliveries, or talk to the florist, or deal with Anton having a crisis about the particular shade of frosting on the cupcakes, so Pen had to step in.

To her surprise, she found it invigorating. Her mom always commented about Pen's inability to focus on one thing and her tendency to flit among a thousand tasks, but with a cascade of small details to deal with, Pen was in her element. She easily swapped between discussing the number of paper napkins twenty people might go through, the logistics of the bathrooms, and what to do with Sally's cute dogs on the big day.

Anton stayed in the kitchens at the café and occasionally sent up samples of food for Luke and Bernie to taste and approve before he went into full-scale production mode. Rob had somehow managed to divide his time between the online cake business, the wedding, and working with the unbroken colt. Pen wasn't sure if he was sleeping at all.

Late one afternoon, after she'd accepted delivery of five folding tables and several hundred fairy lights that someone, probably her, would have to put up, she wandered down to the barn. It hadn't snowed again but there was something in the sluggish movement of the air that told her it wouldn't be long before it did. She looked over toward the mountains, where heavy, black clouds were gathering, and wondered when the storm would hit. Rob's old truck was parked outside the barn. She knew exactly where she'd find him and headed toward the sheltered interior yard, which had walls high enough to keep out the worst of the wind and the weather.

Even though she approached as quietly as possible, both man and horse were instantly aware of her. She sat down on a bale of hay and just watched Rob work his magic. Something about his calmness with the colt transmitted itself right to her. Her shoulders relaxed and the million zinging thoughts in her head quieted down enough for her to breathe more normally.

She hadn't said anything to Rob about the kiss, and he hadn't either, which seemed about right for two people who struggled to communicate, in their different ways. She'd relived it in her head a million times and convinced herself that he'd meant it in a friendly, supportive manner, and that she was a fool to obsess over something so trivial. But her brain didn't care about logic and continued to mull it over even as she got on with other things.

Rob patted the horse and smoothed his hand along

his flanks. After being at the ranch for a few weeks, the colt looked far healthier, but still had a lot of growing to do.

"Can you pass me that second saddle blanket?" Rob asked out of the blue, making her jump. "I forgot to bring it over."

Pen got the blanket, and walked to Rob, careful not to get behind the nervous colt so that she wouldn't get kicked.

"Put it on the ground between us," Rob said. "So, he can have a sniff."

Pen did as he asked and remained still while the horse bent his head to investigate the new and suspicious object. The last thing she wanted was to start moving and freak the colt out. She had a lot of sympathy for his suspicions about everything around him. She'd been the same when she was a kid.

"You can back away now," Rob said. "Thanks for your help."

Pen waited until she resumed her seat on the hay bale before she answered. "You're welcome."

She watched him go through the now-familiar routine of letting the colt get used to the blanket before it was placed gently on his back. This time Rob set the second blanket over the first, placed his hands on the horse's back, and leaned in before stepping away. He repeated the process several times while talking quietly to the horse.

"That's new," Pen said.

"It's about weight transference. I want him to start to

recognize what it might feel like to have a saddle or a person on his back."

"Makes sense." Pen nodded.

Leaving the blankets on the colt's back, Rob led him around the yard a couple of times and then took him back into the barn.

Pen followed and helped Rob settle the colt in his stall.

"He's much calmer now," she commented as she shut the bottom half of the door.

"Yeah, he's doing good." Rob put away the lead rope and the blankets in the tack room. "Slow and steady works like a charm."

"Just like with people," Pen murmured. "I wish I'd had teachers like you when I was in school. Most of them thought throwing me in the deep end would work just fine."

"That's stupid." Rob turned to look at her. "A lot of people still break horses like that."

"Poor horses." Pen shivered. "By the way, my mom said to tell you that you're welcome at our place anytime for dinner."

"You have a nice family."

"Yes." She managed a smile. "I'm very lucky."

He turned toward the exit of the barn, and Pen walked beside him, her hands in her pockets, her head down.

"Doesn't mean they don't have their blind spots," Rob said.

"About what?"

"You, for one."

She stopped and looked up at him. "They love me very much."

"That's obvious, but sometimes love can be . . ." He hesitated. "Kind of limiting."

"What do you mean?"

"Okay, my parents loved me, and yet my dad was one hundred percent against me going to catering school."

"Why?"

"Because he assumed that as his oldest son, I'd follow in his footsteps and take over the ranch when he was gone. He couldn't think of a better life for me."

"But you're a fantastic cook."

"I was." His smile was bleak. "I bet if he was standing here right now, he'd be reminding me that if I'd stayed home like he'd said, I wouldn't have ended up on the streets addicted to painkillers and then in jail. And he'd be right."

"Not necessarily."

Rob raised an eyebrow. "Come on, Pen. Even you can't make something positive out of that."

"You did what you thought was right."

He stared at her for a long time before shaking his head. "That's it? That's all you've got?"

"You're not your father, Rob. You have every right to decide how to live your own life even if you make mistakes." She paused to take a breath. "You don't blame him for what happened to you, so why should he get to blame you for not being a carbon copy of him?"

Rob blinked at her. "That's . . . stupid."

"Oh, great! Now *you're* calling me stupid." Pen turned away.

He caught her elbow and gently turned her to face him. "I didn't say you're stupid. It's just that occasionally, like most people, you do say stupid things."

"It's all the same!" Pen was aware at some level that she wasn't behaving well. "I'm the dumbest person in my family, so thanks for pointing that out."

"Hey." He cupped her chin, his callused thumb tracing her jawbone. "You know you're getting mad at the wrong person, right?"

She positively glared at him and was amazed when he smiled.

"I can't get mad at them. They mean well."

"So did my dad."

"Did you get mad at him?"

"I did better than that. I left home and put myself through culinary school." He kissed the tip of her nose. "And that's what you're doing right now. Proving them wrong."

She tilted her head higher and her mouth met his in a clash of warmth. With a stifled sound, he kissed her, and she kissed him back, her fingers curling into his hair as he drew her tight against him. He just felt right, like the calm at the center of her personal storm, or the answer to all the questions in her world, and she didn't know how to handle that at all.

After what felt like a long time, he eased his mouth free and looked down at her.

"Pen, we should . . ."

She stepped back. "It's okay. I know what you're

going to say—that it was a mistake, that you just feel sorry for me, or that you were being my friend."

He frowned. "I wasn't going to say any of that."

"Good! Then let's just go back to whatever we were doing before and forget this ever happened, okay?"

"Sounds like you're the one with regrets, but that's definitely okay."

"I said it before you got the chance to."

"You *said* it because you realized that kissing an ex-con wasn't a good idea."

"It wasn't that at all!" Pen glared at him. "I was thinking how lovely it was to kiss you and how right it felt."

He took a long time before saying anything. "And I was just thinking it was cold out here and we should get back to the house."

"*That's* what you were trying to say?"

He took her hand and started walking. "I've only lived here for a year, but even I know when it's going to snow."

Pen let Rob tow her up the path toward the house, her thoughts freewheeling like a buzzard on a warm summer day. She noticed he hadn't addressed any of her remarks about how she liked kissing him, but who could blame him? She had no idea how to deal with the feelings she had for him or how to share them without blurting out the first thing that came into her head.

The first light touches of snow drifted down from the leaden sky and melted on her hair and coat. Rob glanced down at her and increased his pace.

"Where's your hat?"

"I left it at the house," Pen confessed. "Your Stetson isn't exactly weatherproof either."

"It's better than nothing."

He drew her into the shelter of the porch, and they climbed the steps together. She glanced back over her shoulder as the snow continued to fall, making the ranch look like a Christmas card.

"I'll make us a drink." Rob had already taken off his coat and boots. "Hot chocolate okay for you?"

"Yes, please," Pen answered automatically, her attention on the snow as she followed him through into the silent kitchen. "Where is everyone?"

"Luke should be back any moment. He's just up the road at the snowmobile barn. Sally's in town at the clinic helping out, and Noah's probably home with Jen and the kids." Rob put a pan on the stove and added milk. "The horses are all in, the cattle are as close to the ranch as we could get them, and we've already built the winter shelters."

"Sounds like everything's in good shape," Pen commented. "Luke must be thrilled to have someone who knows what they're doing while Max is away."

Rob shrugged as he stirred the milk. "I spent my first eighteen years on a ranch. It's second nature to me."

"Do you miss it?"

He stopped stirring. "When Dad and I were fighting, and he wouldn't let me go to school, I began to hate it. I swore I'd never go near another ranch again. But now? I find it kind of comforting, and I enjoy the work."

"More than cooking?"

"I hardly get to cook anymore." Rob added the hot

chocolate powder and a pinch of cinnamon and stirred vigorously. "I miss that, too."

He brought two mugs of hot chocolate over and set them on the table.

"Thank you." Pen took a sip. "It's lovely."

"You're welcome."

"Did you write your holiday cards?" Pen asked.

"Yup. All done."

"Are you sending one to your folks?"

Rob looked at her. "And ruin their Christmas?"

"I think they'd be pleased to hear from you."

"I disagree. My dad is a very proud man."

"You mean he's as stubborn as you are."

She surprised a smile out of him. "Yeah, I guess the apple didn't fall far from the tree." He looked down at his mug. "What the hell would I even say to them?"

"Happy holidays?"

"Funny."

"It's a start," Pen said. "Someone has to be brave." It was her turn to consider her words. "We had something . . . similar happen in our family. We had to wait for our person to realize we loved them regardless and come home."

He looked right at her, and she forgot about the conversation and simply stared into his beautiful brown eyes.

"Why do you keep kissing me?" Pen blurted out.

He blinked. "You don't like it?"

"I do, but I'm confused, and if I try to explain myself, I'm going to sound like a madwoman, and then you're never going to want to kiss me again."

He reached across the table and took her hand, his fingers warm and strong, his calmness wrapping around her.

"I think I know you well enough to get what you mean, so go ahead."

"Really?"

He nodded. "Shoot."

Pen took a deep breath. "I think I have feelings for you, and I'm not sure what to do about that because I have no idea how these things are supposed to work, and I don't understand flirting, or whether someone is just joking, and then I get the wrong idea and look stupid in front of the whole senior year at prom."

"What happened at prom?"

"Oh! Some guy asked me to go with him. I got all dressed up and excited only to get there and find he'd done it as a joke."

His expression darkened. "I hope you kicked his ass."

"I just laughed, pretended I got the joke, and went to the prom anyway," Pen said. "Because, as I said, I probably did misinterpret what he meant."

"I bet you didn't." His fingers tightened over hers. "I wish I could go and kick his ass for you. Does he still live around here?"

"No, he went off to college and never came back, thank goodness. Otherwise, I would've been avoiding him in town for the rest of my life."

"Pen, he's the one who should be ashamed of what he did, not you."

"It's not his fault that I get things wrong," she said earnestly. "Mom explained it to me when I got home that night, and I was crying. She said I needed to be more careful about how I interpreted things or I would get myself into difficult situations."

He went to speak and then stopped.

"What is it?" Pen asked.

"It's not my place to criticize your family, but man, that advice sucks. Making you responsible for everyone else's behavior? That's not okay."

"She was just trying to keep me safe."

"Yeah, I guess in her own way she was." Rob sat back, releasing her hand. "Anyway, back to what you were originally saying."

"Which was?"

His lips twitched. "Whether you're okay with the kissing thing."

"I am okay with it if you can confirm what it means."

"As in, am I kissing you like I'm your friend or something else?"

"Yes, that." Pen nodded.

He studied her for a long moment. "I kiss you because I like you."

"But what kind of like?"

"Like I want to keep doing it even though I know it's a bad idea?"

"Why is it bad?"

He sighed. "Because look at us, Pen. You're . . . amazing. And I'm not."

"Anyone who has overcome addiction and turned their life around is amazing, Rob. And, if you want to keep kissing me, I don't mind at all."

"Then maybe we agree to be honest with each other

as things progress?" Rob suggested. "Make sure we're on the same page?"

She smiled at him. "I'd like that."

"Good."

They were still smiling at each other when Luke came into the kitchen complaining about the weather. He got some coffee and started texting at a furious rate before looking over at Pen.

"I think you should stay here tonight. Mom's just turning in at the gate, and she says the roads aren't safe."

Pen nodded. She knew Luke wouldn't allow her to be in any danger. Driving down to town through the forest was hazardous on a good day, let alone when a layer of ice was forming. And it meant she got to spend more time with Rob, who was okay with the whole kissing thing.

Pen smiled. "Thanks, Luke. I'll text Mom and let her know."

CHAPTER 6

Luke closed the dishwasher door and looked over at Rob. "Why don't you take Pen to see your new place before it gets too bad out there?"

Rob turned to Pen, who was nodding enthusiastically.

"I'd love to see it! Bernie says you've done an amazing job with the remodel."

Sally smiled at her son. "He certainly didn't cut any corners."

"Like Noah would let me." Luke grinned. "He terrified all the contractors just by standing there and scowling so they all produced quality work."

Pen was already moving, and with a sigh, Rob rose to his feet. Luke winked at him.

"Take your time."

Rob was still pondering that wink when he stepped out into the freezing cold and held the door open for Pen. At least this time, she wore her knitted hat, scarf, and gloves. Her chin was buried into the collar of her ski jacket against the erratic gusts of wind. He took her hand without even thinking about it.

"Careful, it's getting icy."

She drew him even closer, tucking her hand into the crook of his arm. He wasn't a particularly tall guy, but she fitted perfectly against his side, and he liked seeing her there. He liked everything about her—the way she smiled at him, the way she made him want to protect her, how her lips tasted of cherries and coffee.

Man . . . he was in so much trouble. How had Little Miss Sunshine gotten into his head and made him want things he really didn't deserve? And he wanted her—there was no room for doubt about that.

It didn't take more than five minutes to reach the old bunkhouse. He dug out his key and opened the front door, stamping his booted feet on the mat as he entered.

"There's not a lot to see." Rob took off his hat and coat. "I think Luke just likes showing off his work."

Pen removed her jacket and looked around with her usual bright curiosity. The front of the space was a combo family room and kitchen with a bedroom and a bathroom at the back.

"It's certainly warm." She'd taken off her boots and was wiggling her toes. Her socks had pink bunnies on them.

"Underfloor heating," Rob said.

She looked over at him. "Are you going to give me a tour?"

"I think you can just about see everything from where you're standing."

"Not when the doors are closed."

"I wasn't expecting guests." He took her hand and walked her past the kitchen. "So, excuse my mess."

He showed her the bathroom first, and then opened the door into his bedroom. "Here you go."

He looked down to see her smile had disappeared. "What's up?"

"It's very . . . sparse."

He shrugged. "I don't own much stuff. I either sold it to get more painkillers, or I lost it when I couldn't pay my rent and the landlord took possession of everything."

She put her palm on his chest. "It must have been awful to lose everything."

"It's just things, Pen. The worst thing was losing myself."

"Oh, Rob." She wrapped her arms around his waist, and he tentatively stroked her hair.

"It's okay."

She looked up at him, her eyes full of tears. "You're right about the possessions, but I'm so glad you didn't give up. Watching someone you love lose themselves to addiction is hard enough, but for the person concerned? It's a tragedy."

"Then it was good that I didn't stay home and inflict all that on my parents," Rob murmured, knowing he should let her go but reluctant to do so, on many levels.

"Do they know what happened to you?"

"They tried to reach out to me. I blew them off."

She studied his face but didn't say anything, which was most unlike her. He found himself wanting to explain.

"I felt like a lowlife. I couldn't bear for them to see what I'd done to *myself*."

She nodded. "I get that. We had to wait until our person reached rock bottom before they asked for help. It was horrible to have to watch that and not interfere."

"One of your family is an addict?" Rob asked. He hadn't noticed any familiar faces at his monthly meetings.

"Not anymore." Pen smiled for the first time.

Rob wanted to tell her that addiction was a lifelong battle but it wasn't his place, so he smiled back at her.

"That's great."

"We still worry, but it's been five years now."

"That's a start," Rob said. "It's always still there for me. I hate taking any kind of drug now."

"I can imagine." Pen stepped away from him and looked around the bedroom. "You could do with some pictures in here."

He'd begun to love the way her mind flitted from one subject to another. It certainly kept him on his toes.

"I'm not great with that kind of thing."

"I noticed." Pen grinned at him. "I'll get my aunt Linda to give you one of her patchwork quilts. You'll need it in the winter."

She headed for the door and Rob followed her, glad that she'd left his bedroom because he'd been imagining gently lowering her down onto the sheets, stripping her naked and . . .

"You need a cat!" Pen called out to him. "And some throw cushions, and maybe a picture or two?"

"Number one, I can't afford much, and two, I'm renting this place, and I don't think Luke will want me gussying it up."

"I don't see you as a gussying it up kind of person,"

Pen agreed. "But a picture might be nice. Do you have photos of your family?"

He considered her for a long moment, took out his wallet, and handed her a small, folded, square card.

"Oh, Rob . . ." Her voice was soft as she looked down at the only photo of his family that had survived his desperate years. "You look just like your dad."

She came toward him, put her arms around his neck and kissed him on the mouth. "Life sucks sometimes, doesn't it?"

He didn't bother to answer but kissed her back, his hand in her hair, holding her right where he needed her. She pushed on his chest, and the next moment he was sitting on the couch, and she was on his lap.

He groaned as the kiss became more frantic and allowed his hands to wander all over her body while she returned the favor with her usual enthusiasm. Eventually, he eased back and looked up at her.

"If we don't stop now, I'm going to want more."

Her beaming smile made him want to smile in return. "Like as in everything? I've never done that before, but I think I'd like to do it with you—that is, if it's something that you'd be interested in, but if you aren't—"

He realized he should've just kept kissing her because the thought that he'd be her first lover was making him want to howl like an alpha wolf.

"Pen."

She stopped talking.

"I think we should take this slow," he suggested. "There's no rush."

She nodded, her expression intent. "There are bases, right?" She wrinkled her nose. "That's a baseball thing. I think I made it to second base once, but that's about it, and to be honest, I'm a bit hazy on the details, and I do like a list. Perhaps you could write it out for me?" She looked at him expectantly.

"I think we can work it out ourselves," Rob said. "And just do what comes naturally."

"Have you done it before?"

"Yeah."

He tensed, hoping she wouldn't require all the details because he wasn't proud of some of the things he'd done in his lost years.

To his relief, she smiled. "That's great! You can keep me on track!" She touched the front of his flannel shirt. "I would like to see more of you. Is that okay?"

"Only if I get to see you, too." Rob couldn't quite believe what he was saying, but he didn't want to disappoint Pen even a little bit, and he was getting quite fond of how direct she tended to be. "All you have to remember is that if you don't like anything, just speak up and I'll stop."

She nodded. "And the same goes for you, too."

"I think I'll like everything you do to me, sweet pea."

She started unbuttoning his shirt and then frowned. "You have a T-shirt underneath."

"It's freezing out there."

"I suppose it is." She paused. "In the interest of disclosure, I have three layers of clothing on, including a thermal cami."

"Camo?"

"Camisole." Pen mock frowned at him. "Now, please focus and take off your shirt and your T-shirt so that I can finally get a look at your tattoo."

Rob raised an eyebrow. "It's my tattoo you're after?"

"Among other things," Pen said. "I can multitask."

Rob sat forward, took off his flannel shirt, and pulled his T-shirt over his head.

"Oh." Pen stared at his chest.

"Not to your liking?" Rob asked, his hand reaching for his shirt. "I can—"

Pen leaned in and used the tip of her tongue to trace one of the tattooed wings before kissing his skin.

"It's a phoenix," Rob said even as she continued her explorations.

"Mmm."

"I had it done when I worked at a Michelin-star restaurant and thought I'd made it."

She briefly looked up at him, her blue eyes shining. "It's perfect for you."

He curved one arm around her waist and caressed her hip bone, making her shudder.

"Sometimes I wish I'd saved the money. It would've come in useful."

"You would probably have spent it on the wrong things anyway." Pen kissed his throat. "Can I see the back?"

He obligingly sat forward again, and her hands wandered over his flesh, making him acutely aware of the tightness of his jeans and his increasing desire to strip her naked. Her hips rolled against his, and he tried not to groan.

"What's wrong?" She sat up straight.

"Nothing I can't handle." He gestured at her to keep going.

She glanced down at his jeans, and he bit back a yelp as she touched his fly.

"This doesn't look comfortable. Would you like me to—"

His hand closed over hers and stopped her fingers. "No. I'm good."

"Oh, did I do something wrong?" She bit her lip. "I just thought—"

"I don't want to rush things," Rob tried to explain. "And you unzipping me might end up with me rolling you onto your back."

"And doing what?" Pen asked.

"What do you think?"

"Making love to me?"

Rob nodded, his attention riveted to her face and the utter sincerity of her gaze. No one had ever looked at him with such trust and appreciation in his life.

"How can you look at me like that?" he said hoarsely.

"Like what?"

"Like you want me."

"Because I do," Pen said. "I can't think of anything I'd like more in my life."

Pen held her breath as a conflicting wave of emotions went across Rob's normally impassive features. She wasn't going to lie. She did want everything he was willing to give her because she was surrounded by his calmness and strength, and somehow it was becoming increasingly important to her. Her fingers returned to stroking his skin as if they couldn't stop wanting the sensation of being connected to him.

He took a deep breath. "I want that too, but we're going to take it slow."

"Then can you slowly take your jeans off so I can see all of you?"

He groaned. "Pen, you'll be the death of me."

"Got to give a lot of credit to Wrangler," Pen said. "They sure make sturdy jeans."

A laugh shook through Rob. "And you're still not getting into them—yet."

Pen gazed at him. "Then can we just . . . cuddle a bit?"

He nodded. "That sounds great." He slid his hand behind her neck. "Come here, sweet pea, and kiss me."

Two hours later, Rob walked Pen back to the main house and left her with a last lingering kiss at the guest bedroom door before heading back out. He'd had the best time cuddling up with Pen on his couch, listening to her chat away and just being with her. He'd never had that kind of connection with a person before in his life. He wasn't sure how he felt about it and was terrified of doing it wrong.

Luke was in the kitchen, and Rob stopped to say good night.

"Do you think the road will be okay for us to get to work tomorrow?" Rob asked.

"Yup, it's eased right off, so the roads should be

clear," Luke said. "I'm keeping my fingers crossed for the big day."

"At least no one has far to come," Rob said. "You and Bernie both being local."

"That helps," Luke agreed. "But sometimes we do get cut off completely." He sighed. "Maybe I should've been less selfish and had the wedding in town. I guess I wanted to get married in the same spot my parents did."

"Nothing wrong with that." Rob remembered to try to be sociable. "I think my parents did the same."

Luke put his mug in the dishwasher and turned it on. "I know you're going to be busy with the logistics on the day, but you're still a guest. We both want you to celebrate with us."

"That's . . . very kind of you," Rob said. "Bernie's an amazing person."

"She says the same." Luke grinned. "And I think Pen's got a soft spot for you."

"Yeah. We've been working together a lot on the wedding."

"I noticed."

Rob met Luke's amused gaze. "She's good at her job, and I respect that."

"It's okay. I'm not warning you off or anything." Luke paused. "Pen's perfectly capable of dealing with her own love life."

"She's"—Rob tried to put into words how he felt and trusted Luke to hear him out—"way too good for me."

"That's also up to Pen," Luke said. "But you'd better not mess her around."

"I would never do that."

Luke nodded. "I know, which is why I'm kind of trying to be subtle and encouraging you without actually coming out and saying it."

"That's what you're doing?"

"Obviously not my strength but, hey, I'm willing to try because I like both of you."

The fact that people actually thought he was likable was difficult for Rob to fathom, but he couldn't deny that it gave him hope.

"She kind of crept up on me and made it impossible not to like her," Rob confessed. "She's just a really good person."

"Yeah, she is," Luke said. "So don't screw this up."

Rob nodded and walked through to the mudroom to put on his boots and jacket. He had a weird sense that he'd been given the seal of approval from both his bosses. What he did with that, and how he'd ever manage to deal with Pen's amazingness, was currently beyond him, but for the first time in a long while he wanted to try.

Outside the cold had settled into something more bearable, and the snow had stopped. As he went down the steps the frost-dusted boards creaked and groaned beneath his booted feet. He paused to look up at the clear, black sky and appreciate the constellations of stars clearly visible above him. The vastness overhead always reminded him of how small and insignificant his worries were, and he needed that tonight.

Could he find a way to make things work with Pen? Rob blew out a breath. The last few years had taught him a lot about meeting life's challenges headfirst, not blaming others or relying on props to see him through a problem. What it hadn't done was teach him how to accept that good things might happen, which was a whole new ballgame.

All he knew was that he had to protect Pen's heart at all costs and that he'd never forgive himself if he hurt her in any way. He should leave her alone, but something inside him kept telling him that she was the *one*— that if he let her go, he'd regret it for the rest of his life. He hadn't felt hope for so long that he didn't trust the feeling, but he'd have to be brave, and that was the most difficult thing of all.

CHAPTER 7

Pen couldn't look away from the joy on Bernie's face as she made her vows to Luke in front of their families. She'd chosen to wear her grandmother's wedding dress, which was full-skirted, 1950s-style cream satin with a boat neck. She also wore a fluffy knitted shawl around her shoulders to keep out the cold, and had her red hair piled on top of her head, crowned with a tiara.

Luke had looked stunned when she'd appeared, and Pen had tried very hard not to cry. She'd always known Bernie had a thing for Luke, but it had taken him a lot longer to work things out, with some help from his friends. Noah was acting as his best man and looked as formidable as ever in casual western wear, which was the preferred choice of all the men present except Jake, who'd gone for a tailored jacket and shirt.

Pen had hung hundreds of fairy lights around the family room, creating a magical grotto decorated in a holiday theme of red, gold, and white, which everyone had exclaimed over as they'd entered the space. For the first time in years, she'd felt proud of herself.

Jake nudged her and leaned in close. "You did good, Sis. No hitches so far."

"Tell me that after the reception," Pen murmured, "and I'll love you forever."

Her gaze turned to Rob, who had seated himself on the other side of the aisle. He wore a pressed blue shirt and khaki pants and looked his usual serious self. She knew he must have a million things going on in his head involving the wedding catering, but none of it showed. She tried to return her attention to the pastor's sermon, but her thoughts drifted off again. The next tricky part was persuading the guests to leave the family room so that they could set up the tables for the reception. She poked Jake in the arm.

"Will you help me clear the room after the ceremony finishes?"

"What do you want me to do? Strip naked or something?"

Pen rolled her eyes. "Just use your charm."

"I can do that. Where am I sending everyone?"

"Into the dining end of the kitchen."

"Thank heavens it's a small wedding," Jake commented. "And as it's just family, I can holler really loud, like I'm moving cattle."

"Don't you dare," Pen whispered.

Her mom pressed her finger to her lips and frowned at them. Pen immediately stopped talking, and Jake grinned.

"Sorry, Mom."

Pen surreptitiously checked the time as the pastor continued. Anton was going to have a fit if all his carefully laid plans for the meal were put out, but what could she do? It was hardly polite to stand up and make "get on with it, buddy" gestures at the pastor, who'd known her since birth. She glanced up as Noah, who was also checking his watch, frowned at the pastor, who immediately stuttered and started to wind things up. For once, Pen was grateful for Noah's intimidating presence as the wedding concluded with the bride and groom enjoying the traditional kiss.

She immediately jumped to her feet, grabbed Jake's hand, and moved to the front of the room.

"What a wonderful ceremony," Pen spoke as loudly as she could above the chatter. "Now, if you would all make your way into the kitchen, we'll set up this room for the wedding buffet."

No one except Rob moved. Jake grinned down at her.

"I've got this, shrimp."

He whistled loudly and then cupped his hands around his mouth.

"Everyone move on out into the kitchen. Don't make me have to set Sally's dogs on you."

There was a general laugh, and people did start to move.

Pen rushed ahead to make sure that the trays of beverages set up on the temporary bar between the kitchen proper and the dining room and mudroom were in place. She welcomed everyone and offered them a drink while behind her, chaos reigned in the kitchen, which she tried to ignore.

Bernie must have told the whole family that Pen

was her wedding coordinator because they all knew. Everyone wanted to chat, and she received lots of compliments, which surprised her. Even her mother had something nice to say. When everyone had a drink in their hand, Pen checked that Luke and Bernie were still busy with the photographer and went into the family room, where Rob and Kaitlin from the café were busy setting up the tables and unfolding chairs.

"I can do this if either of you are needed elsewhere," Pen said as she put red tablecloths on the tables and found the boxes of decorations, gold plates, and silverware she'd prepared earlier.

"Thanks." Kaitlin hurried off while Rob stayed where he was.

Pen set a candle centerpiece in the middle of each table and checked off each item.

"It looks good," Rob said from behind her.

"Five more to go." Pen grinned at him. "I can do it if Anton needs you."

"To be honest, when he's in full diva mode, I'd rather keep out of his way," Rob said. "And you're doing great. Luke and Bernie won't be out of the photographer's clutches for a while yet, so we've got time."

Pen picked up the second box and started assembling the next tabletop. Bernie and Luke had wanted a holiday theme, and she'd tried to deliver exactly that—which hadn't been hard because it was her favorite time of the year. As the wedding was only two days before Christmas, finding things hadn't been a problem, even in their remote location.

"Gift bags!" Pen looked around. "Where did I put them?"

"Gold things with tassels?" Rob asked. "I saw something like that in Noah's old bedroom when I was getting changed."

Pen ran toward the door. "I'm so grateful I won't even ask what you were doing in Noah's bedroom."

"It's the designated catering-staff space," Rob called after her. "No need to get all squirrelly."

Pen opened the door and saw the chaos caused by several people changing in a small room. She picked her way through to the closet, where the gift bags sat on one of the shelves.

By the time she got back, Rob had already done two more tables. He glanced over at her. "Where do you want the bags?"

"One on each place setting," Pen said. "I can do that."

Rob didn't stop working but he did frown. "Anton wants to put the appetizers out, so that won't work."

"I thought it was a buffet."

"The main part is, but the appetizer goes on the table to slow them down while we get the buffet service organized."

"Fine," Pen huffed. "I'll stand them up beside the champagne glass."

"Or you could wait and hand them out at the end," Rob suggested. "I mean that's what normally happens, right?"

"At children's parties maybe, but not necessarily at weddings," Pen tried to explain. "There are things in there they might need."

"To eat with?"

Pen glared at him, which made him pause.

"I am not having this discussion with you right now. They need to be on the table and that's where they will be!"

Rob held up his hands. "Okay, you're the boss."

Pen was still muttering under her breath when Rob finished the last table and headed for the door.

"I'll check in with Noah about timing and get right back to you."

"Thank you."

He smiled. "You're beautiful when you're angry."

Pen might have given him the finger when he turned away, but she'd never admit it. She wanted everything to be perfect and was cross with herself for not consulting with Anton beforehand about something so basic. She carefully set each bag on the table, finishing with the special ones for the bride and groom.

Rob came back.

"All good to go. Anton's ready, the wait staff are ready, and Noah says he'll start sending the guests back this way in five minutes if that's okay with you."

"That's great." She met his gaze. "And thanks for the help and I'm sorry for . . . what I said."

"Sweet pea, I've worked in some of the best restaurants in California, and I've heard far worse."

"Still, it wasn't nice of me to get mad at you for my mistake," Pen countered.

"You're under a lot of pressure right now. So don't beat yourself up, okay?"

"Easy for you to say."

He kissed her forehead. "You have no idea."

He headed back to help with the buffet, which was being set up in the kitchen. Pen heard Noah's loud voice, and the guests all emerged into the hallway and spilled into the family room.

"Your names are on your plates," Pen called out. "Please take your seats while we await the arrival of the bride and groom."

For once everyone listened to her, and thirty or so people sat down. Noah looked over at her.

"I'll go get Luke and Bernie."

"Thank you." Pen gave him her best smile. She wondered if he'd be interested in a side job as a wedding herder, because he sure seemed good at it.

"It all looks beautiful, Pen."

Noah's wife, Jen, came in with her son, Sky, held firmly by the hand. Sky was loudly asking where the TV had gone, reminding Pen strongly of Noah.

"Thank you." Pen pointed at the table closest to the door. "I put you on this side with me, in case you need to make a quick getaway."

"Perfect!" Jen said. "Because Sky's ability to sit still is zero, and Noah will be too busy worrying about his best man speech to catch him if he runs off." She patted her round stomach. "I'm not that fast anymore. Goodness knows what I'll do when I have two to wrangle."

Pen stepped out of the way as Sky did a little twirl and tried to escape only to pause when he saw Noah blocking the exit. Noah cleared his throat and stood aside as Bernie and Luke came into the room bathed in smiles.

"May I present to you Mrs. and Mr. Nilsen."

Everyone stood and applauded as the bride and groom took their seats alongside their parents and Noah. Pen sat down as well and watched with some trepidation as everyone checked out their gift bags. She only released her breath when she realized the bejeweled crowns and hand-knitted elf caps were a big hit all around. She'd even made personalized ones for Luke, Bernie, Noah, and Sky, which Jen in particular seemed to find hilarious.

Noah stood up again, and everyone immediately stopped chatting.

"When you're done with your appetizer, please proceed to the kitchen, in an orderly fashion, where the buffet awaits you."

Pen found herself nodding obediently and wishing she had half Noah's authority.

"The wedding speeches and toasts will commence after dessert and beverages are served, thank you."

Pen ate her appetizer fast, realizing it was the first thing she'd eaten all day, and rushed out to the kitchen where a serene scene awaited her. Anton and Rob had donned fresh whites and stood ready to serve with Kaitlin.

Anton gave her a thumbs up. "Ready when you are, boss."

Pen glanced over her shoulder to see Noah escorting Luke and Bernie through the door, followed by a very determined-looking Sky. She leaned against the wall and watched everyone file past her, offering help if they needed it, and generally making sure the line was running smoothly from her side of things.

Eventually there was no one left to serve but her and the kitchen staff. Anton called her over.

"Come and get something to eat. You've earned it."

Rob loaded up a plate with all the things she liked and handed it over. "Go and sit down. We'll be there in a minute."

Rob made sure everything was in order for Kaitlin, who had volunteered to stay at her station while everyone else ate and went to wash up. Anton glanced at him as he did the same.

"You like that girl, don't you?"

"Pen? Yeah."

"She likes you, too."

"So she says."

"I don't think she's the kind of woman to play games, so I guess she means it." Anton paused. "It's about time someone saw the good in you."

"She sees the good in everyone."

"Yeah, it's her gift." Anton smiled. "Are you going to stick around and take her seriously?"

Rob hesitated, and Anton kept talking. "She knows what you did?"

"I told her everything."

"Then she really does like you." Anton patted his shoulder. "And there's no reason why you can't make her happy."

"Except I've made a career out of doing the exact

opposite," Rob said. "What if I screw this up? I'd never forgive myself if I hurt her."

"The fact that you're thinking like that makes me believe you'll get it right this time. You've got to promise me you'll at least try."

Rob met his friend and mentor's gaze. "I can do that."

"Then good. Let's go and eat."

Pen sat in a happy daze of exhaustion as the family room was transformed yet again into the smallest dance floor in the world. The old plank floor made from trees felled right where the house now stood had probably seen its fair share of celebrating over the past generations and would now embrace another memory.

"You doing okay?"

She looked up to see Rob at her shoulder.

"Just taking it all in."

He sat down beside her and took her hand. "You must be exhausted."

"I am a bit tired," Pen acknowledged. "But I'm trying to stay in the moment so that I can remember it next time someone tries to tell me I can't do something."

"That's a great idea," Rob said gravely. "I could do with some of that in my life."

"I'll tell you when you're doing great." Pen smiled at him.

"And I'll do the same back. Do you want to dance?"

Pen eyed him. "In front of everyone?"

"I don't know what Anton's been telling you, but I'm not that bad a dancer."

"I meant, like, in front of your friends and my family?"

His faint smile died. "Okay, yeah, I guess that was stupid of me. You probably don't want your family knowing anything about me." He eased his hand free and stood up. "I should really be getting back to help Anton, anyway. I just wanted to make sure you were okay."

He left before Pen could untangle her words into a coherent sentence and make sense of what he'd implied from her reply. She jumped to her feet and bumped straight into Jake, who took hold of her elbow.

"Are you okay? Was that guy bothering you?"

"That guy is Rob. We work together. You already met him at our house."

"That makes it worse."

Pen blinked at him. "What?"

"Do you want me to tell him to back off?"

"Why on earth would you do that?"

Jake sighed. "Okay, let's start again. If that guy is bothering you I'll go and have a quiet word with him."

"He's my friend."

"You sure about that?"

"One hundred percent sure." Pen met her brother's skeptical gaze. "I absolutely adore him."

Something in her tone must have alerted Jake to her being more serious than he had anticipated.

"Like, in really adore him?"

"Yes." Pen smiled.

"Like, as in boyfriend material?"

"Absolutely."

Jake looked down at her. "Okay."

"What?"

"Nothing." He patted her shoulder. "I need to sneak outside and have a smoke. Cover for me."

"Like Mom doesn't know," Pen said. "And you should give it up, anyway."

"I know. Kev says the same." Jake smiled. "I guess I just have an addictive personality, and this feels like the lesser of a lot of evils."

After watching him go through rehab twice, Pen wasn't going to argue with that.

"It's snowing."

"Then it serves me right if I come down with pneumonia or get buried in a snowdrift." He winked at her and headed for the door, pausing briefly to speak to their mother on his way out.

Pen gave him five minutes and then walked through to the kitchen, but there was no sign of Rob. Anton was just packing up the last of his things.

"Are you looking for Rob?"

Pen nodded.

"He went back to his place to change his clothes. He'll be back in a minute."

"Thanks," Pen said.

"No, thank you."

"For what?" Pen asked.

"Seeing him for what he is and liking him anyway."

Anton smiled at her. "Rob deserves to be happy, and so do you."

"Pen?"

She turned at the sound of her mother's voice.

"Hey, Mom. Are you having a good time?"

As Anton turned away to continue packing up, her mom came over to her.

"It's been wonderful—although I knew Bernie would insist it was perfect."

Pen looked at her mom. "I'll take that as a compliment. Bernie wanted to enjoy her day without the stress of organizing everything, which is where I came in, so I'm glad you've enjoyed it."

"There's no need to get all defensive, sweetheart. I'm sure Bernie was grateful for your help, but claiming you did it all is a bit far-fetched."

Pen took a steadying breath. "I did do it all, Mom. Ask Bernie if you don't believe me."

Her mom chuckled. "Don't be silly. If I ask Bernie of course she'll give you all the credit."

"Because I deserve it." Pen held her mom's gaze. "I wish you wouldn't do this."

"Do what?"

"Assume I'm not capable of achieving anything."

"That's not what I'm doing at all!"

"Yes, it is, and it hurts, Mom. I'm twenty-eight, and I'm getting tired of being treated like a kid."

Her mom drew herself upright. "All your father and I have ever wanted is for you to be happy, Pen, and if we're a tad overprotective because of your . . . problems . . . then that's because we love you."

"I know you love me."

Pen was beginning to wish she hadn't said anything. Every time she tried to stand up for herself it ended with her mom being upset and Pen having to expend all her energy comforting her for having such a difficult daughter.

"Then maybe before you start attacking me, you'd remember that." Her mom's voice trembled.

"I'm not—"

"And how hard we worked to help you overcome your issues."

Pen pressed her lips together and looked away, her gaze inadvertently meeting Anton's, who was trying very hard not to be present. And who could blame him?

"I have to go," Pen said. "I'm not sure when I'll get home. As Bernie won't be here to tell me what to do, I'll have to muddle through on my own."

"Pen, don't be silly, darling . . ."

She turned away, her pride in her accomplishments deflating with every step, her doubts about her abilities shouting loudly in her mixed-up, muddled brain. She wanted to run away, but she couldn't do that because it would prove her mom was right. And she had a responsibility to Bernie and Luke to finish the job they'd hired her to do.

She found a smile somewhere and went back into the family room where Noah was dancing with Jen and Sky while still managing to check his watch. He looked straight at Pen.

"Luke and Bernie should be leaving now."

Pen nodded. "They're already getting changed. I'll get an update on their departure time."

"Thanks." Noah cleared his throat. "You've been excellent all day."

Jen winked at her. "Take a moment to savor that positive comment, Pen. Noah doesn't say that to everyone."

"I wish he'd tell my mom," Pen murmured as she walked down to Sally's suite, where the bride and groom were getting ready to leave on their honeymoon. "She might actually believe him."

She knocked on the door and realized she still hadn't had a chance to talk to Rob. But the wedding had to come first. Once they'd waved Luke and Bernie off, she'd find him and talk things through.

Rob paused on his way back to the house as a hint of smoke wafted past him. His gaze immediately went to the barn, but everything looked serene, and it was unlikely a fire would start during a snowfall. Nevertheless, he changed tack and walked down the slope. Years of living on a ranch meant he wasn't prepared to take a chance and make a small problem a much bigger one.

As he approached the barn, a shadow moved near the fence facing the paddock.

"Hey."

Rob recognized Pen's brother, Jake.

"Hey." Rob gestured at the cigarette between the other man's fingers. "I smelled smoke and came to check that the barn wasn't on fire."

Jake grinned at him. "I might not have been born

in a barn, but I do know it's important to completely extinguish my cigarette when it's done." He took another drag and blew out the smoke. "I'm trying to quit so I limit myself to one a day, but I must confess, I still enjoy every poisonous, deadly moment."

Rob couldn't help but smile.

"I gave up two years ago, so I hear you."

"And you've stuck to it?" Jake looked at him. "That gives me hope."

Rob shrugged. "I have what's known as an addictive personality. I can't just do one of anything."

"Same." Jake sighed as he finished the cigarette and ground the butt under the heel of his boot until there was nothing left to see. "Pen says you work for Bernie."

"Yeah, I mainly run her online delivery business and help create new menu items in the test kitchen."

"If you don't mind me saying, you don't look like a typical pastry chef."

"I grew up on a family ranch like this one. My dad thought I'd take over when he retired."

"Nothing like rocking the boat and upsetting your family's expectations of you, is there?" Jake sighed. "My parents are great, but that didn't stop me doing a lot of stupid shit and nearly killing myself along the way."

Rob suddenly remembered Pen mentioning a family member who'd gone through a similar journey to his own.

"I can relate," Rob said.

"I hate myself for that, you know?" Jake looked out over the frozen pasture. "I mean, it's bad enough ruining your own life without dragging everyone else down with you."

Rob couldn't have agreed more but he stayed quiet and let the other man speak.

"They all pretend everything is fine, but every so often I still see it in their eyes, the fear that I'm going off the rails again, and that this time they won't be able to stop me from destroying myself. And sometimes I guess I feel that way, too."

"Do you go to meetings?" Rob asked.

"Yeah. If I hadn't agreed to do that, my partner, Kev, wouldn't have moved in with me." Jake smiled. "It's amazing what you do for love."

Rob nodded. He already knew he wanted to be a better person for Pen.

"I guess I should go back before my mom organizes a search party." Jake shivered. "And it's getting cold out here."

Rob started walking alongside Jake, his gaze on the house where Pen was probably still working hard to make everything right. He'd been taken aback when she hadn't wanted to dance with him, but he guessed it made sense. No one would be particularly keen to introduce an ex-con as their boyfriend, particularly to an overly protective family like Pen's.

Jake glanced over at him. "Pen had to deal with a lot of crap when she was growing up. She found me in my bedroom once, when I'd overdosed and had to call 911. She was around twelve at the time."

"That's tough."

"And you know Pen. She wants to help everyone." Jake smiled. "Sometimes too much."

Rob stopped in his tracks. "Are you trying to make some kind of point here?"

"I guess I am." Jake grimaced. "I don't want her to think she has to save everyone all the time."

"And you think she's trying to save me?"

Jake met his gaze steadily. "I wouldn't want you mistaking her feeling . . . *bad* for you for something else."

Rob went to speak, but Jake kept going.

"And I'm not trying to be mean, Rob, I just know from my own experience that working out who *says* they want to help you as opposed to who actually does isn't easy, especially when you're an addict. We all have trust issues, right? It took me three years to believe Kev actually meant a word he said to me, and even now I still have my panicked moments."

"Pen's a good person. I'd never do anything to hurt her."

Jake nodded. "Then let's just keep it that way."

They continued on to the house in silence, Rob's mind in chaos as he digested Jake's obviously well-intentioned warning. The thing was—there was nothing he could disagree with. Pen was the kind of person who loved to help others. Had she seen that desperate need in him and tried to give him the same support she'd given her brother? Was it as simple as that? But she'd told him she wanted more and that she liked him. . . .

Just as Jake went to open the kitchen door, Noah

came through it and held it open, his keen gaze scanning Jake and Rob.

"Clear the decks. Bride and groom on the move."

The wedding party, headed by Bernie and Luke, spilled out of the open door in a burst of colorful chatter, warmth, and excitement.

Rob stood back as the bride and groom were kissed, hugged, and sent on their way with cheers and waves. It wasn't until the brake lights of their truck had disappeared into the darkness that Rob noticed Pen was missing.

Half of the guests decided to call it a night and departed, which should've made it easier to find her. As Rob checked each room, Pen's mom came into the hallway.

"Have you seen Pen, Rob?" she asked. "I assumed she'd be coming home with us."

"Knowing Pen, she won't be leaving until everything's back in place," Rob said.

"Surely someone else can do that?"

"It's her job. I'm not sure Pen would let them," Rob said. "She's something of a perfectionist."

"Pen?" Diana's brow wrinkled.

"She's done an amazing job with the wedding, Mrs. Jones. You must be so proud of her."

"I'm always proud of her." There was a note of uncertainty in her voice Rob hoped meant she was thinking a bit more about how she viewed her daughter.

"I think I overheard Sally asking Pen to stay over, for the company," Rob said.

"Then we'll be off. If you see her, will you let her know?"

Rob nodded, and Diana headed out, calling to her husband and Jake to follow her to their truck. He found Sally in the kitchen making herself a drink. Her smile faded as he approached her.

"What's wrong?"

He shrugged. "Nothing to worry about, I'm just looking for Pen. Did she leave with someone already?"

"She said she'd stay overnight to make sure everything was restored to normal, but I haven't seen her for a little while." She lowered her voice. "Anton said she and her mom were having quite the argument in the kitchen earlier."

"Her mom is . . . overprotective."

"She apparently refused to believe Pen had managed the whole wedding."

"Seems on-brand," Rob murmured. "Is Anton still here?"

"He's just finishing packing his truck."

"I'll go talk to him."

"And find Pen," Sally called out to him. "That's the most important thing."

CHAPTER 8

Rob hurried outside again and found Anton just closing the cover of his flatbed truck.

"Hey, you haven't got Pen in there somewhere, have you?" Rob asked.

"Nope." Anton jiggled his keys. "I just saw her heading down to the barn."

"The barn?" Rob frowned. "You mean she missed Bernie and Luke leaving?"

"She said goodbye and then snuck out the back while they went out the front." He paused. "She was arguing with her mom earlier."

Rob looked up where the snow was now falling steadily, shielding the emerging moon and the darkness of the skies in a white swirling mist.

"Did she at least have her coat on?" Rob asked.

"Yeah." Anton got into the truck, where Kaitlin was already sitting. "I'll leave her in your hands, Rob. Don't mess this up."

Rob was tired of people saying that to him. He knew he was a screwup. He didn't need everyone pointing it out. It just made him doubt himself even more. He zipped up his jacket, pulled his hat low, and started down to the barn. The wind had picked up and cut across his face with an icy chill that made his teeth chatter. There were lights on in the barn, but that was normal, so he had no way of knowing whether Pen was actually there or not.

He let out a relieved breath as he entered the barn and the scent of warm hay surrounded him. He saw Pen immediately. Despite still wearing her blue, polka dot party dress under her ski jacket, she was leaning on the lower door of the unbroken colt's stall, talking softly to the animal.

Rob already knew that neither Pen nor the horse responded well to loud noises, so he waited until he was close before he cleared his throat. Pen still jumped.

"Hey." Rob kept his tone light. "Your mom asked me to let you know that she and the family were heading out."

"Good," Pen said without turning her head.

"Okay," Rob said cautiously. He leaned against the wall and eyed her profile. It was weird not to see her smiling. "Sally's hoping you'll stay and keep her company. I think she's going to miss Luke not being around."

He wasn't sure how to proceed, but even his stupid brain was flashing a big "with caution" sign.

"I always intended to stay to make sure everything was cleaned up," Pen said.

"That's basically what I told your mom—that you'd be making sure you'd done your job."

She slowly turned to look at him. With a shock he

realized she might have been crying. Her smile appeared, then quickly disappeared.

"Thanks for sticking up for me, but I doubt she heard you. She'll never believe I'm capable of anything."

"Then I guess all you can do is keep proving her wrong." Rob held her gaze. "She doesn't get to define who you choose to be."

She looked back at the colt. "It's easy to say that but putting it into practice is hard." She sighed. "It's like she's killing me with kindness."

"I get it. You should come back up to the house. It's getting cold out here."

"I'll be there in a while." She turned toward him. "Are you sure my mom's gone?"

"I saw her drive off. Jake was still arguing with her about leaving you behind."

Her smile returned. "He's always been my hero."

"Some hero." The words were out of Rob's mouth before he realized it. "Hey, can you forget I said that? I'm tired, and my mouth is working faster than my brain."

Pen raised her chin. "I'm not sure I can."

Rob shoved his hands into his pockets and looked skyward. "I don't want to fight with you, okay?"

"Did Jake come and talk to you? Is that why you're mad at him? I told him not to."

"He's your brother. He's got a perfect right to check me out, and to be fair, he had some valid concerns."

Any expression left Pen's face. "You discussed my 'problems' with my brother? You let him tell you how to deal with me?"

"*Hell* no," Rob said. "We discussed—"

She talked over him. "And what did you both decide, Rob?"

"Nothing." He frowned at her.

"Let me guess. You decided poor little Pen didn't know her own mind and needed you and her big brother to protect her from the stupidity of her own decisions."

"That's not how it went at all." Rob tried but failed to keep his cool.

"However, it went, Rob, I don't appreciate you going behind my back to buddy up with my brother."

"I didn't." He glared at her now. "We talked about how difficult it is to have an addict in the family."

"And then he warned you off."

"I'm still here, aren't I?"

"Because now you feel sorry for me." Pen turned toward the exit. "Maybe that's what this has been about all the time."

"That's not fair."

"As my mom always tells me, life isn't fair, Rob. I wanted you to see *me*, not the screwed-up version my family sees."

"I've *always* seen you, whether I wanted to or not!" Rob said. "Do you think this has been easy? To trust someone and hope she doesn't just feel sorry for an ex-con because she's a good person?"

She started walking away from him. "Maybe we've both been fools."

Rob flinched. She might as well have slapped his face. "I thought you'd be braver than this."

She didn't stop, and he cursed under his breath as she

disappeared into the darkness. He kept feeling like he'd missed something—that they hadn't been having the same fight—and he didn't know how to fix it. Not that there was anything to fix. She'd made that very clear. It felt like his heart was snapping into a million icy pieces. He took a couple of deep breaths, checked that everything in the barn was in place, and decided to go to bed.

If Pen wanted to talk to him, she knew where he lived. He stomped back up the hill and unlocked his front door. True to her word, two days ago, Pen had dropped off several throw cushions, a photo she'd taken of Rob and the rest of the café team, and one of her aunt Linda's quilts. She'd been making his house into a home, and he secretly loved it—except now all his doubts had returned, and he'd blown it.

His gaze went to the stack of holiday cards he'd written in a feeble attempt to express his thanks for everything the local community had done for him since he'd arrived lonely and hurting the previous year. He sorted through the envelopes, stopping at the one with Pen's name on it. He hadn't sealed the flap. He took out the card, which showed a paint horse pulling Santa's sleigh.

He sat at the kitchen table and got out his pen. There were things he wanted to say to her that he might never get the opportunity to say out loud again, so he'd write them in the Christmas card and hope she understood how thankful he was to have met her.

After he finished writing, he took out a blank card and studied it for a long while before opening it and uncapping his pen.

To Mom, Dad, and family.
Wishing you all the best.
Roberto.

He studied the words and added a p.s. along with his cell number.

I am in a good place. Thank you for everything you did for me and I'm sorry for what I put you all through. I appreciate your love and care and wish you nothing but the best.

It was probably too late for the card to make it by Christmas Day, but it would get there eventually. As Pen had pointed out—everything had to start somewhere. And if they didn't choose to acknowledge him, he was cool about that, too. There was no obligation on their side; it was more about him acknowledging the hurt he'd done.

But was it enough? He took out his cell and tapped in the number to his dad's farm office, which he still knew by heart. He swallowed hard as he listened to his mom's recorded voice telling him to leave a message or call back during regular business hours. He almost chickened out, but he pictured Pen's face, and it steadied his nerves.

"Hey, it's Roberto. I just wanted to wish you happy holidays." He paused. "I miss you guys, and one day I hope to have the opportunity to make things right with you—if that's something you'd be okay with."

There was a lot more he wanted to say, but most of it needed to be done face-to-face. He ended the call and checked his messages. There was nothing from Pen, which wasn't surprising. The thought of not having a connection with her made his heart hurt. At some point, when she was willing to talk to him again, he'd apologize, and mean it. He couldn't allow himself to think about what he'd do if she no longer wanted him.

With a sigh, Rob went to take a shower. Today had been . . . a lot. All he could hope for was a better tomorrow.

Pen walked into the ranch house and immediately burst into tears. Luckily there was no one around to see her so she was able to cry her heart out. She'd never seen Rob so coldly furious. He'd looked as if she'd betrayed him, and that didn't make any sense at all.

"Pen!" Sally came around the corner with her dogs trotting at her heels. "Are you okay? What on earth happened?"

"I think Rob and I have broken up."

"Oh, sweetheart." Sally enveloped her in a hug. "Come and sit down and tell me all about it."

Pen followed her into the family room, which had been miraculously restored to its former purpose. The Christmas tree stood in one corner, and the toy box sat beside it. The only thing remaining from the wedding were the twinkling fairy lights Sally had wanted to keep for the holidays.

"Noah moved the couches back when you were out," Sally remarked as they sat down. "He's very strong."

"Thank goodness." Pen's nose was so stuffed up from crying that she sounded like she had a cold. "I thought I'd have to do it myself."

"You did an amazing job today, sweetie." Sally patted her hand. "Everyone enjoyed themselves immensely, and Luke and Bernie were thrilled to bits."

"Thank you. I had a lot of help."

"I told your parents they should be proud of you."

Pen nodded, not wanting to get into that right now.

"So what's up with you and Rob?"

"He's mad at me."

"Rob? I've never seen him get mad at anyone, especially you."

"It might be because I accused him of listening to my brother warning him off."

Sally was quiet for a few moments.

"Shouldn't you be mad at Jake for interfering?"

"Oh, I'll be talking to him, don't worry."

"Is it possible Rob just listened to Jake to be polite, and that he won't let it affect his judgment?"

Rob's words flashed through Pen's mind. *I'm still here, aren't I?* Was that what he'd been trying to tell her? Was that why he'd gotten so mad when she'd ignored him?

"I suppose it's possible," Pen said slowly. "Although it doesn't matter now because I've already ruined everything."

"Things can be fixed, sweetie. That's part of having a relationship. And if they can't, you'll only know that after you've been brave and talked things through."

"If Rob will ever talk to me again." Pen bit her lip.

"Pen, that man adores you. He'll listen." Sally patted her shoulder. "Now, it's been a long day. You'll feel much better after a good night's sleep."

A yawn shuddered through Pen, and she stood up. "You're right. I shouldn't have argued with him when I was tired and upset with my mom. It was bound to go badly." She smiled at Sally. "Thanks for listening to me, and I hope you aren't missing Luke too much."

"He'll be back before I know it," Sally said. "I'm just thrilled that he and Bernie have made things work."

Pen kissed Sally's cheek and went to the guest bedroom. She sat on the bed and picked up her phone to text Jake. Sally would probably advise her to leave it until the morning, but she didn't think she'd sleep until she contacted her brother.

Why did you talk to Rob when I specifically asked you not to?

I didn't.

He said you talked.

We did.

Pen scowled at her phone. Was Jake being deliberately annoying? The bouncing bubbles told her he was typing again so she waited.

I met him outside the barn when he was making sure I wasn't a fire hazard. We talked about a lot of things.

Like me.

You came up, but you weren't the focus of our conversation. We mainly talked about addiction and how it hurt people we loved. He's not a bad guy, sis, he's trying to be better just like I am.

Pen considered his words for quite a long while.

So you approve of him?

I didn't say that. ☺ He's still an addict and that's never going to be easy to live with.

Kev lives with you.

Kev loves me. ☺

Pen wasn't going to get into that with her brother. She still hadn't told Rob how she felt beyond her usual gibberish, but the amount of hurt she was currently feeling made her think she cared about him a lot.

I didn't tell him to back off, sis, I swear.

I bet you kind of did, Jake. You were just more subtle about it.

He responded with an angel and a shrug emoji which confirmed her suspicions.

I don't want you to have to go through that, Pen. You had enough heartache growing up with me.

Pen took a deep breath.

I think that's up to me, isn't it? I'm no longer a kid and I'm quite capable of making up my own mind—not that it makes much difference because, congrats, Jake, you scared him off anyway.

Pen was just about to put her phone away when he texted back.

Sweetheart, if I put him off that easily, he's not the man for you anyway.

She didn't reply. How could she? There was an element of truth in what he'd written. Jake had a core of steel that had helped him pull himself out of the depths of addiction and make something of his life, and he expected others to do the same.

Pen turned her phone face down. She had to sleep. Tomorrow might not fix all her problems as Sally hoped, but at least it was the fresh start she desperately needed after the ups and downs of the wedding day. She couldn't control what Rob wanted to do, but she could at least clear the air with him and make sure they hadn't been arguing about different things. She'd jumped to the conclusion that Jake had told him to back off, and everything had gone downhill from there.

The least she could do was try to explain and leave it to Rob to decide if he could forgive her. She was just about to get into bed when something else occurred to her. Maybe Rob should be asking for her forgiveness if he'd taken Jake's warning to heart and decided she wasn't worth the risk.

I'm still here, aren't I?

They'd promised each other to be honest, and that was what she would do. What the outcome would be she wasn't sure, but Jake was right about one thing: If she and Rob stood any chance of making it together, they'd have to be brave.

CHAPTER 9

Christmas Day started with a snowstorm that made the town look like a Christmas card, but Pen wasn't feeling particularly festive. She'd politely ended all conversations with her mom and Jake about what had gone down at the wedding, and neither of them were happy with her. To her surprise, it felt good to have established some boundaries, and she reminded herself to do it more often.

By the time her large family gathered together, ate a huge lunch, and started distributing presents, she was feeling quite lonely. Everyone else had a partner, and even though she knew the teasing was meant with love, she was tired of smiling at all the jokes about her single status. She almost wished she'd stayed up at the ranch to keep Sally company while Luke and Bernie were away, but Sally had Noah, and Jen, and Rob. . . .

"Hey." She looked up to see Jake standing in the doorway of her bedroom. "Why are you hiding up here?"

"I'm not hiding. I just came up to find a book for cousin Finn."

"That was half an hour ago."

She shrugged. "It took me a while to find it."

"It's not like you to mope, sweetheart."

Pen picked up the book and went toward the door. "I lost track of time. You know what I'm like."

Jake didn't budge, so she had to look up at him. "What?"

"You really like him, don't you?" Jake asked.

Pen dropped her gaze to the book. "I should get this to Finn before he leaves."

Jake sighed. "I know you think I let you down, but you can talk to me, shrimp."

"I guess I know what you're going to say, so what's the point?" She smiled at him. "Will you stop towering over me and get out of my space?"

He stepped back. "I just want you to be happy."

"And I'm tired of everyone in this family thinking they get to decide what that means. If I want to have a relationship with Rob then that's what I'm going to do, okay?"

"That's better." Jake grinned at her. "Fight for your man."

Pen groaned and pushed past him. "I don't know how Kev puts up with you."

"He loves me." Jake gave her a mischievous grin. "He makes me want to be a better person."

Pen went down the stairs and paused in the wide hallway. Her mom had opened the doors between the dining room, front parlor, and kitchen to provide space for the whole family to gather together. Two Christmas trees sat twinkling away at opposite ends of the house, and the space smelled of spices, baked ham, and her aunt Linda's special Christmas brownies, which Pen was fairly certain contained some lethal orange liqueur.

She set the book down on the hall table and back-tracked to the kitchen, which was empty. She found her keys, coat, and backpack and went out the back door. The snow had stopped, and everything was silent and still around her. She took one last look at her family through the windows and got into her four-wheel-drive truck.

She took a moment to text Jake.

Off to see Rob. Tell Mom not to worry x.

She was halfway up the county road toward Nilsen Ranch when her phone lit up with a thumbs up emoji followed by about a hundred hearts. The county had already been through and salted the road, so it was safe to drive. Pen tried to think about what she was going to say to Sally and Rob when she gatecrashed their Christmas Day, but nothing came to mind.

She'd have to make it up as she went—which was her usual mode of operation anyway. She didn't think Noah would throw her out, but you never knew. And what if Rob didn't want to see her? It would be awkward as hell.

"Stop it, Penelope," she said out loud. "Focus on the road."

She had the gate code for the ranch memorized after her frequent visits for the wedding planning and got through without incident. The old logging track through the forest to the ranch house was bumpy but still well-defined. She slowed down and reminded herself to breathe deeply and not get ahead of herself. She glanced over at the neatly wrapped presents peeking out of her backpack on the passenger seat. Even if Rob wanted nothing to do with her, she could still deliver the presents and leave.

Dusk was settling over the forest and wisps of mist swirled through the tree trunks like fingers reaching for her truck. She was almost relieved when she turned the last corner and the light from the cluster of houses and the barn was revealed.

She parked her truck behind Rob's and gathered her belongings. It was time to make her own decisions and live with the consequences.

Rob had never been the life and soul of any party, being too shy as a kid, too out of control as a teen, and lately, too careful not to draw attention to himself as an addict and an ex-con. If it hadn't been for his worries about Pen, he had to admit, it had been the best Christmas in years. Anton had joined Sally, Noah, Jen, and Sky for the day, meaning the food had been out of this world, and the company exceptional.

He didn't have to explain himself or try too hard because they not only got him, but they seemed to like him despite the fact that he wasn't at his best. No one had said a word about Pen, and he appreciated that because his head was full of images of her laughing at him, kissing him, and arguing with him while he missed her like crazy.

He'd also had a chance to talk to Anton about Bernie's

plans to take the online business statewide and how he felt about that. As someone who'd been burned by bad business deals, Anton understood where Rob was coming from and didn't belittle his concerns, which was refreshing, and gave Rob a lot to think about.

Jen had just gone to put Sky down for a nap in his old room when the screen door creaked open and banged shut. Everyone else still digesting lunch in the family room looked up.

Noah was instantly on his feet. "Are we expecting anyone, Sally?"

"Not unless Bernie's had enough of Luke already and left him in Reno," Sally joked.

"Hello?"

It was Rob's turn to stiffen as he recognized Pen's hesitant voice. Sally grinned at him.

"Hey, Pen! We're all in the family room, come on in!"

She came in clutching her backpack, her cheeks flushed from the cold and her hair in two high pigtails tied with tinsel. She wore a cherry-red sweater with a short plaid skirt and woolen stockings. Rob had never seen anything more beautiful in his life.

"Hi!" She gave a little, awkward wave. "I thought I'd drop your presents off."

To everyone's credit no one questioned her dubious decision-making as she carried on talking.

"Except I didn't know Anton would be here—which was silly of me because Rob wouldn't have let him spend the day alone, and as he's up here now, of course, Anton would come, too."

"Don't worry about me," Anton said.

"I do have something for you, but I left it at the coffee shop." Pen paused. "But I forgot you weren't working that day, and I think it just stayed there."

"It's all good," Anton reassured her. "I hope you've got something for Rob."

Now everyone, including Pen, was looking at him, and for once he was glad his tan skin tone meant he didn't blush much.

"I have something for everyone," Pen said, beaming.

She set her backpack on the coffee table and sat on the floor to take things out. "This one is for Noah, this is Jen's, and Sally, here's yours."

She handed out various squishy-shaped parcels.

Noah unwrapped his immediately and regarded the contents. "This is useful. Thank you."

"You can't go wrong with a knitted scarf and a hat," Jen agreed as she revealed her own pink-and-blue patterned set.

"I made one with sheep for Sky." Pen handed over another parcel. "And a tiny one for the bump."

"Thank you!" Jen rushed over to give Pen a kiss.

Sally unwrapped her yellow hat with applique sunflowers. "I love it, thank you." She paused. "Did you make something for Rob?"

Rob, who was busy gawping at Pen like a teenager with his first crush, jumped.

"I'm . . . good with whatever she wants to give me."

"Really?" Pen looked right at him, and his mouth went dry.

"Anything." He held her gaze. "Not that I deserve it, because I'm an idiot, but—"

Noah cleared his throat. "Is this about to get personal? Because we don't mind if you need some privacy."

"Noah." Jen rolled her eyes. "Just let the woman give the man his present, okay?"

Pen handed over a square package, her gaze solemn. "I hope you like it."

Rob's fingers were trembling as he carefully unwrapped the present to reveal a framed photograph.

"Wow . . ." He let out a breath. "It's great."

Jen looked over his shoulder at the picture of him and the young colt in the pasture. "Did you take that, Pen?"

"Yes, when neither of them was looking," Pen said. "I took quite a few, actually, but that was my favorite."

"I can see why." Sally joined the conversation. "They look so in sync, it's remarkable."

Rob was still staring at the picture Pen had taken as if seeing himself for the first time.

"Do you like it, Rob?" Sally asked.

Rob set it carefully on the seat beside him and turned to Pen. "Can we talk?"

She nodded, and he took her hand and went toward the kitchen. Behind them, Noah was still yacking. "See? I said they needed some privacy, and I was right."

Rob went out onto the veranda, turned around, and drew Pen into a tight hug.

"I'm sorry."

She didn't resist him, which was a good sign.

"For what?"

"Being an ass."

She looked up at him. "That's not very specific, and anyway, I—"

He cut her off with a kiss full of rough longing and need, and . . . with a sigh, she kissed him back, her hands in his hair.

Eventually, he raised his head, his voice hoarse. "I don't like fighting with you." She shivered slightly, and he glanced up at the sky. "Let's go back to my place, okay?"

She nodded, and they ran across the yard to the other side of the barn, where the old bunkhouses were situated. He'd left a light on, so it was an easy matter to step inside, find her a towel for her hair, and turn up the heat. By the time she returned, he'd set a match to the log fire and sat on the couch, leaning forward to warm his hands.

"Come here." He patted the seat beside him, but she shook her head.

"Can I sit opposite you? If I'm sitting too close, all I think about is kissing you."

"I kind of like that option."

"That's because you don't want to hear what I have to say."

He met her gaze. "Correction: I'm afraid of what you're going to say."

She didn't laugh, which was good, and nodded instead.

"I'm the one who should be apologizing, Rob. I made some assumptions about you and Jake that weren't fair."

"To be honest, I wasn't exactly in the best frame of mind when I came to find you, either," Rob admitted. "I would've taken anything you said the wrong way."

"I was feeling the same." She sighed. "I'd just had an argument with my mom."

Rob made himself hold her gaze. "And I was thinking how hard it is for an addict's family and how difficult it would be to love someone like that."

"Because of Jake?" Pen asked.

"Yeah, but he was right," Rob continued. "I didn't know you had to call 911 when he overdosed."

Pen's gaze was clear. "I saved his life. That's all I cared about. and what I choose to remember."

"I just . . . suddenly thought you didn't deserve to have to face that risk with me. And when you got mad about me talking to Jake, I thought maybe I was right, because you'd realized it, too."

"I thought Jake had warned you off when I asked him not to, which is why *I* was mad." She grimaced. "Of course, he did warn you off in a subtle way, but I didn't realize that until afterward."

"So, we were both kind of right and kind of wrong," Rob said slowly. "We've got to get better at this communicating stuff, Pen, or we'll never make it."

"Wait." Pen sat up straight. "You weren't planning on breaking up with me?"

He frowned. "Hell, I thought you'd already done that part."

"I didn't actually say the words."

"You stormed off."

"I didn't 'storm.' I just left the barn."

Rob raised an eyebrow. "Okay, you ran out on me. It felt like you meant it."

She scowled at him. "It was a very long day. I was tired, you were tired, and my family were being obnoxious to both of us. Is it surprising that we ended up arguing with the wrong people?"

"You mean each other?"

"Exactly." She nodded. "They're the ones who should be begging *our* pardon."

"I don't want to do anything that takes you away from your family, Pen," he said carefully. "I'd never forgive myself if you had to choose."

"Rob . . . they'll have to make that choice for themselves. I've already chosen." She smiled at him. "And I'm with you."

His words stuck in his throat, but he had to tell her the truth. "I'd be the luckiest man alive to have you in my corner. And I'd do my best to never let you down or cause you to regret that decision."

"I like the sound of that. Can I come and sit with you now?"

He stood up and opened his arms. She skipped over to him, narrowly avoiding the coffee table and flung herself against him with such force that they toppled over onto the couch. Rob looked up into her blue eyes and smiled.

"I think I'm in love with you, Pen Jones."

"You think?" She kissed him. "Then I'll have to try harder to take those doubts away because I'm sure I love you to death."

He rolled her onto her back and grinned down at her. "Merry Christmas, Pen."

She cupped his cheek and grinned back. "You're the best present I've ever had."

"Oh!" Rob raised his head. "I have to give you your card."

"Now?" Pen complained as he got off the couch and went over to the table. "Can't it wait?"

She couldn't believe how happy she felt, as if a choir of heavenly angels were singing loudly in her head.

"I want you to read it." He held the card out.

Pen opened the envelope and took out the card, pausing to admire the paint horse on the front. Rob had very clear loopy handwriting that was easy to read.

"Dear Pen," she read out loud. "Thank you for making this the best year of my life. I don't have much money, but I do have a gift for you—will you choose a name for the colt? I just know you'll get it right. Love, Rob."

She took a shaky breath and looked up at him.

"It's . . . so *sweet* of you to trust me with this."

He shrugged. "I can't think of anyone better."

She reached for his hand and found it waiting for her. "Thank you."

"There's something else," he hesitated. "I sent my parents a Christmas card and then I called and left a message."

"That was very brave of you."

His smile was crooked. "You told me someone has to take the first step. I thought it should be me."

"I bet they'll be thrilled."

"We'll see." He squeezed her fingers. "And while I'm laying everything out there, I'm not sure if I want to continue in the catering business. I might want to be a cowboy again."

"You could do both," Pen suggested. "Otherwise Luke and Bernie might be having their first married fight."

His smile was so warm, she almost melted.

"One thing I love about you is your optimism, and your belief in me."

"That's two things," Pen pointed out. "But you're welcome."

Rob cupped her chin and looked deeply into her eyes. "You brought the sunshine back into my life, and I never want to live in the dark again."

Pen blinked back her tears. "And you're the calm center of my universe."

He gently kissed her mouth. "Then let's keep being honest with each other and build on that, okay? Because I very much want to share every Christmas with you from now on."

"Agreed. Now should we get back to the house before Noah explodes with curiosity?"

Rob chuckled. "That would be messy." He pulled her to her feet. "And, if we don't get out of here soon, I'm going to be wanting to do more than kiss you."

"I wouldn't mind."

He set her hat on her head and helped her into her coat. "We're going to do this the old-fashioned way."

"Ooh, you're going to come 'courting'?"

"Yup." Rob closed the door, and they walked back through the snow-blanketed pathways and trees. "With flowers, and sitting in the front parlor, and everything."

The silence was immense. Pen took it all in and sent up her thanks to the universe for all her blessings. Their path might not always be easy, but she had a feeling that with the help of their community and their love for each other, she and Rob would have a very happy ever after indeed.

And if anyone deserved it more than them, she'd be very surprised.

HER CHRISTMAS
COWBOY

DELORES FOSSEN

CHAPTER 1

"Kidnapped anyone lately?" asked the man behind Reese Darnell.

Reese froze and then had to immediately unfreeze so she could turn around and face the person who'd just posed that question.

Well, heck.

There were embarrassing things from her past that she wasn't anxious to relive, but this tall, dark-haired guy with the dreamy blue eyes had just brought up the World Series of embarrassing moments.

Zack Caldwell.

He was still just as tall, just as dark haired, and his eyes were just as dreamy blue as she recalled. Rock star looks, all showcased by his great-fitting jeans, a gray shirt, and boots. A cowboy to the core.

Cowboy plus, she quickly amended.

Along with being her former "captive," Zack was apparently now the sheriff of this small town of Loveland, Texas. Either that or the shiny sheriff's badge pinned to his shirt was some kind of prop meant to add to the humiliation that had flashed from her hair roots to her toenails. Along with the humiliation, there was also something else doing some flashing.

A whole lot of heat.

Mercy, she'd felt attraction for hot guys before, but this seemed to be attraction on steroids. Lust at first sight. And her face might have been registering that, too. Hard to tamp down this kind of carnal kick. Of course, this particular kick was coupled with the whole embarrassment thing.

She glanced around the squad room of the Loveland PD and hoped no one was witnessing this humiliating trip down memory lane. There were four deputies in or near their desks, and the perky looking receptionist-dispatcher wearing an elf outfit. The deputies and the elf seemed to be going above and beyond to do anything other than look at their boss and her.

Which meant they were probably listening to every word.

Reese hoped one of them didn't volunteer to arrest her.

"Well?" Zack muttered, one of his dark eyebrows lifting. "Are you here to kidnap me?"

Normally that wouldn't have been a serious question, and it might not have been now, but sadly, he did have the right to ask. Because, hey, she'd succeeded at kidnapping him before. Technically anyway.

Reese attempted a smile, one that she hoped dismissed the whole kidnapping thing for what it was: A Texas-sized mistake.

That particular blunder had happened six years ago when Reese had attended a *Fifty Shades of Grey* masquerade party at the pub owned by her then-boyfriend,

Paul. On that night, Reese had donned a trench coat over her skimpy lace undies along with the requisite mask, and she'd threaded her way through the partiers to a dark corner where she thought she'd spotted Paul in his own mask.

Emphasis on *dark*.

She had launched herself at her man and immediately proceeded to do very naughty things to him. It had started with some murmuring in his ear. Specifically, *I've kidnapped you and now you're my plaything*. Reese had followed that declaration up with a French kiss that was long, hot, and deep. Her captive had gone still for a couple of seconds, then responded with a long, hot, and deep kiss of his own. It hadn't lasted though, because he'd eased away from her and dropped the bombshell question.

Uh, who are you?

The kisses, touches, and dirty murmurs had come to a quick halt, and what had followed could only be described as utter humiliation, complete with garbled apologies. And snapping her trench coat shut.

During the garbling she'd learned he was Zack Caldwell, an old friend of Paul's who'd just dropped by to catch up and had been provided with a mask for the party. Zack was someone who should have been merely an embarrassing blip in her memory.

Even now though, Reese could recall the taste of him.

Not good.

And the reminder of that *not good* was enough to prompt her to clear her throat, shove aside the lustful heat, and get down to business. She took out the PI license that she'd already shown the dispatcher.

His eyebrow lifted again. "During your short stint as a kidnapper-dominatrix, you were a paralegal."

That must have been something Paul had mentioned to him, because Reese certainly hadn't volunteered anything like that. Once she'd realized she hadn't been French kissing her boyfriend, she'd gotten the heck out of there. Unfortunately, not before Paul had appeared and demanded to know what was going on. After rattling off an excuse of mistaken identity, Reese had left to try to restore a shred of her dignity. Then she'd put the whole ordeal behind her.

Except for remembering way too much about Zack's taste.

"I got my PI license three years ago, and one of my cases brought me here to Loveland," she responded, trying to sound professional. "I didn't know you were the sheriff," she added in a mumble. If she had known, she would have tried to do all of this over the phone or internet.

"I've been sheriff for the past five years. I was a deputy here before that," he explained.

She'd heard Paul mention the deputy part, and somehow Reese had stopped herself from doing any searches on social media for Zack, even after Paul had told her Zack's name. For one thing, Reese hadn't wanted to relive her humiliation by poring over the man's details.

"We can talk in my office," Zack said, tipping his head to an open door trimmed with twinkling Christmas lights.

Actually, every door, wall, and desk in the place had them, along with some tinsel and, oddly, small posters of a red-lipsticked mouth pursed for a kiss. They'd been taped up about three feet apart and had been strung with lights to accentuate them, like mini movie marquees.

Reese stepped into a room where Christmas reigned. A floor-to-ceiling tree in the corner. Another smaller one on a filing cabinet, and shiny silver sleighbell ornaments scattered on any and all available surfaces. She made a cursory count of six baskets that had big red bows on the handles and were filled with pine cones and holly. The room smelled like cinnamon, candy canes, and coffee.

"My mom did some decorating," Zack muttered as he followed her gaze. "She's a fan of the season."

Clearly. But it wasn't just Christmas stuff in here. There was a poster of the kissing mouth like the ones in the squad room. Beneath it was a sticky note with the number 162.

"So, what's the case you're working on?" Zack asked, motioning for her to take a seat. He didn't sit. He sort of leaned, resting his rather superior butt against the edge of his desk.

Reese released the breath that'd been pent up in her chest. Good, they were going to move away from memories of kidnapping, superior butts, and French kissing and go on to business.

"Happy Harry," she said, and then realized she needed to back up a bit. "I'm trying to locate this man," she added, taking out her phone to show Zack the picture she'd copied.

As pictures went, it sucked. Plain and simple. It was a grainy shot of a man and woman taken on a beach. The woman had a big beaming smile, but at the exact moment the photo had been snapped, a seagull had seemingly divebombed the man, who was in the process of ducking and batting it away. Even with the enhancement of the image, the only part of him that was visible was his chin and right ear. Because he was wearing a hat, you couldn't even see his hair.

Zack looked at the picture, frowned, and his eyebrow lifted again. "Please tell me you have a better photo of this guy."

She had to shake her head. Her great-aunt Sylvia had lost everything in a house fire thirty-four years ago, around the same time Reese was born.

"I do have this though." Reese took out a copy of the document from her purse. "It's a marriage license for my great-aunt Sylvia Darnell and Harry Smith. AKA, Happy Harry."

Reese watched as Zack read through the license, which thankfully didn't suck in print quality. The info was clearly visible. Just over sixty years ago, when her great-aunt had been nineteen, she'd married Harry Smith, who'd been twenty.

Or rather he had claimed to be.

Harry hadn't been exactly Honest Abe about, well, anything.

Reese took out a thick envelope with more documents. "Those are two more licenses showing other women that Harry Smith wed in the decade following his marriage to my great-aunt. For these, he used the surnames Miller and Jones, but both of them called him by his nickname, Happy Harry. And since he didn't divorce any of these women before he married the next one, that means that while Harry might indeed be happy, he's also a serial bigamist."

Zack met her gaze, and she saw the flat look of a cop's skepticism in the dreamy blue of his eyes. "How do these women know it's the same man?"

Oh, this was not going to be fun to answer. "Poly-orchidism," she said, pronouncing it the way she'd practiced from hearing it on the internet.

His look went even flatter. Not a surprise to her. "What?" he asked.

She huffed and spelled it out. "Balls. He has three of them, and it's a very rare disorder."

That didn't erase his flat look, but his eyebrow rose again. "Do the other two women have better photos of him? Not of his balls," he tacked on. "But pictures of his face?"

Reese had to shake her head. "Both women were furious when Happy Harry walked out on them, and they ended up destroying any and all photos and memorabilia. One by dumping the stuff into an old outhouse on her family's property, and the other by throwing them into the Gulf of Mexico."

"And how exactly did these women find out about each other?" Zack pressed.

Reese gathered her breath and gave him a thumbnail. "An online group for women who've had painful or embarrassing episodes in their lives. Don't," she warned him when that eyebrow rose again. "I'm not part of the group. My great-aunt Sylvia is, and apparently after months of chatter, the two women and my aunt figured out their painful and embarrassing episodes were caused by the three-balled Happy Harry."

She hadn't meant to be so blunt with the last part, but Happy Harry riled her to the core. And he probably hadn't stopped with the trio of broken hearts that she knew about. There could be others.

"Did any of these women end up divorcing this guy?" Zack asked.

"The other two did, but it took them years, since they couldn't find him to serve the papers, and the final decree for wife number two didn't happen before Happy Harry married wife number three. My great-aunt didn't go through with a divorce. She was with him for two years, and when he left, she insisted that she never wanted to risk another broken heart."

He nodded, glanced over the marriage licenses again. "What makes you think he's here in Loveland?"

"All three women recall him mentioning he was born here. Of course, that doesn't mean he came back here, but I thought it was a good starting point." Reese took out another piece of paper and handed it to him. "Those are the names of six possible candidates. All were born here in Loveland about eighty years ago, give or take five years, and have given names that are variations of Harry. Henry, Hank, Hal," she supplied.

"How'd you come up with all of these?" he asked.

"Not easily. I did a lot of internet searches, land records, mentions on social media, newspaper articles, and birth and marriage records on ancestry sites. I was even able to access some old school files." She paused. "Do you know them?"

He set the copies of the licenses on his desk to take the paper, and after glancing at it, he nodded. Then sighed. "I have to ask: What do you intend to do with this man if you find him? If you're looking for an arrest, it's possible the statute of limitations will prevent that."

"I don't want him arrested," Reese was quick to say because she'd already discussed this with her great-aunt and the other two women. "I just want him to explain to his wives why he did what he did." She put wives in air quotes. "I want to try to give them some closure." She paused. "Are all six of those men still alive?"

"They are," he verified. "I'm guessing you'll want to pay these men visits?"

"Absolutely." Reese stood and gathered up the licenses she'd shown him. "I just didn't want to start knocking on doors without talking to you first. Or rather, talking to the sheriff. I didn't know it'd be you," she added. If she had known, she might have skipped the nicety of letting the locals know they had a PI on their turf.

He nodded as if he totally got the gist of what she hadn't voiced. "Some of those men aren't likely to answer their doors, much less talk to you," Zack said. "I'll drive you out to the first couple of names on the list."

Her first instinct was to decline his offer, to put some distance between her and the source of her embarrassment. But then she thought of unanswered doors. Thought of how some people might react to a stranger trying to question them about their past.

Or their number of testes.

"Thank you," Reese said.

Zack gave another of those sighs that made her feel as if she were nothing but a pain in his superior butt, and he took a black Stetson off a wall peg. Just then, the dispatcher appeared in the doorway.

"What is it, CiCi?" he asked.

"Sorry," she muttered, not sounding at all apologetic but rather giddy. Now that Reese got a better look at her, she could indeed confirm the woman was wearing a Santa's elf outfit with Doc Martens. "Sorry," she repeated. "I just wanted to give you this." She thrust a sticky note at Zack, then bobbled around like a toddler hyped up on Christmas cookies.

Zack sighed again, went to the poster on the wall, and replaced the "162" with the new note. It read "163."

"Shia Franklin and Lizzy Gonzales," the dispatcher announced and clapped her hands. She then glanced between Reese and Zack. "Hey, you two—"

"No," Zack said, cutting her off.

Reese waited for him to explain what he'd just declined, but instead he slid on his Stetson and tipped his head, indicating she should follow him. Zack led her out a side entrance and into the small parking lot where she'd left her own car.

The blast of winter air hit her, and she felt her foot skid a little on a patch of ice. Sometimes winter in this part of Texas could be more like spring, but that wasn't the case now. Loveland and the rest of the area were going through an actual cold spell, with an ice storm in the forecast. It was the reason Reese had booked a room at the town's quaint inn, called the Love Nest. The reason, too, it had taken her a while to walk through the small parking lot, since parts of it had been like a skating rink.

"One sixty-three?" Reese asked just as Zack asked, "So, how did things work out with Paul?"

Reese was reasonably sure his answer would be a lot more interesting than hers. "You're Paul's friend so you must know," she said.

Zack shrugged and led her to a silver truck. He did the gentlemanly thing of opening her door and helping her in. The helping turned out to be more than just a hand on her back though. The step up was high, and apparently her boots weren't made for ice because she skidded again.

And Zack caught her.

A full-fledged catching, with his arms going around her and pulling her against him to anchor her. Body to body. A reminder that they'd had a similar experience when she'd kidnapped him.

She remembered his taste again, too.

Yeah, this wasn't good, and the ice wasn't helping. As she tried to maneuver, she just kept slipping, which created a whole lot of body smushing and bumping. Apparently, his boots were ice friendly because he finally scooped her up and set her on the seat of the truck.

"Paul," Zack said, obviously picking up the conversation where they'd left off, and he wasn't breathing nearly as hard as she was. "Every now and then I'll get a text from him, but other than that, he and I have sort of lost touch." He closed her door and went to his side.

Reese waited until he was in the truck before she responded. "Paul and I lost touch, too." She shrugged. "Well, we did after we divorced four years ago."

Zack started the truck but didn't drive away. "I'm sorry," he muttered. But then he stopped, shook his head, and turned in the seat to face her. "Actually, I'm only sorry if you are."

"I'm not," she blurted before giving some thought to his comment. "Why? Did you know that Paul would turn into a control freak with a penchant for lying about his so-called business-only relationships with his wait-staff?"

All right, she should have given that comment more thought, too. For Pete's sake, why was she spilling her guts to this man?

"Yes," Zack said. "And I'm sorry you didn't know."

"Oh," Reese muttered.

Zack frowned and shook his head as if he couldn't believe he was about to do some blurting of his own. "What happened during that fake kidnapping was un-nerving for me, too," he said.

Reese winced. "I'm so sorry—"

"Not that kind of unnerving," Zack interrupted. He stared at her with those take-me-for-a-spin eyes. "I considered calling you and asking you out. The only thing that stopped me was because it would have been poaching on a so-called friend."

Oh, she wished he had poached, but thankfully, she didn't blab that out. Perhaps because her mouth had stopped working. Possibly her breathing, too. That had everything to do with the intense gaze Zack had on her.

"I'll admit I've given a lot of thought to those kisses," he went on, the testosterone coming off him in waves now, like a high-powered sprinkler. "And I haven't been able to forget you."

The heat came rolling through that cold truck, and it was hot enough to melt any nearby ice patches. Hot enough to send off alarm bells in her head, too. Reese knew she wasn't a woman eternally wounded by bad love as her great-aunt was. But she also wasn't a dive first, think later kind of person either.

Judging from his scowl and muttered profanity, neither was Zack.

He cleared his throat, put the paper with the names on the seat between them, started the truck, and dragged in a breath deep enough to supply air to multiple folks. "All right," he said. "Let's go pay a visit to my grand-dad."

That yanked Reese right out of the heat haze. "Your granddad?"

He nodded and tapped his finger on the paper before he started driving. "Harry Miller. He's the first name on your Happy Harry list."

CHAPTER 2

Zack had figured the bulk of his workday would be consumed by fender benders on ice-slick roads, escaped livestock, and pressure to keep hiking up that one sixty-three number. He certainly hadn't thought the day would include a search for a man with three balls and an encounter with a woman who'd rocked his world.

A cliché, yes, but an accurate one.

Those kisses with Reese had become his benchmark for all kisses since then. And none had lived up to the ones that had happened in that dark corner of the pub. Even now, Zack could feel the heat from them. Even now, he could feel the way she'd fit against his body. But it was sort of obvious from her startled expression that she wasn't thinking of heat or kisses.

Well, maybe not.

Zack thought she might indeed be mulling over such things, and perhaps reliving them, but at the moment she was dealing with the shock that his grandfather's name was on her list.

"You think your granddad could be Happy Harry?" she asked.

"No," Zack couldn't say fast enough. "But then, no one probably wants to think of a grandparent as a serial bigamist with an extra ball. So, you'll meet him and hopefully rule him out."

Zack was almost certain about that ruling-out part, just because he didn't want to believe his granddad was capable of being a bigamist. But he was a cop, and even slim possibilities had to be considered.

"Uh, has your grandfather ever said anything about being married more than once?" she asked.

"No." He backed out of his parking space, feeling the shimmy of the tires on the ice. There shouldn't be much ice on the roads because of traffic, or rather what constituted traffic in a small town, but Zack took it slow, easing out onto the street. "My grandmother passed away two years ago, and they'd been married for nearly sixty years."

"The Happy Harry I'm looking for could have had a life, and a wife, here for all that time. My great-aunt and the other two women said he was away on business a lot. That's one of the reasons it took them so long to realize he wasn't coming back."

Zack had plenty of questions about Harry, but he went with a general fill-me-in approach. That way, he'd get to hear the sound of Reese's voice while he drove. "What else did they say about Harry?"

Reese gathered her breath and pushed a strand of her dark blond hair from her cheek. "Apparently Harry used different stories. With my great-aunt, he claimed he was an artist. For wife two, he said he was in the wholesale antiques business. He told wife three he was a cattle broker."

Zack frowned because there were some possible nuggets in those three accounts. His granddad did indeed like to doodle and draw, and according to what Zack had heard, Zack's great-grandparents had once owned a junk store that had possibly sold antiques. Added to that, his grandfather was a rancher and had worked and owned his small cattle ranch since long before Zack was born.

"None of the three women come from money," Reese went on, "and according to them, neither did Harry . . ." Her words trailed off when Zack reached the center of Main Street.

Judging from the way Reese's eyes widened again, she'd missed this particular part of Loveland, probably because she hadn't driven any further than the police station. Well, she was sure seeing it now. The town had been doused in, well, kisses.

Specifically, Christmas kisses.

There were dozens of posed kissing mannequins, some limbless, lining the sidewalks. They were all wearing Christmas outfits and were nestled between antique lampposts decorated with lights, holly, and tinsel.

And then there was the massive banner strung across Main Street.

WILL YOU KISS ME?

The question was printed in Christmas red with mounds of glistening fake snow beneath it. Beneath that was an electronic display that flashed the number "163."

"Uh, what's going on?" Reese asked.

Now, it was Zack who took a deep breath. "The current mayor and her assistant came up with this idea of breaking a record to generate publicity for Loveland as the so-called romance capitol of Texas. Most records are, well, let's just say impossible for a small town to break, so the aim is to do a group photograph with as many kissing couples wearing Christmas outfits as possible."

"One hundred and sixty-three couples," she muttered in a lightbulb over the head tone.

He made a sound of agreement. "Which totals three hundred and twenty-six, and is about a tenth of the total population. The mayor would like everyone to participate."

Especially him, since he was the sheriff. But Zack had no desire to do any kissing for the sake of publicity.

"Are you sure your grandfather will be home?" Reese asked, taking in the south end of Main Street.

There was just as much Christmas fanfare and flavor here as on the rest of the town's main road. Kissing dummies interspersed with inflatable Christmas figures. Santas, elves, reindeer, and polar bears. It was a testament to some serious decorating skills—or perhaps just plain luck—that this section of the street managed to look festive instead of just plain tacky.

"He'll be home this time of day," Zack verified, pausing to use his hands-free to call in a fender bender that he spotted in the parking lot of the Petal After Petal Flower Shop.

"Uh, should we give your granddad some kind of heads up that we're coming?" she asked.

He heard the nervousness in her voice, and it made him smile. She wasn't out to hurt anyone, which told him that she had deserved better than Paul. Then again, that wasn't much of a stretch.

"No heads up needed. He'll be glad to see us," he said as he continued the drive out of town. "FYI, after the fake kidnapping, I considered telling you that Paul was a cheater, but that had a whole tattletale vibe to it. Plus I couldn't be sure I didn't have an ulterior motive in wanting you to break up with him."

Her mouth tightened, letting him know something else about her. Paul had hurt her, and that meant Reese might have washed her hands of romance. He hoped not though, because Zack was beginning to see this as his second chance to get to know the woman who'd kissed his lights out.

With that thought drumming in his head, he turned at the sign announcing they had just arrived at the Happy Trails Ranch. He could tell from her little gasp that she'd connected the dots of Happy Trails to Happy Harry, and Zack had to admit it was an eerie coincidence, but it was also an accurate name. It had been a very happy place when he'd grown up there with his mom and maternal grandparents after his father had died when he was ten. Happy Trails had given Zack a deep love of the land.

And his granddad.

Because his grandfather had no doubt heard the sound of the approaching vehicle, he already had the door open before Zack pulled up in front of the two-story white Victorian. Normally, Harry Miller looked like the quintessential eighty-two-year-old grandpa, with his sugar-white hair, generously wrinkled but rosy face, and his slightly hunched posture.

Today, though, he didn't hit the quintessential mark. Zack's granddad was wearing a green herringbone suit that was clearly a size too small for him and from a long-ago fashion era. The pants fit him more like leggings, and the gold buttons strained against his chest and belly. Even the matching hat—yep, someone had obviously thought it wise to make matching headwear—was perched too high on his thick mat of hair, making Zack think of old photos he'd seen of Laurel and Hardy.

"Just a guess, but this isn't gonna work, am I right?" his granddad asked when Zack stepped out.

"That depends on what you're aiming for," Zack said, heading for the passenger-side door. But then Zack stopped talking, shook his head. He couldn't think of a single instance in which the outfit would work.

His granddad sighed but didn't seem distressed by the obvious conclusion. "Oh, well. It was worth a try. Your mom wanted me to see if it would fit for the Christmas Eve Kiss . . ." His words trailed off when his attention landed on Reese as Zack helped her from the truck.

"Granddad, this is Reese Darnell," Zack said. "Reese, this is Harry Miller."

"Pleased to meet you, sir," she muttered just as his granddad repeated her name.

"Reese?" he questioned. "Wasn't that the name of the woman who kidnapped you a couple of years back?"

Reese looked at Zack and frowned. "I didn't tell him," he assured her. "But I did mention it to my mom, and she must have spilled it to him." Along with countless others, meaning that particular incident wasn't going to be much of a secret in Loveland.

"Come on in out of the cold," his granddad insisted. "Let me get out of this garb, and I can pour us all some coffee."

"Please, don't bother with the coffee, Mr. Miller," Reese said, but she was talking to the air, since his granddad had already scurried off. Age clearly hadn't slowed him down much.

Reese sighed and glanced around, taking in the place. Zack did as well, though he knew every inch of this living room and the other rooms in the house. Even though the furniture and furnishings had come into and out of fashion, it looked and felt cozy and comfortable. Like home.

A fire flickered and popped in the hearth, and the fragrance of the wood mixed with the smells of sugar and cinnamon. Obviously there'd been some baking going on.

After Reese had made a cursory glance around the room, she went to the massive stone fireplace, specifically to the framed pictures that lined the eight-foot-long mantel. She leaned in, studying the wedding picture of

Zack's grandparents. Maybe looking to see if there was any resemblance to the man in the grainy photo on her phone.

"That's my Grandmother Fiona, the one who passed away two years ago," Zack explained, moving next to her. He tapped the next picture, which was of his own parents' wedding. "My mom and dad. My dad died when I was ten."

Her gaze went to his. "I'm sorry. I lost my parents in a car accident when I was twelve, so I know how hard it must have been."

It had indeed been gut-wrenchingly hard. "My grandparents made it easier for me. I'm guessing your great-aunt took away some of the pain for you?"

She nodded. "My grandparents weren't able to take care of me, so I ended up with Sylvia." Reese smiled a little. "She's my hero."

Which explained why Reese was so eager to find justice for her. Zack was pretty sure she wouldn't find that at the Happy Trails Ranch, but it was possible one of the other names on the list would pan out. He just didn't know which one.

Reese smiled again when her attention turned back to the remaining photos. It was basically a montage of his life. "Newborn," he said, tapping the one of him nestled in his mother's arms, and then he moved on to the others. "First day of school. Junior rodeo, saddle bronc competition. Prom. High school graduation. Another rodeo, adult this time, in the cutting horse competition."

"Very much the cowboy," she muttered, and there

was a wistful tone to her voice. Their eyes met for a moment, and he saw something that pleased him.

Heat.

So Reese had a thing for cowboys. Or maybe for him?

Her grumbled mild profanity let him know it was maybe both and that she wasn't happy about it. That could be because of their unconventional first meeting, but for Zack, that mishap had just got them over a hurdle. The first kiss had happened and was amazing. Now, after seeing Reese again, he knew he wanted a second kiss from her. And maybe more.

She turned her attention back to the remaining photos, and Zack filled her in on them. "Graduation from the police academy." And the final one. "Sheriff." He paused a moment. "My mom is their only child, and I'm their only grandchild, so I get centerstage on the mantel."

"What used to be here?" she asked, tapping the three-inch gap between the police academy shot and the one of him pinning on his sheriff's badge.

"A wedding photo," he answered.

He saw a flash of disappointment in her eyes, and her gaze flew to his hand. No doubt looking for a ring. Which wasn't there.

"My ex and I divorced nearly two years ago," he provided. "No kids, no lingering baggage. How about you?" Though he knew the no kids part because of the snooping he'd done on Reese, it wasn't always easy to ferret out baggage.

"Little to no baggage," she volunteered. "I went through a phase where I wanted to hit myself over the head for not seeing what Paul really was. Then, I chalked it up to lesson learned."

"Good," Zack said. Because this meant there was a clear path to . . . exactly what he wasn't sure, but he decided to test the waters. "Want to grab some lunch after you've talked to my granddad?"

She blinked and opened her mouth. He could practically see the "no" that she was about to voice. But it didn't come. Instead, she sighed. "I'm here for just one day," she murmured.

"Just one day when you have to eat," he pointed out. Their gazes hooked up again. And held. Zack felt the stir of heat once more and wished they were past any and all hurdles so he could test the attraction.

"Oh, good, you're asking Reese out on a date," he heard his granddad say in what had to be the worst timing in the history of such things.

Apparently the man had broken speed records, because he had not only changed into his normal clothes, but he was also carrying a small tray with three cups of coffee and some cookies.

"That's good," his granddad added, smiling at Reese. "It's been a while since Zack's been on a proper date. Sugar? Cream?" he tacked on, easing the tray onto the coffee table.

"No, thank you," Reese said. "I drink it black."

"So does Zack." His granddad made that sound as if

it were a huge connection between Reese and him. A common-ground kind of thing to build a relationship on.

Zack sighed and took one of the cups. Clearly, he was going to have to dissuade his granddad's match-making attempts. Yes, he wanted to see more of Reese, but he didn't want her to go on the run to avoid pressure.

"Reese has some questions she needs to ask you," Zack said, hoping the quick change of subject would distract him.

His granddad's eyes brightened. "About the two of you going to the Christmas Eve Kiss Ball together?"

"No." Zack had no trouble being firm about that particular event. Even if he did attend out of a sense of duty, it wouldn't be for the kissing. "It's about . . ." He stopped and motioned for Reese to jump in.

She did after she had a long sip of coffee. "Sixty years ago, a man married my great-aunt Sylvia Darnell and then disappeared from her life. She's recently learned that this man subsequently married two other women."

His granddad just stared at her. And stared. Then it seemed to hit him. "Oh, and you think I did that?" He chuckled before Reese could respond, and the chuckle turned into a full belly laugh, one that had his granddad actually flopping back on the sofa.

Reese didn't laugh, and eventually his granddad noticed that she hadn't joined in. While wiping tears of laughter from his eyes, he sat upright and faced her. "It wasn't me. I married my Fiona when we were eighteen. She was the only woman I ever kissed, bedded, or married."

He smiled, his gaze landing on the photo on the mantel, and it took him a couple of seconds to put aside the clearly good memories he was recalling. "What made you think the man was me?" he asked Reese.

"The name," she readily provided. "And the fact you were born here in Loveland." She paused. "The Happy Harry who married my aunt had a condition . . ." She stopped, looked at Zack, who took up the explanation.

"Three balls instead of two," he spelled out.

"Oh, my," his granddad muttered while he shook his head. "I assure you, I only have the two. Can you imagine how tight in the crotch pants would fit if you had three?" he asked in a whisper.

"I suspect plenty tight," Zack agreed, and because he knew Reese would want more info, he asked the question for her. "Do you know of anyone from around here who has that extra bit?"

His granddad's headshake was quick. "Sorry, no, that's not the sort of thing that comes up in conversation, But if anyone had mentioned something like that, I'd remember."

Again Zack agreed, and he handed his granddad the list. "Can you think of anyone whose name isn't there? It'd probably be a variation of Harry and someone around your age. Maybe someone who had a job that took him out of town a lot."

His granddad studied the names. Frowning, he shook his head as if dismissing them, and then he seemed to have an ah-ha moment. "Homer Smith. His real name is Harry Smith, Jr.," he explained to Reese. "Folks called him Little Harry, and I can tell you, that got him teased a lot, so he started calling himself Homer. It stuck."

"Homer," Zack repeated in a grumble. Well, that was another name he hadn't wanted added to this list. Reese must have picked up on his disapproval because she looked at Zack. However, he didn't get a chance to explain because her phone rang.

"It's my great-aunt," she muttered. She stood, moving to the other side of the room as she answered it. Even though she didn't put the call on speaker, it was impossible for him not to get the gist of the conversation.

"Yes, I made it to Loveland," Reese said. "But, no, I haven't found him yet." A pause. "I'll definitely keep looking." Another pause, longer than the first, and her shoulders went a little stiff. "Can't you talk them out of that? I mean, I might find him with my next interview . . ." A third pause. "Oh, I see. Well, okay, I guess, but please make it clear to them that Happy Harry might not be here in Loveland."

Several seconds later, after an "I love you" and goodbye, Reese turned back around to face them. "The two women once married to Happy Harry have decided to come to Loveland." Judging from her expression, Reese wasn't a fan of their decision. "I just don't want them to be, well, overzealous or anything, if they do find him," she added.

Zack groaned and got to his feet. "When will they get here?"

"Tonight," she said with a sigh. "And Aunt Sylvia is coming with them."

He was sighing, too. "You're satisfied my granddad isn't the bigamist?"

She nodded.

"Good." Zack took a pen from the drawer in the end table and crossed Harry Miller off the list. "All right, let's go," Zack said. "We'll visit the person Granddad just gave us."

"Homer Grange," she muttered.

Zack made a sound of agreement. "But most folks around here call him by a different name." He paused a heartbeat. "We're going to visit Santa Claus."

CHAPTER 3

So, Santa Claus hadn't turned out to be a serial bigamist after all, and Reese was thankful for that.

Homer Grange, aka Santa Claus, was a sweet, round-bellied man who donated much time, energy, and money to making kids happy by doing year-round Santa appearances. After spending ten minutes with him and Sunny, his wife of fifty-five years, Reese had ruled him out as a candidate for Happy Harry. It had helped, too, when Zack had posed the question of a possible birth defect of the genitals, that both a red-faced Sunny and Homer had whispered confirmations that he had "nothing strange going on down there."

Reese sipped her coffee in the small sitting area of her room at the inn and looked at her list again. The day before, Zack and she had managed to get through four names. All now eliminated and crossed out. The other two men hadn't been home, so the plan was for Zack and her to return today and finish up. It was possible those visits would be completed before lunch, which meant there'd be no reason for Reese to linger around Loveland.

Except there was. Sort of.

Sylvia and the other two wives had delayed their trip to Loveland because of icy roads and would be arriving sometime that morning. Reese wanted to be there to give them an in-person update about the search. And, darn it, Reese wanted to linger around for Zack, too. Even if that wasn't a smart thing to do.

She'd meant it when she had told Zack she had little to no baggage about her divorce. Of course, she'd always be ticked off at Paul for not keeping his jeans zipped. She'd always be a little riled at herself, too, for not seeing the truth about him sooner. But there was also some wariness in her now that hadn't been there before Paul.

Before she'd fake kidnapped Zack and kissed his lights out.

It was that wariness that was whispering to her to take things slow, to look for red flags that could turn into a lying, cheating, scummy situation.

Okay, so maybe she had more than a smidge of baggage.

Reese might have mulled that over more, but she was interrupted by two sounds. Her phone dinged with a text, and there was a knock on the door. While she went to the door, she glanced at the short message from Sylvia.

We'll be there soon.

She responded with a thumb's up emoji, opened the door, and felt a tsunami of lust when she saw that her visitor was Zack. He was carrying a silver tray with more coffee and some breakfast pastries.

"Patty said you hadn't eaten yet," Zack said, referring to Patty Muldoon, the owner of the inn.

The reason she hadn't eaten breakfast was because it was a meal she usually skipped, but Reese was ready to make an exception this morning. "Thanks," she managed once she got her mouth working. Mercy, the man had that hot cowboy cop deal down pat, and it was hard for her to remember those baggage smidges whenever she was around him.

She stepped back so he could come inside, and he set down the tray, the maneuver giving her a good view of his great-fitting jeans as they stretched and pulled over his equally great butt. Yeah, no trace of baggage while gawking at that.

He turned, and maybe in response to her expression, Zack flashed a grin that could be classified as foreplay. They stared at each other for several moments with the heat zinging between them, and Reese was well aware they were in a small room with a bed just a few yards away. She had to shake her head to clear it and then move away from him just so she could think.

Nope. That didn't help. She still couldn't think and wasn't sure she could even breathe. But she forced herself to tip her head to the list of Happy Harry candidates and muttered, "Two more to go."

"More," he provided, doling out another dose of that smile that only Zack and the Greek god of sex and hotness could have managed.

Because her brain was fuzzy, it took a moment for

that to sink in, and she watched as he took her pen from the table and jotted down four more names.

She shook her head. There was a Buddy, Buck, Jinx and Butch. Reese sighed. "I take it all of those are nicknames."

Zack made a sound of agreement. "Four brothers. And none of them owns land or has done anything to land them in newspaper articles or internet searches."

"They didn't show up in school records either." Reese wondered how many more additions there might be.

He nodded. "They were born here, but when they were still little, their parents apparently moved them and their five sisters just outside of Loveland, to a ranch owned by a family member. The ranch was eventually left to all of them, but it's deeded to a family trust. The first two are still on the ranch, the third lives here in town with his daughter, and the fourth is at the retirement village about four blocks from here."

"So I'm back to six names," she muttered.

Zack grinned again. "Guess you're stuck with me for a while longer."

Yes. And suddenly that seemed wonderful and unnerving at the same time. "I spent two hours this morning doing internet searches on you," she confessed. Along with that, Patty had talked nonstop about him when Reese had gone downstairs to get some coffee.

No smile this time, but he studied her eyes. "I did the same on you."

She sighed again and voiced her concern. "Things are moving very fast, and after what happened at the masquerade party kidnapping, you probably think I'm a lot more adventurous than I am."

"Well, it was adventurous," he admitted, "but I definitely didn't get the sense that it was something you did on a regular basis."

"First and only," she confirmed. "I wasn't much of a risk taker before Paul, and I certainly haven't been since."

He made a sound to indicate he understood that.

"Added to that," she went on, "I'm only going to be here a very short period of time. Maybe only a day or two at most."

Zack made another of those got-that sounds. "I might have a fix for that."

Reese frowned, not at all certain she wanted a fix. Part of her just wanted to get swept up in this scalding hotness while the logical part of her muttered cautions. In the end, she'd want to heed those cautions but have the memories and pleasure of the swept-away part.

"Accelerated dating," Zack said, causing Reese to give him what she was certain was a puzzled look. "Those kidnap kisses created a heat that isn't going away, so let's use it to move forward. Today, we can cram multiple dates into one." He motioned toward the pastries. "Breakfast together is our first date. The second date could be lunch. Third could be a stroll through town this afternoon to take in the Christmas decorations. Tonight could be the fourth date for dinner."

His gaze locked with hers, and oh, the heat came and added to the sizzle that was already there.

"I'd think after the first date, we'd kiss, don't you?" he asked in that dreamy voice that made her melt.

The melting, however, came to a halt when there was another knock at the door. Talk about lousy timing. "It's probably Aunt Sylvia," she grumbled, going to the door and opening it.

But it was not Sylvia. This was a slim fifty-something-year-old woman wearing a red coat and a Santa hat. She smiled at Reese, but then her attention zoomed in on Zack. "Patty said you were up here," the woman said, and then extended her hand in greeting to Reese. "I'm Naomi Caldwell, Zack's mother and the current mayor of Loveland."

"Uh, I'm Reese Darnell," she managed. She definitely hadn't expected a visit from his mom.

"Reese?" she repeated, a light coming into her blue eyes that Reese could now see were a genetic copy of Zack's. "The woman who fake kidnapped you?"

Reese groaned, her gaze cutting to Zack. "Exactly how many people know about that?"

"Too many," he muttered just as his mom volunteered, "He talked about you a lot. Well, what a wonderful coincidence you're here in Loveland, the romance capitol of the state."

"Stop matchmaking, Mom," Zack warned, but then he went to her and brushed a kiss on her cheek. "Why are you here?"

"Oh," the woman murmured as if she'd just now recalled the reason for her visit. She extracted a yellow sticky note from her purse. "Dad told me about your search for Happy Harry, and he came up with these names to add to your list of possible candidates. Most moved out of Loveland but are still in the county."

Reese took the note, looked at the five names, and didn't bother to groan when she saw there weren't any duplicates. She'd started the morning with two possibilities, and now she was up to eleven. This search was moving in the wrong direction.

Naomi tapped the first name on the list. "Hank Byers."

"The Easter Bunny," Zack grumbled. He looked at Reese. "He dresses up like a big rabbit for the town's annual egg hunt."

Great. What was next? The Tooth Fairy?

"Gotta go," Naomi said, turning to leave. She added a final parting remark from over her shoulder as she strolled away. "You two should definitely do the Christmas Eve Kiss Ball."

"No," Zack was quick to say, but when he looked down at Reese, she thought he might indeed have some kissing on his mind. Just not the public kind. Or one brought on by mistaken identity or a fake kidnapping.

"On the accelerated plan, this is probably the tail end of our first date," he said, his voice unleashing all that hotness again. "So, are you up for a first date kiss?"

Reese figured it was a good idea to think this through. But she didn't. Nope. Apparently, she was ready to ditch the whole notion of moving too fast because she didn't give Zack a verbal answer.

Her answer was a kiss.

She slid her hand around the back of his neck and pulled his mouth down to hers. Of course, she didn't have to pull hard because he was already heading in her direction.

At the touch of his mouth to hers, the slam of heat was instant. And the pleasure. Like all the best things possible rolled into one. He tasted like wonderful, high caloric things. Like her deepest fantasics.

Like Zack.

No, she hadn't forgotten this. Hadn't forgotten the taste of him. She had no idea how this cowboy managed to stir all of her senses at once, but he did. Stirred and sent them flying.

One touch, and she wanted more. He gave her more, all right. Zack slipped his arm around her waist and eased her to him so that along with being mouth to mouth, they were body to body. All that delicious pressure mixed with the other delicious things, and it occurred to her that this kiss was accelerated, too. It was racing forward, urging her to escalate the heck out of this moment.

But that didn't happen.

"Well, well," Reese heard someone say. Not just any ol' someone though. Her eyes snapped open to see her great-aunt Sylvia standing next to Happy Harry's other two wives. All three women were looking amused.

Reese moved away from Zack as if he'd scalded her. Which that kiss just might have done. She cleared her throat to make introductions so she could then consider finding a hole to stick her head in.

"Uh, this is my great-aunt Sylvia, Maeve Hopkins and Arabella Simon," she managed. "Ladies, this is Sheriff Zack Caldwell."

Reese silently groaned when she saw the spark of recognition in her aunt's eyes. The kiss had dulled her thoughts so that she'd forgotten something very important.

That she hadn't kept her mouth shut about a specific incident in her past either.

"Zack?" Sylvia repeated. She turned to the other women. "This is the guy I was telling you about. The one Reese faked kidnapped and kissed. Well, well," Sylvia repeated, turning back to Zack and Reese. "Are you two picking up where you left off?"

CHAPTER 4

"I don't have three man things," Hank Byers, aka the Easter Bunny, whispered to Zack. Hank pointed to his nether region in case Zack hadn't gotten the point.

He had.

Along with Hank's denial that he'd ever married any woman but his late wife, Dorothy, he refused to claim an extra testicle either.

"But I do have a birthmark on my right butt cheek," Hank went on, his tone as if he were discussing the weather. "Of course, it looks nothing like a man thing. It's more like that pile of cartoon poop that people put in their texts, but . . ." He stopped, his wrinkled forehead bunching up. "Can't remember why I thought you should know that."

Zack was figuring the same thing and so wished Hank hadn't put the image in his head of the Easter Bunny sporting a poop emoji. He stood and glanced at Reese, who had discreetly moved to the other side of the room so that Zack could ask the delicate question about balls. Now that Zack had his answer, he gave her the nod so she could rejoin him at the table in Hank's kitchen.

"Hank isn't Happy Harry," Zack relayed to her.

Hank gave an apologetic shake of his head. "I sure wish I could help."

"You did," Reese said, "by eliminating yourself. Now we can take you off the list."

True, but during the course of their pre-balls conversation, Hank had given them two more names of possible candidates. At this rate, it might be Valentine's Day before they got through them all.

And that caused Zack to smile.

It wasn't a hardship to spend time with Reese, and spending time was exactly what they'd been doing for the past two days. He'd managed to spend all those hours with her by using some of his vacation days. That hadn't stopped work calls though, but thankfully his deputies were keeping them to a minimum. No doubt because word had gotten around about the Happy Harry search and Zack being joined at the hip with the PI.

Joined at the hip had been necessary since it had taken a full day to track down the four brothers—Buddy, Buck, Jinx and Butch—and to check their names off as well. Zack hadn't detected any deceit whatsoever in any of their comments or body language. Ditto for another candidate, Harry Johnson, who'd been on Reese's original list.

They said their goodbyes to Hank and stepped back out into the cold. "Where to next?" she asked, looking over her list.

He tipped his head toward Main Street. "To Seasonal Delights."

She eyed him with caution. "Is this an accelerated date or a potential Happy Harry interview?"

"Both." He gave her red scarf an adjustment and stood shoulder to shoulder with her so his body heat would stave off some of the cold.

Zack dismissed the idea of putting his arm around her since their mere presence in the center of town would fuel enough gossip without adding PDA. He didn't mind the gossip and had accepted it was inevitable in a small town, but he figured Reese probably wouldn't want said gossip getting back to her great-aunt.

"By my calculations, this is our fifteenth date," he said as they strolled away from Hank's.

"Fifteenth?" she questioned.

He nodded. "I'm counting all meals, all Happy Harry interviews, and dreams," he tacked on.

Her gaze flew to his, and Zack figured she was about to say something about dreams not counting, but Reese nodded. He could see she was fighting a smile, too. "Any chance I showed up in your dreams?"

She lost the fight with a smile but then regained her straight face. "Things just seem so intense."

"Not for a fifteenth date," he pointed out.

"It's still forty-eight hours, plus the thirty seconds or so when I kissed you at the masquerade party." She paused, waiting for someone to walk by before she continued. "Aren't you bothered by it?"

"Some," he admitted. "But I've been thinking about

you a long time, so I guess that's numbed any objections the logical part of my brain might dish up." He shrugged. "Added to that, there's no pressure here. At the end of the interviews, you can just walk away."

He was hoping like the devil she wouldn't do that, but he was already working out a contingency, just in case.

"You live only an hour away in San Antonio," he continued to spell out. "So, if accelerated dating doesn't work for you, then we can maybe try things the old-fashioned way."

A whole lot of tension faded from her expression, leaving only that beautiful face. Of course, Reese was beautiful with or without tension, but it was much more fun seeing her gazing at him as if he were the fix to a problem instead of the problem itself.

Zack felt a kick of heat. Tried to rein it in, and he figured Reese was doing some reining as well. Both of them failed, because at the same moment, they ducked into a narrow alley, and their mouths met.

Instant hunger. Instant pleasure.

And there was probably that whole added element of doing something a tad bit forbidden. Of course, their entire kissing history had that element to it. First, at the masquerade party and then when her great-aunt had walked in on their lip-lock.

Despite his body urging him to take this particular kiss so much deeper, Zack held back. Good thing, too, because he suddenly became aware of the absence of chatter coming from Main Street. From the corner of his eye, he saw they once again had an audience. This time it was one of his deputies, Brenna O'Sullivan, and her fiancé, Theo Cameron, who just happened to be Zack's good friend.

Both Brenna and Theo seemed plenty surprised, probably because Zack was doing that whole PDA thing, but then Brenna grinned. "Shouldn't you be saving that for the Christmas Eve Kiss Ball?" she joked.

Zack scowled, his only response because he had no intention of explaining that a hot spontaneous kiss was one thing but a staged one just didn't feel right. He wanted to get lost in a kiss, didn't want to think of photographers, angles of the shots and the hundred and sixty-six other couples who'd be kissing around him.

"By the way, your great-aunt Sylvia just played the take one, give one and found gold," Brenna said, shifting her attention to Reese. Obviously, there was no need for Zack to make introductions, but judging from Reese's blank look, there was a need to explain.

"One of the shops has a big window display of wrapped Christmas gifts, and anyone can take one from the mix as long as they add one. That way, everyone who wants a Christmas surprise can have it."

"What a nice tradition," Reese concluded but then shook her head. "How'd my aunt win gold?"

It was Brenna who picked up this part of the explanation. "Harrison Harvey, who owns Seasonal Delights, always puts some extra special gifts into the mix. Your aunt just pulled out a fourteen karat gold necklace."

No way had Reese missed the part about Harrison, especially since they were on their way to see the man.

"Uh, did my aunt happen to meet the owner?" Reese asked.

"Maybe," Brenna muttered, and because she was a good cop, she no doubt picked up on the concern that had landed in Reese's eyes. Because if Sylvia had indeed come face to face with her bigamist husband, then things might not be all merry and bright.

Zack muttered a goodbye that was almost as quick as the one Reese doled out, and together they hurried out of the alley and toward the shop. They were still a good ten yards away when Zack heard a strange sound— maybe a moan, maybe a sob.

That got them moving even faster, and when they broke through the crowd that had gathered, he spotted Sylvia in the doorway of Seasonal Delights, and she was staring at something in her hand. The other two wives were staring as well, but Harrison couldn't have been the center of attention because he was nowhere in sight.

"Oh, Reese," Sylvia said when she saw her great-niece. The woman's face was lit up as if it were, well, Christmas. "Isn't it beautiful?"

The tightness eased in Zack's chest when he realized the sounds they'd heard were of the happy variety, and that Sylvia and her companions were ooh-ing and ahh-ing over a gold angel necklace.

"It is," Reese assured her, taking in both the necklace and the shop itself.

Just inside the door was a large red Santa's bag sitting on a table. It was stuffed to the top with wrapped gifts. To the left of it was a box of prewrapped presents that people could purchase if they wanted to do a gift exchange and didn't want to bring one they'd bought elsewhere. Because Zack knew how this worked; he was aware there'd be discreet price stickers on the bottom of those presents, ready for purchase, but the buyer wouldn't know exactly what they were purchasing. The presents in the Santa bag had small stickers, too, so that the person could opt for something more suitable for a man, woman, boy, or girl.

"I got this," Maeve said, showing off a thin silver chain bracelet.

"And I got this." Arabella turned to the side to show them the colorful butterfly barrette in her hair.

Reese did some brief ooh-ing and ahh-ing and then followed it up with a quick question. "Any chance you've seen the shop owner?" she asked Sylvia, Maeve, and Arabella.

All three women shook their heads, and Sylvia's expression grew serious. "Why? Is he possibly Happy Harry?" she asked in a whisper.

"We're here to interview him," Zack settled for saying. He, too, responded in a whisper, though he was certain that by now everyone in town knew what Reese and he were up to.

Sylvia opened her mouth as if she might want to be in on that interview, but then she gave her head a little shake and looked at the other two women. "While they're talking to him, why don't we go ahead and pop down to the civic center and get our names on the Christmas Eve Kiss Ball board?"

Zack noticed Reese's blank look. "The board?" she asked.

It was the tall, willowy Arabella who answered, and she began to show just as much enthusiasm as Sylvia had for the necklace. "If you want a kiss partner for the big photo being taken at the ball, you add your name to the board, and the mayor's assistant will find you a match. The number's up to one hundred seventy-four, and it just keeps on growing. Isn't that wonderful?"

Reese's blank look continued. "Are you saying the three of you are going to participate in the Christmas Eve Kiss Ball?"

The three women nodded in unison. There was plenty of glee in those gestures, too.

"But the ball isn't for three days," Reese pointed out. "We could be done with the interviews before then. We might have found Happy Harry."

That caused some of the merriment to fade, and Zack wished he could read minds, because it seemed to him these three women weren't so hellbent on finding the man they'd all married. Then again, maybe they'd just hit the pause button on those particular feelings so they could have a little fun. This seemed like an unexpected Christmas adventure to them.

"I'm guessing once the interviews are done, you'll be going back home?" Sylvia asked Reese, but then the woman glanced at Zack. "Or will you stay and spend time with Zack?"

"I'll be going home," Reese muttered, but then she tempered her words by adding, "That's the plan anyway. I need to get back to work on a couple of other cases."

"The ones you've been doing on the internet?" Sylvia pressed, and she looked at Zack again. "Reese does a lot of work online."

He'd guessed as much, but he didn't want to put Reese in a corner. If she wanted to leave, she should go.

Not permanently though.

Well, not if he had a say about it, anyway. He'd let Reese get away once before, and he didn't want it to happen again.

Zack was about to suggest they just get through the interviews and then they'd cross the bridge of "what will Reese do next?" when he spotted a man coming out of the office behind the checkout counter.

"That's Harrison Harvey," Zack said, tipping his head in the man's direction. He frowned, though, when he saw that Harrison wasn't alone. Zack's granddad and one of their other ruled-out interviewees, Hal Franklin, were with him. It wasn't a shock to see the three together since they were lifelong friends, but Zack would have preferred this chat with Harrison to be audience-free.

"Zack," his granddad greeted, and the moment seemed to freeze when his attention and Harrison's landed on Sylvia, Arabella, and Maeve. Worse, the women seemed to have frozen as well.

Hell.

Was this it? Was Harrison actually Happy Harry? Or had Reese and he been wrong to cross Hal off the list?

Harrison, Hal, and his granddad snaked their way through the jam of Christmas shoppers and made their way to the wives. None of the six was sparing Reese or

Zack a glance. Nope. It was as if the rest of Loveland had disappeared except for those six octogenarians.

"You're Reese's aunt?" his granddad asked, and once Sylvia had nodded, he extended his hand. "I'm Harry Miller, Zack's grandfather."

Sylvia flushed a little. She started to say something, stumbled over her words, flushed some more, and then managed to make introductions. "This is Maeve Hopkins and Arabella Simon."

"Harrison Harvey," the man interjected, and he was flushing, too, while he fixed his gaze on Arabella. Hal was doing some gaze fixing of his own on Maeve.

Even though Zack considered himself to be plenty smart, it still took a couple of seconds for this to sink in. All the flushing and freezing wasn't because Happy Harry had been outed. This was attraction. It could hit out of the blue and had miserable timing, but here it was.

"Uh, how's it going with the project you're working on?" his granddad asked Zack. The man was obviously trying to be discreet, probably in case the wives hadn't known the reason for this trip to the shop, but they clearly did.

"None of these men is Happy Harry," Sylvia assured Zack.

"Yeah, I got that," he said, taking out his copy of the list so he could strike out Harrison's name.

As he did that, Harrison cleared his throat and glanced around. He must have decided what he had to say required more privacy than the forty or so customers who were milling around because he motioned the group to follow him to his office. They did, all of them, and Harrison didn't utter a word until they were behind closed doors.

"Your granddad told me about this Happy Harry search," Harrison explained, "and I think I might know someone who could, well . . . fit the description." He went behind his desk and jotted down a name that didn't ring any bells for Zack.

Harry Floyd.

"Harry was born here in Loveland, and we played football together when we were in junior high," Harrison went on. "He lived out on Sawmill Road, but his family moved away when he was around sixteen or so."

"And what makes you think this guy could be Happy Harry?" Zack asked.

Harrison winced, stalled, and then stalled some more. And that's when Zack knew what Harrison was hesitant to say. They finally had the name of their three-balled man.

CHAPTER 5

"BLTs, popcorn and chocolate covered strawberries," Reese supplied.

"Tacos, fried chicken and key lime pie," Zack said.

They both made sounds of approval at the other's choices of favorite foods. It was all part of the accelerated dating plan. A way of getting to know each other better and to pass the time while they waited to hear from Harry Floyd.

"All-time favorite movie," he threw out from the list they'd made while eating an amazing shepherd's pie lunch from Desi's Diner that had been delivered to her room at the inn.

"*Love Actually*," she answered.

"*Lord of the Rings*." That came from Zack.

They made more sounds of approval, something that'd happened for each and every item. Then she glanced at her phone again.

"A watched phone never rings," Zack said.

She had to smile, but she was feeling plenty of frustration as well. Frustration and a massive stewpot of other feelings. In fact, Reese had so many things swirling around in her head and body that it was difficult to think straight. Then again, thinking straight was always a problem when she was around Zack.

For now though, she couldn't blame her frustration on any kisses. Or because she was gawking at his amazing face or body. Or because she was conflicted about the attraction simmering between them.

Nope.

The list topper of the moment was the frustration of waiting for a call back or even a visit from Happy Harry. After Harrison had given them the man's name, Reese had used the PI databases on her laptop to locate him in Bulverde, Texas, which was only a short drive from Loveland. Armed with that info and his phone number, she had called him three hours earlier. When he hadn't answered, she'd left a message for him to contact her ASAP, telling him that she was a friend of a friend and was staying at the inn in Loveland.

What she hadn't mentioned was the number of his testes or the fact that he could be the bigamist she'd been searching for. Reese had hoped that the somewhat vague message would spark enough interest for the man to either return her call or show up in person. So far though, nada.

"Favorite childhood memories," Zack read from the list.

That snapped her attention away from her phone, and while she was trying to figure out which one to choose, her attention landed on something outside her window. She spotted her great-aunt, Arabella, and Maeve near the ice-skating pond, and they weren't alone. Zack's granddad, Harrison, and Hal were with them, and they were all putting on skates.

"Good grief," Reese muttered. Her first instinct was to hurry down there and warn Sylvia that she could fall. But then, she saw the beaming smile on her great-aunt's face. In fact, there were smiles all around.

"What the heck?" Zack grumbled when he saw what she was looking at. "To the best of my knowledge, my eighty-two-year-old grandfather has never ice skated in his life." He took out his phone, maybe to call his granddad and issue a *be careful* type warning, but then he sighed and slipped his phone back in his pocket. "I guess the right attitude to take about this is live and let live."

"Yes," Reese muttered, but she winced when Sylvia's arms windmilled as she stepped onto the ice. Reese was fairly certain that her great-aunt had never ice skated either, but thankfully Zack's granddad was able to keep them both on their feet.

Two by two, the others crept out onto the frozen pond. More arms windmilled, and their bodies bent at odd angles, but there were also smiles. Lots of them. And Reese saw something else: The way Sylvia was looking at Zack's granddad.

"Maybe there's something in the air here to make people . . ." she started but then trailed off. She'd nearly blurted out *fall in love*, and there was no way she intended to say that in front of Zack.

For starters, it might send him running. Yes, he seemed more than okay with this accelerated romance, but that didn't mean he wanted to hear the *L*-word. And there was the flip side to saying something like that: Reese didn't want to hear the *L*-word either. Two and a half days wasn't nearly enough time for . . . she stopped again.

"What exactly is going on between them?" she asked, tipping her head to the ice skaters. "And what's going on between us?"

Smiling, Zack moved closer and slid his arm around her waist so they were side by side and still looking out at the skaters. "Between us can be here and now. It can be just this. Or it can be—"

He stopped, winced, and muttered some profanity when his granddad slipped and landed on his butt. Sylvia fell too, and that created a mini pileup. Reese held her breath, but there didn't appear to be any injuries. However, there was a lot of giddy laughter, and the skaters created such a happy winter wonderland scene that others stopped to take some photos.

Reese forgot about her phone watching, her concerns about the romances going on, and just enjoyed the moment. She looked at Zack, glad that the moment included him.

"It can be just this," he repeated, brushing his mouth over hers.

She felt the heat skyrocket and waited for him to deepen the kiss, along with finishing his *Or it can be*. No finishing though because his phone dinged with a text. Muttering some more profanity, Zack read the message.

And did more cursing.

A lot more.

At first she thought it had something to do with their search for Happy Harry, but when he showed her the text, she saw it was from someone she certainly hadn't expected.

Paul.

Just heard from someone in Loveland that you're seeing Reese. Paul messaged. WTH? I know you can't be mixing it up with my ex. I don't think there's a statute of limitations on poaching on a friend's ex.

Reese felt another surge of heat, but this wasn't from the pleasure of Zack's mouth. It was from a shot of scalding-hot anger. She looked at Zack through narrowed eyes. And his eyes were narrowed, too. She saw that he, too, had anger flaring through him.

Good.

"Should I remind the cheating piece of crap that he doesn't have a say in what you and I do?" Zack threw out, but then he waved the reminder off and went with a much shorter, more direct response:

Piss off, Paul.

Reese laughed before she even knew she was going to. "I think I'm a little bit in love with you for doing that," she blurted.

Shock roared through her just as anger had done moments earlier. "Oh, crap," she muttered. "I shouldn't have said that."

She would have no doubt started babbling to try to explain, well, something, but all thoughts of babbling and explanation faded when Zack pulled her to him and kissed her.

Any and all kisses from Zack were hot, but this one was a chart topper. He put plenty of intensity into the pressure of his mouth on hers, and with a few clever moves and the flick of his tongue, he made her forget all about texts from pond scum exes. All she could remember was that she really enjoyed doing this with him.

He deepened the kiss, pulling her even closer until it wasn't just his mouth persuading her but also his body. And what a body it was. All those muscles that managed to feel both snuggle-worthy and hard at the same time. Her own body was especially pleased with this newfound contact, and Reese instantly wanted more.

Zack gave her more.

He turned her, moving them away from the window until her back was against the wall. Now that she was anchored, he pressed himself even harder against her, firing up the heat until an ache started in the center of her body and started to spread.

Zack lowered his mouth to her neck, landing some kissing there while he slid his hand between their bodies to her breasts, which had definitely started to long for attention. Zack gave it to her. First by cupping her and then by touching his mouth to the front of her shirt. Yes, there was fabric between her nipples and his mouth, but the shirt suddenly felt thin and flimsy.

He continued kissing, moving his lips over her throat and letting his warm breath stir up even more heat before he came back to her mouth. The problem with a really good kiss and some amazing touching was that it couldn't just do a run in place. Nope. It created a need to go further. It caused an urgency to wash over her, causing her breath to go thin and her heart to race.

For a moment, Reese thought the sound she heard was her racing heart, but when Zack stopped kissing her and lifted his head, she realized what it was.

Someone was knocking on the door.

Zack muttered some profanity and looked ready to do whatever it took to get rid of the interruption.

"Sheriff Caldwell?" a man called out.

Zack stepped back, and she gave him a questioning look. "I don't recognize the voice," he muttered.

He was clearly frustrated, but he was also the sheriff, so this wasn't a knock he could just ignore. Zack went to the door and threw it open to reveal their visitor: A man with thinning gray hair and a portly build.

"Reese Darnell? Sheriff Caldwell?" the man asked, and the moment he got confirming nods, he added, "I'm Harry Floyd. And I understand you're looking for me."

CHAPTER 6

Zack definitely wasn't pleased with the interruption, not when Reese and he had been trying to reach new heights of lust. However, he could only hope they could aspire to those new heights later, since they really did need to deal with this visitor.

A visitor who could potentially end Reese's reason to be there.

That was something Zack decided to ponder later. For now, there were questions that had to be asked. Before he could launch into a few or ask the man to come in, Harry Floyd did his own verbal launching.

"I got your phone message," he said, directing his words at Reese, "and I gathered up a few things and drove right over." He tipped his head to a shoebox he had tucked under his arm and then quickly added, "The lady at the desk gave me your room number and told me you were up here with Sheriff Caldwell."

It didn't surprise Zack that info like that was known and divulged. Heck, it was possible everyone knew exactly who this man was and had perhaps even tried to discern if the crotch area of his jeans was unusually crowded. Zack couldn't keep himself from doing the same, but there was nothing obvious.

"Come in," Zack offered, figuring the man would be more forthcoming with details if there was at least some privacy.

Harry muttered his thanks and stepped in. "I know you aren't really a friend of a friend," he added to Reese. "I called a few people that I'm still in touch with here in Loveland, and they told me what was going on."

So, Zack didn't need to fill him in on what could have been startling news. Reese and he kept their attention pinned on their visitor, trying to gauge his reaction. They didn't get much time to do that, though, because there were some new knocks at the door.

"It's me," Sylvia called out.

Zack rolled his eyes, and Reese sighed. Harry's visit would be far more complicated with Sylvia there, but Zack doubted the woman would just go away. He opened the door and saw it wasn't just Sylvia, though, but Arabella, Maeve, and their three ice-skating partners. Thankfully, they'd all removed their skates before coming in.

"I saw him in the parking lot," Sylvia blurted. "I saw Harry . . ." Her words trailed off as her gaze landed on the man. She gasped and pressed her hand to her now-trembling mouth.

Maeve had a similar reaction. "Harry," the women said in unison.

Zack felt both relief over now having the case solved and disappointment that Reese would likely soon be leaving. Both emotions were short-lived, though, as

Zack shifted into cop mode, in case one of the women tried to go after their bigamist husband. Thankfully, though, Maeve and Sylvia just seemed to be in shock. Ditto for their skating partners. But Arabella was frowning and shaking her head.

"What happened to the little scar on your eyebrow?" Arabella asked, walking closer to Harry.

"A scar?" Reese, Zack, Maeve, and Sylvia asked in unison.

Arabella nodded. "Happy Harry had a little scar that he got when he was mowing the lawn and a small rock flew up and hit him."

Arabella had been wife number three, so that explained why the first two hadn't known about it.

"I never had a scar," the man insisted, but he didn't seem especially surprised by the question. He sighed and gave each woman a long look before turning to Zack and Reese. "I've only married one woman," Harry went on. "That was fifty-two years ago, and I'm still married to her."

Zack played a quick mental connect the dots. The women had clearly recognized this man. Or rather they'd recognized his face. So that left an obvious conclusion.

"Do you have a twin brother?" Zack asked.

Harry nodded and turned what appeared to be an apologetic gaze at the wives. "My twin brother, Elwood, had a scar." He pointed to a spot on his right eyebrow. "And he had this habit of calling me Serious Harry and himself Happy Harry."

That brought on a lot of different responses. Sighs.

Soft gasps. Headshakes. Worried groans. What Zack didn't see, though, was any trace of anger. Good. He didn't want any venom aimed at this man because of his brother.

"Elwood left home when he was sixteen," Harry went on. "He'd gotten into a big argument with our dad, and he basically ran away. It was a decade or more before he even came back for a visit. He had the scar then." He paused. "That was the last time I saw my brother."

During that decade, Elwood could have married, and deserted, all three wives. The timing fit, and the scar added to the validity of this man's twin being Happy Harry. But the bigamist had another distinct feature. Maeve asked the question before Zack could.

"Did Elwood have three man things?" she pressed.

Harry nodded, which brought on more of those sighs and gasps. It was a first for Zack to have an ID confirmed by an extra testicle, but since he was certain now that they had the right Happy Harry—or rather, Happy Elwood—he could start questioning Harry.

"When your brother came home for a visit, did he happen to mention he'd married three different women?" Zack asked.

Harry quickly shook his head. "No. He mentioned a girlfriend, but she wasn't with him."

Hell, that could possibly mean there was a fourth wife if Elwood had continued his string of saying *I do*.

"About twenty or so years ago, I got a visit from a woman named Sadie, who was looking for Elwood. She said he was using the surname Johnson then but that she'd found his birth certificate and used it to find me. Sadie said Elwood and she never married, but they were together for five years before he up and left her. She thought I might know where he was. I didn't," Harry said. "But Sadie gave me this box of stuff Elwood had left at her place."

Harry took the shoebox from underneath his arm. "There are cards and letters in here that my brother wrote to various women, but he obviously never sent them. There were no addresses or surnames, so I didn't know how to get in touch with the intended recipients to pass them along." He paused again and handed the box to Zack. "The women's first names are Sylvia, Maeve, and Arabella."

Suddenly the box became the center of attention, so Zack set it on the table and opened it. Since he wouldn't be bringing charges against Elwood, there was no need to treat the letters as evidence that would have to hold up in court. He poured out the contents, fanning through them, and saw that each envelope was indeed marked with one of the women's names.

The wives looked pleadingly at Zack, and he stepped back so they could retrieve the envelopes intended for them. He only hoped there wasn't something heart-crushing inside. That was why he didn't ask his grand-dad, Harrison, or Hal to leave. The wives might need some TLC once this ordeal was over.

"Do you know where Elwood is?" Zack asked Harry.

Again, Harry shook his head. "I haven't seen or heard from him in over fifty years, but I did get some news about him." The women stopped the envelope sorting to look at him. "I'm sorry, ladies, but I'm pretty sure my brother is dead."

CHAPTER 7

"The first time I saw you, my heart danced in my chest," Sylvia read aloud from one of the letters. "It was love at first sight."

Reese rolled her eyes but kept her mumbled profanity to herself. Well, most of it anyway. Every now and then, a muttered "BS" escaped.

She hated watching her great-aunt go through this emotional wringer, but she was hoping the letter was also giving Sylvia some closure. Or rather, that the closure could start. For now, she figured, Sylvia just had to finish reading what her so-called husband had left behind and then process it.

Arabella and Maeve were no doubt doing the same thing, but they'd chosen to go through their stashes in their own rooms at the inn. Harry, Harrison, Hal, and Zack's grandfather had opted to give them privacy by heading back to their own homes. Zack had left as well, to go to his office so he could try to track down a death certificate for Happy Harry under whatever name he had been using.

That left Reese with her great-aunt, and Reese tried

to keep her emotions in check while she watched and listened to Sylvia read and cry her way through the envelopes. Three had been birthday cards, and those had simply been sweet and sentimental with no real personal greetings. He'd simply signed them "Love you, Babe. HH."

The carefree tone had made it hard for Reese to keep her emotions in check, especially when she'd realized HH had likely bought and signed some of the cards while he'd been married to other women. Ditto for the two "Just Thinking of You" cards. And the anniversary one? Well, three BSs had escaped her clenched teeth.

Sylvia had made it through the cards with tears and her own muttered anger and then had moved on to the letters. In these there was some personalization. Lines and lines of it, and while it had been hard for Reese to stomach, she was glad Sylvia was reading them aloud.

"Love at first sight," Sylvia repeated in a tone that made it clear she was giving that some thought. "Yes, it was, I suppose," she added in a mutter, and continued to read. "Everything between us happened so fast, and it didn't help that we were so young. We didn't stop to think. We dived right in."

Reese mentally muttered more profanity, but of course, she couldn't stop herself from thinking about Zack and her. Things were indeed moving fast between them, too. And they had also done some diving in. Was that a mistake? It didn't feel like one, but then, things were nowhere near the marriage stage for them. But the heat was continuing to simmer and soar.

Part of her wanted to just enjoy the soaring, the heat.

Another part of her, that cautious part that had been hurt by Paul's antics, wanted things to slow down. That part of her wanted to guard her heart. At the moment, she wasn't sure which of those two forces would win out.

"Do you regret it?" Reese asked. She figured her great-aunt would wonder what she meant by that. However, Sylvia seemed to grasp her question.

"I'm not sure. The hurt is still there. It's a mix of rejection and knowing that I should have figured out something was wrong before he left me." Sylvia stopped and shook her head. "But I didn't see it coming. I honestly didn't. I thought everything was wonderful between us, and that our marriage and love would last forever. I think that's why the cut was so deep when he left and didn't come back."

She watched as her great-aunt blinked back tears. Sylvia carefully refolded the letter and placed it back in the envelope. She stood. "I think I'll go back to my room, drink some wine, and take a long bubble bath."

Alarm shot through Reese. "Maybe now isn't a good time to be alone."

Sylvia managed a smile, and she kissed Reese on the cheek. "I'll be fine. I just need a little time to myself." She held up her envelope stash. "Time for not only what's in these, but also for the fact that I might never be able to confront Harry . . . Elwood," she corrected.

"Do you think it'd be easier if you had been able to confront him?" Reese wanted to know.

Her great-aunt seemed to give that some thought and shrugged. "Perhaps." She looped her arm through

Reese's, and they went to the door. When Reese opened it, she saw Zack standing there.

His back was resting against the wall, and he was reading something on his phone. His body language indicated that he'd maybe been there for a while.

"Did you find anything on Elwood?" Sylvia immediately asked him.

Zack shook his head. "Two of my deputies are very good at internet and database searches. They're both working to try to find anything. Since he was known to use aliases, the search might not be a quick one."

Sylvia nodded as if that were the answer she'd expected. She smiled again, and this time it was Zack's cheek she kissed. "I'm going to my room, but I didn't want Reese to be alone. She's worried about me," her great-aunt added in a secretive whisper. She turned to head down the hall but then stopped and met Reese's gaze. "Don't let anything in these letters stop you from going where your heart leads you."

Reese nearly blurted out that it wasn't her heart doing the leading here. It was the heat from this blistering attraction to Zack. An attraction she could feel even now, when she was indeed worried about her great-aunt.

"Call me or come back if you decide you don't want to be alone," Reese insisted. She watched Sylvia walk away, and that's when she saw Zack's grandfather waiting down the hall outside of Sylvia's room. The woman greeted him with a warm smile and, yes, a kiss on the cheek.

"So, maybe she won't be alone after all," Reese muttered, and Zack and she went into her room. She looked at him. "Please tell me your granddad is a good guy."

The corner of Zack's mouth lifted. "He is. One of the best. He won't push but will be around if your great-aunt needs him to be." He paused a heartbeat. "If we do manage to come up with a death certificate for Elwood, Sylvia, Arabella, and Maeve may be shaken to the core."

"Yes," Reese muttered. It was something she'd already considered, and she was bracing for it. Hopefully the three wives were preparing themselves as well. She gave one last glance down the hall but didn't see either her great-aunt or Zack's granddad, so she shut the door.

"Was there anything in any of the cards or letters that might help with the search for Elwood?" he asked.

She sighed again. "No." Then she huffed, "Apparently, Elwood's heart danced in his chest when he first saw Sylvia, and he claimed it was love at first sight. Yeah, right."

"And Sylvia's take on that?" Zack pressed.

Reese really didn't like admitting this. "She more or less confirmed it. I think that's why she doled out that really bad advice to us about going where the heart leads."

He smiled, took hold of her, and eased her into his arms. Not the best time for it, with this firestorm of emotions coursing through her. Or so she thought. But Reese instantly felt most of the tension slip right out of her body. Leave it to Zack to manage such a miracle.

"I just don't want Sylvia to be hurt by anything else she learns about the man she married," she muttered.

Zack made a sound of agreement and continued to hold her. He was no doubt giving her a chance to vent. To spill out more of her worries. And she could have.

But she didn't.

Reese eased back enough so their gazes could meet.

Then she silently cursed. Because she could have sworn her heart did do some dancing. She had to be wrong about that. Or maybe the revved-up heartbeat was because of the spike in heat when she looked at his face.

Despite her own earlier mental warning about being close to him, she leaned in and kissed him. Of course, that bounced up the heat even more, and the dreamy feel of pleasure slid through her, canceling out the worry. Making her believe that trusting her heart was indeed the way to go.

A sound rumbled in Zack's chest. A sound to let her know that he was pleased with the kiss. Pleased and aroused.

Yeah, she was right there with him.

Reese deepened the kiss and got a fresh kick of heat from the taste of him. It was as if pretty much everything about Zack, including his taste, had been designed to pleasure her. There'd definitely been no disappointments in that area, and it felt as if he were taking them up a ladder with amazing things waiting at the top.

He added his own zing and deepened the kiss. Added the pressure of his body as well when he inched her against the wall. Good thing, too, because she wasn't sure she could feel her legs. But, mercy, she could feel everything else, and that's what counted.

Zack gave her memory a refresh when he kissed her neck, and he managed to find just the right spot to make her feel as if she had stepped up another rung on that ladder. The heat stirred inside her. Building, building, building. Until the kiss became hard and hungry. Until she wanted so much more.

He gave her more, of course. After all, this was Zack,

and *more* was his specialty. As he brought the kisses back to her mouth, she felt his hand between them, and he moved his clever fingers under her shirt. Bare skin on bare skin.

Another step up that ladder.

It occurred to her that if she was going to stop, it had to be now. If she was going to attempt to guard her heart, she should do it before things went any further.

She didn't.

Reese decided in that instant that she would indeed take the advice to follow her heart, and her heart was saying to latch on to Zack and this moment and just enjoy everything that was happening. That's why she went after his shirt as well.

They did some fumbling with their clothes, mainly because neither of them wanted to pause the kissing long enough to make things easier. Easier didn't hold a candle to steamy, hot kisses. And touching. Yes, there was some of that, too, once the shirts were off.

Reese ran her hands over the muscles of his back and returned the favor of kissing his neck. She got a welcome response from him—that husky groan of pleasure. So she did it again. And again. And she might have continued to torture him if he hadn't rid her of her bra and done some torturing of his own on her breasts.

There it was. More steps on the ladder.

The heat and need created a demand for more, of course. That was the problem with really good kisses and touches. They started off as wonderful sensations but then snowballed into a demand for something else. Release from the pressure cooker heat that was building.

Apparently Zack was right there with her on that because he scooped her up in his arms and carried her to the bed. He kissed her again when he eased her down onto the mattress and then moved back.

Reese cursed the loss of heat from his body. Or at least she did until she saw that she had an amazing peepshow going on right in front of her. Zack was stripping off his boots and socks, then his belt, then his jeans.

Then, his boxers.

Oh, yes. An amazing peepshow.

It occurred to her that no one should have such amazing DNA, the combination of such a hot body and face, but she was thankful for it. Because she was definitely reaping the benefits here.

The benefits increased when he shimmied her out of her pants and panties, and he gave a scorching look of approval before he reached down and retrieved something from his pocket. A condom. Thank goodness he'd remembered it because Reese certainly hadn't.

Zack finally moved onto the bed with her, bringing back all that amazing heat. Enough heat that Reese figured it counted as at least six ladder steps, but he apparently wasn't easing up on generating fire because he started right back up kissing her. And this time, he did some additional exploring.

He trailed his mouth from hers, to her breasts, where he dallied for a while and soon had her moaning in pleasure. He didn't stop there. Zack kissed her stomach, continuing to move lower and lower until he reached the inside of her thighs. Then, he gave her a kiss that

Reese was sure she'd remember for the rest of her life. Talk about an avalanche of good, steamy sensations.

Yep, she'd remember this.

And she might have rolled Zack on his back and returned the favor, but the man outmaneuvered her. He put on the condom while he lit more fires by kissing his way back up her body. With every inch, she felt slam after slam of pleasure, rendering her speechless. Thankfully, Reese no longer cared about such things as speech. She only wanted one thing.

For Zack to give her release from this intense heat.

He got started doing just that by easing inside her. This next wave of sensation was the strongest yet, but he stilled a moment. And looked at her. Just looked. It might have gone on, oh, forever, if she hadn't lifted her hips, taking him in even deeper. That seemed to snap something inside him, and it revved up the urgency and need for both of them.

With each thrust, Reese could feel herself moving up those steps. She wanted to hang on, to draw this out as long as possible, but there was no way her need would allow that. It had to happen now. Zack understood that, too, because he gave her exactly what she needed— hard, fast strokes, moving against the most sensitive part of her body. Giving and taking everything both their bodies demanded.

Reese moved up, up, up. Until she reached the top. Until she could take no more. And then Zack gave her exactly what she needed to finish.

CHAPTER 8

Judging from the little moans of pleasure that Reese was still making, the sex had been amazing. It certainly had been for him, and while he wasn't moaning, he was enjoying the feel of her naked body snuggled to his. He was savoring her scent, too. And the steady beat of her heart against his.

He stopped mentally naming things since, heck, there was no part of this he wasn't enjoying.

Reese and he had been dancing around their attraction since the moment she'd stepped into the sheriff's office, and he'd hoped it would eventually lead them to this. No way could he regret it.

But Reese might.

He figured they'd have to deal with that soon enough. She wasn't big on taking risks, and landing in bed with him was exactly that. A risk. And she might decide it was a mistake that couldn't be repeated.

Zack scowled as that dismal notion wormed its way through his thoughts. This could be it. Instead of their lovemaking being the big start he wanted with her, it could end up being the finale.

"I'm trying not to overthink this," she muttered, snuggling in even closer to him. "How about you?"

The overthinking was already happening, but Zack kept that to himself. In fact, he kept everything verbal to himself, located her mouth, and kissed her. It was an instant cure for his worries. An instant cure for a lot of things, since kissing Reese drowned out all the other stuff.

Well, everything but the knock at the door.

Reese and he groaned in unison, and while obviously neither of them wanted to get up, it could be her great-aunt or his grandfather. That got both of them hurrying off the bed and racing to gather up their clothes and get dressed. They were still in the process when there was another knock. And still scrambling when there was a third knock.

"Does it look as if we've just had sex?" Reese asked, yanking on her shoes and finger combing her hair.

Yeah, it did, but Zack didn't verify that. Instead, he kissed her again and followed her to the door. She opened it not to Sylvia or his grandfather, but to a man he recognized. Or rather he thought he did until Zack noticed something different about the familiar face.

A tiny scar running through the man's eyebrow.

This wasn't Harry Floyd but rather his twin, Elwood. Aka Happy Harry.

Judging from the slight gasp from Reese, she had figured out his identity as well. She shook her head and stared at the man as if she was trying to figure out what to say. "We've been looking for you," she finally managed.

Elwood nodded. "My brother made a bunch of calls to try to track me down, and a couple of the people he spoke to called me to let me know that both the sheriff and a lady PI were searching for me. I went to the police department, but the nice deputy there told me you were probably both at the inn." He held out his hands to Zack in a cuff-me gesture. "I'm here to turn myself in."

Zack sighed. "Are you admitting to being a bigamist?" he asked.

"I am." Elwood didn't hesitate. "And I'm ready to take my punishment."

Zack eased the man's hands back down. "I'm not arresting you." But then he stopped and rethought his statement. "Unless you've married another woman in the past seven years."

Elwood smiled, but there didn't seem to be any humor in it. "Nope. I had a partner, sweet Bessie, for nearly thirty years, but she flat out refused to marry me. She passed away last Christmas." He paused, squared his shoulders. "If you're not going to arrest me, then would it be possible for me to speak to Sylvia, Maeve, and Arabella? The clerk said they were all staying here."

Zack looked at Reese to see how she wanted to handle this, and she took out her phone. "I'll have them meet us. But not here," she muttered, glancing back at the rumpled bedcovers.

"There's a small, private, party room downstairs," Zack suggested, and when he got a confirming nod from Reese, the three of them headed in that direction while she made calls to the three wives.

"I'm guessing they're gonna be real mad at me," Elwood muttered.

"I think that's a good assumption," Zack said. "Mad and hurt."

Elwood winced. "Yeah. I'm sure I did cause them plenty of hurt."

The man didn't say anything else as they went to the party room. When they moved past a pair of six-foot-tall artificial Christmas trees, the motion-activated firs started to bounce and sing. Not the same song either. A tinny version of "Here Comes Santa Claus" clashed with "Frosty the Snowman."

Thankfully, when they moved deeper into the room, the trees stopped, and the room grew quiet again. The perky Christmas decorations didn't create an ideal venue for a showdown, but Zack figured a showdown was coming.

And fast.

They'd hardly gotten into the room before he heard the sound of hurried footsteps, and Sylvia arrived. His grandfather was with her, but he stayed back in the doorway.

The trees sprang to life again, their fake fir branches slapping with the up and down movements while they moved onto another pair of songs: "Jingle Bells" and "Holly Jolly Christmas."

Frowning, both Sylvia and his grandfather moved away from the trees to silence them, and Zack made a mental note to tell the inn owner to try to sync the decorations or move one elsewhere. The performances of the songs were bad enough without the lyrics running together.

"Happy Harry," Sylvia murmured when her attention finally landed on their visitor. The shock was in her voice and all over her face. She touched trembling fingers to her mouth and went a few steps closer to Elwood before she froze in place.

"Sylvia," Elwood greeted. "You're as beautiful as you always were."

Zack groaned—he was pretty sure that wasn't the right thing to say. It wasn't. Anger flared in Sylvia's eyes, and she likely would have hurled some insults at Elwood if there hadn't been more footsteps. Seconds later, Maeve and Arabella hurried in with Hal and Harrison. Like his grandfather, the men stayed near the door. Maeve and Arabella went to stand alongside Sylvia.

And in doing so, set off the blasted trees.

"We Wish You a Merry Christmas" and "Santa Baby" made up this unwanted round. The newcomers quickly figured out they had to move away to stop the cacophony, and they did.

"Has the lying scumbag said why he cheated on all three of us?" Arabella snarled, clearly more riled than Sylvia. But Maeve was having a different reaction. She seemed to be on the verge of tears.

"Not yet," Sylvia supplied.

Elwood took a step toward them. And then immediately retraced that step when Arabella shot him some stink eye. "I don't have an explanation or an excuse," he admitted. "Not one that'll help any of you understand why I did what I did."

"No explanation," Arabella snarled in a *duh* tone. "Well of course you don't. Because there's nothing you can say that'll explain or excuse squat."

"I was in love with all three of you," Elwood blurted.

That didn't light the same fury fuse as his remark about Sylvia being beautiful. Nor did it prompt Arabella to snap or spew anything. The three women just stared at him.

Elwood dragged in a long breath before he continued. "It's true. I met all three of you at different times in my life. Sylvia, when I was so young and didn't have a care in the world. Love at first sight that swept me away."

Sylvia made what seemed to be a sound of agreement, but since her eyes were still narrowed, she probably wasn't about to dole out any forgiveness.

"I had three of the best years of my life with you, Sylvia," he went on, pinning his attention on her, "and then I got some bad news. Cancer of the lymph nodes. These days it's known as Hodgkin's disease. I'd watched my own daddy die from it and didn't want to put you through that, so I left."

Hell. Some of the color drained from Sylvia's face, and now she looked on the verge of crying.

"But you didn't die," Reese quickly pointed out. Obviously, she wasn't ready to let go of her anger.

Elwood shook his head. "I went through two years of treatment, but the doctors told me even though I was in remission, it could return. I'd hoped Sylvia had moved on with her life by then, and I sort of spied on her to make sure that was true. You seemed happy enough. And by then, I'd met Maeve." He shifted his gaze to her.

"I was a nurse at the hospital where he was being treated," she muttered. A tear escaped and slid down her cheek. "He said it was love at first sight."

"It was," Elwood insisted.

Arabella rolled her eyes. "And you thought being in love excused you from telling Maeve the truth that you were already married?"

"No, it wasn't an excuse," he admitted. "But I got swept away. We had two wonderful years together before the Hodgkin's returned."

That dried up Maeve's tears, and her jaw tightened. "And you disappeared."

"Because I didn't want you to have to nurse me. I thought you should have someone whole, someone who could love you as much as you deserved."

Silence fell over the room. Everyone was probably trying to decide whether they should sympathize with Elwood or do some kind of verbal tar and feathering.

"And then you moved on to me," Arabella snapped, clearly in the tar-and-feather corner.

Elwood sighed again and shifted to her. "Yes. After another year of treatment, I was in remission again and took a job working at the dude ranch your daddy owned. And, yes, love at first sight," he volunteered, causing everyone in the room to huff. "I know it sounds impossible, but it was true. I took one look at you, Arabella, and I knew I didn't want to draw another breath without you."

Even Elwood seemed to realize he'd gone too far. with that flowery account because he winced.

"My daddy would have run you off the ranch if he'd known you were already married to two women," Arabella pointed out.

Elwood made a quick sound of agreement. "And that's why I didn't mention it. By then, Maeve had moved on with her life, too, and she'd filed for divorce."

"But I hadn't gotten a divorce because I couldn't find you," Maeve said.

Elwood nodded. "I knew eventually the divorce would happen, so I married Arabella. What I did was wrong," he quickly added. "Like I said, there's nothing I can say that'll excuse my actions."

"You're right about that," Sylvia said, just as Maeve muttered, "Absolutely nothing."

"Damn straight," was Arabella's contribution, and she continued with a question. "So did you grow a conscience or another ball when you decided to leave me, too?"

"No." That was all Elwood said for several long moments. "I left because I knew eventually I'd have to tell you the truth, and I took the cowardly way out and just disappeared. I figured you'd get on with your life too, and that you'd be better off without me."

A fresh round of anger slid over Arabella's face. "I would have been better off if you hadn't asked me to marry you when you already had two wives."

Both Maeve and Sylvia nodded and made soft, sad sounds of agreement. Elwood made his own sound and muttered an "I'm sorry," before he headed for the door.

No one stopped him, but Elwood got plenty of glares as he made his exit, activating the trees, which jumped into the same song at the same time. Zack supposed it was sort of a Christmas miracle. The firs contributed an odd kind of farewell serenade to this miserable moment as they belted out "All I Want for Christmas Is You."

Reese wanted to say something, anything, that would make the situation better. First, though, she had to wait for those darn trees to quit singing, and then she had the silence she needed. First to think, and then to come up with something that would remove that sad, stark look from Sylvia, Maeve, and Arabella's eyes.

But nothing came to her.

Absolutely nothing.

They all knew that Elwood had screwed them over six ways to Sunday. They all knew this couldn't be fixed. So, on a heavy sigh, Reese just went to the three women and gave them all hugs. Zack and the other three men stayed put, maybe in fear of setting off the singing trees, or perhaps because they were even more uncertain than Reese about offering comfort.

"I feel like such an idiot," Maeve muttered, shaking her head. "I should have sensed something was off and not married him."

Sylvia made a sound of agreement. Arabella grumbled something about a three-balled bastard.

"You didn't know," Reese said. "You trusted the man you loved." She had some firsthand experience about that, and Sylvia must have filled Arabella and Maeve in on her failed marriage because they all gave her brief pitying looks.

"But I should have known something was off," Mae

insisted, and she looked at Sylvia. "At least he wasn't married to anyone else when he proposed to you."

Her great-aunt nodded. Sighed. "It crushed my heart when he left."

That brought on more sounds of agreement and more pitying looks between the women.

"Are you okay?" Reese asked.

"No," the women said in unison.

Sylvia no doubt saw the concern in Reese's eyes because her great-aunt patted her cheek and attempted a smile. "I'll be fine. I just need . . ." She stopped, glanced around, and aimed one of those half smiles at Zack's grandfather. "I'm sorry, but I really need to go home."

"So do I," Maeve was quick to say, and Arabella added her own agreement.

"I'll be fine," Sylvia repeated, her gaze slipping to Zack for a moment before returning to Reese. "You stay here and enjoy, well, the moment."

The suggestion settled like a lead weight in Reese's stomach. *The moment.* The relationship with Zack that suddenly seemed as if it had moved way too fast and was way too intense. The one that could lead to a crushed heart of her own.

Yes, lead weight.

And even if it hadn't been there, Reese was well aware of something else. She couldn't just let her great-aunt go home to spend the holidays alone. No. Sylvia needed family right now.

The three women walked away, no doubt heading to their rooms to pack. Hal, Harry, and Harrison followed them, but their heads were hanging, as if they had all come to the conclusion that there was nothing they could do to fix this situation.

The trees launched into "I Saw Mommy Kissing Santa Claus" and "Grandma Got Run Over by a Reindeer." Reese didn't even attempt to compete with that. She just locked gazes with Zack and waited for the noise to die down.

"You're going with them," he said, and it wasn't a question. His statement only added more weight to her stomach. He wasn't objecting, wasn't trying to convince her there was another way.

"I need to take some time," Reese forced herself to say.

He nodded, leaned down, and brushed a kiss on her mouth. It would have been chaste coming from any other man, but Zack didn't do chaste. And that was yet another reason she should take some time. It was impossible to think straight with so much heat, need, and hope swirling around inside her.

Zack pulled back from the kiss and smiled. A smile that didn't make it to his eyes. "Take that time," he muttered. "And if . . ." He stopped, and something came into his expression that she couldn't interpret. "Take that time," he repeated, and then added, "Merry Christmas, Reese."

As she watched him walk away, she realized that it was the first time those two words, *Merry Christmas*, had sounded like a goodbye.

CHAPTER 9

Zack stayed against the back wall of the civic center while he sipped a beer and watched the giggling, giddy guests stream in for the Christmas Eve Kiss Ball.

Emphasis on Christmas. The decorating committee had clearly wanted to make sure no one forgot the occasion—there were holiday decorations everywhere. Holly wreaths, twinkling lights, and at least a dozen trees—thankfully none of the singing variety. The music had been left to a DJ, who was now in the process of playing a soothing rendition of "Silver Bells."

Some of the guests were actually slow dancing to it but most were eating, drinking, or hanging out with friends. Like the room, everyone was dressed for the occasion in holiday colors. Santa hats and elves' shoes were in abundance. So was mistletoe, thanks to the mayor's assistant, who was at the door handing out sprigs of the stuff that had been formed into dangly balls attached to sticks, like lures on small fishing poles. Presumably this was so even a short person could get enough height to hold the plant over the head of the person they intended to kiss.

Of course, the thought of kissing reminded him of Reese.

Everything did. Simply put, he just hadn't been able to get her out of his mind. Zack wasn't so sure it was the same for her. Yes, she'd texted him multiple times over the past three days since she'd left. Messages to let him know she was okay and to ask how he was doing. But she hadn't said anything yet about returning. Nor had she issued an invitation for him to go see her.

Zack wanted to give her the time and space she obviously needed, but he felt lost without her. Ironic, since their romance had been a whirlwind by anyone's standards. In the span of a week, they'd gone from testing second-chance waters to landing in bed. Now, he had to hope that Reese didn't have so many regrets about the fast pace that she wouldn't let him back into her life.

A burst of extra-loud giggling caught his attention, and he saw most of his police force coming in with their kissing partners. Clearly they were in a festive mood, and since Zack didn't want to bring them down, or have them ask again how he was doing, he stepped back into a narrow hall that led to some storage rooms and a back exit he figured very few people would be taking that night.

Despite the fact he was now in extra-dim light, his mother spotted him from across the now-crowded dance floor, and she gave him a perky wave. She was the main reason he was here. He wanted to support her, and it was expected of him. That's why he'd spent nearly a half hour mingling, saying hello and doling out Merry

Christmases. If he'd stayed away, it would have fueled the gossip even more.

If "more" was actually possible.

All of Loveland was gabbing about the three-balled bigamist who'd crushed the hearts of three women. Elwood's name was mud here, but Zack figured the man was wallowing in misery over what he'd done. Zack hoped he was anyway. Wallowing and then maybe also moving on; he had that same hope for the wives Elwood had abandoned.

The main doors opened again, and Zack saw his grandfather come in with Hal and Harrison. Somehow, his granddad had managed to squeeze into the green suit he'd been wearing when Zack and Reese had interviewed him. Amid the abundant Christmas decorations, the suit no longer seemed as gaudy or outdated.

His granddad and his two friends took the mistletoe balls and cups of Christmas punch as they strolled toward the stage to watch the photographer setting up for what would soon be the big group-kissing shot. Zack would make sure he took a couple more steps back into the hall for that. He was only in the mood to kiss one woman, and she wasn't there.

He caught sight of his mother again as she made her way onto the stage and to a microphone. "Merry Christmas, everyone," she gushed, and she got plenty of greetings back. "This is your heads up. All the kissers need to be on the dance floor in twenty minutes for the big picture."

That was his cue to move even further into the hall, and he was in the process of doing just that when the door behind him opened. A gust of wintery air rushed in. And so did someone else. He'd barely managed a glimpse of the person from over his shoulder when someone took hold of him.

He stiffened. Then he smiled when he saw his captor. Reese, wearing a red dress that hugged all her curves and a glittery Santa hat.

"I've kidnapped you, and you're now my plaything," Reese said, putting his back against the wall and pressing her body to his. "And you can't escape because I have this." She dangled a mistletoe ball over his head.

Zack heard a smattering of giggles and looked to see his mother, granddad, Sylvia, Maeve, Arabella, Harrison, and Hal all grinning at him.

"My accomplices," Reese muttered. "You can arrest them later."

He'd be thanking them, but for now, he had something he needed to do. He kissed Reese, and oh, it had some Christmas magic to it. Then again, any and all kisses with her fell into the magical realm. No mistletoe needed.

Reese melted into the kiss while she melted against him. Suddenly his arms were filled with her, and it occurred to him that nothing had ever felt quite so right.

He kissed her and kissed her, letting the taste and feel of her seep into every part of his mind and body. Yeah, this was potent all right, and they didn't ease back from the kiss until oxygen became an issue.

"I was hoping you'd come," he managed to say.

"Wouldn't have missed it." But then she stopped, shook her head. "Okay, I almost missed it. I was to make sure Sylvia was okay, and while I was waiting and worrying about her, she called your granddad this morning, and they came up with this plan."

Zack smiled and didn't miss the little nudge she gave his body with hers. "They orchestrated a fake kidnapping?"

"No, their idea was just to have me show up here and surprise you. The kidnapping was my idea. I thought maybe I could get it right this time and you wouldn't have to ask me who I was."

"Uh, who are you?" he teased.

She nipped his bottom lip with her teeth and sent a shot of pure fire through him. Then again, the fire shots had already started with that kiss. And just the sight of her.

"I'm the woman who wants to get to know you a whole lot better," she spelled out.

"Good." He kissed her again. "Did you get enough thinking time?"

She nodded. "I accelerated it, like our dates. And, yes, I know that's risky, especially for me, but it felt like a bigger risk if I didn't take this risk with you. Am I using the word risk too much?" she asked, smiling.

"Just the right amount," he assured her. "I've also been doing some accelerated thinking, and I'm miserable without you."

She grinned. "Music to my ears, and that's why I got u this." Reese plucked out a little card from her tiny se and handed it to him.

his card entitles the bearer to fifty dates and another pping," he read aloud. He raised his eyebrow at the t.

"Three kidnappings will make me a serial offender," she spelled out. "I'm thinking you'd have to . . . detain me or something." Her kiss let him know that the detainment would be very enjoyable indeed.

It was hard for Zack to hold back on the kiss, but he reminded himself that they were in a public place. Soon, though, he intended to get Reese behind closed doors. For now, he took the pen he'd seen in her purse, turned the card over, and started writing.

"Your Christmas present," he explained. "This card entitles the bearer to fifty dates, unlimited kisses, and a detainment or two."

Their gazes met, held, and her smile was filled with joy and hope. And lust. Because, hey, lust was their default.

"What happens when we run out of fifty dates?" she asked.

"We do fifty more," Zack was quick to say. "And then sometime during that, we make a big deal about how we fell in love at second sight."

He braced himself in case Reese froze with deer-in-the-headlights shock over what he'd just said. But she didn't. "Love at second sight works for me," she muttered, and she moved in to kiss him again.

A sudden flurry of movement and voices stopped them. "It's time," his mother's voice said over the microphone. "Everyone on the dance floor for the big kiss."

Reese took hold of his hand and pulled him out of the hall and into the crowd. They were surrounded b at least four hundred people, but to Zack it felt as if it were just Reese and him. Just this moment. This kiss.

He slipped his arm around her waist, pulling her to him, and he caught another flash of the joy on her face as he moved her closer. Closer. Closer.

Their mouths met just as they murmured in unison, "Merry Christmas."